Caroline's Choice brings home the intense need of forgiveness. Martha Rogers has written a compelling story of love and redemption.

—DIANA LESIRE BRANDMEYER
AUTHOR OF *HEARTS ON THE ROAD*

Caroline's Choice by Martha Rogers is a delightful tale of adventure and romance, of coming of age and making choices. An enjoyable read and a nice opportunity to escape to another time and place, where the hardships of prairie life were offset by the simplicity of the era.

—KATHI MACIAS
SPEAKER AND AUTHOR OF *VALERIA'S CROSS* AND
THE EXTREME DEVOTION SERIES

The fourth book in Martha Rogers's Winds Across the Prairie series rejoins us with past characters we've grown to love and draws us deeper into the lives of Caroline Frankston and Matt Haynes. At twenty-seven, Caroline decides life in Barton Creek *isn't* going to lead to either romantic or professional success. It takes her leaving for Oklahoma City, a new career, a new suitor, and a frightening accident to awaken both Matt and Caroline to what they really want in life. Rogers spins a lively, sweet tale sure to please fans of American history and the sometimes-winding road to romance.

—TRISH PERRY
AUTHOR OF *THE PERFECT BLEND* AND
TOO GOOD TO BE TRUE

Martha Rogers has done it again! *Caroline's Choice* is a story that will leave the reader begging for more. A must-read!

—RHONDA GIBSON
Y OF A CHRISTMAS

D1417486

Caroline's
Choice

MARTHA ROGERS

REALMS
A STRANG COMPANY

Most Strang Communications Book Group products are available at special quantity discounts for bulk purchase for sales promotions, premiums, fund-raising, and educational needs. For details, write Strang Communications Book Group, 600 Rinehart Road, Lake Mary, Florida 32746, or telephone (407) 333-0600.

Caroline's Choice by Martha Rogers
Published by Realms
A Strang Company
600 Rinehart Road
Lake Mary, Florida 32746
www.strangbookgroup.com

Cover design by Nathan Morgan
Design Director: Bill Johnson

Visit the author's website at www.marthawrogers.com.

Library of Congress Cataloging-in-Publication Data
Rogers, Martha, 1936-
  Caroline's choice / by Martha Rogers. -- 1st ed.
      p. cm.
  ISBN 978-1-61638-193-6
  1. Young women--Fiction. 2. Oklahoma City (Okla.)--Fiction. I. Title.
  PS3618.O4655C37 2011
  813'.6--dc22
                                        2010037998
E-book ISBN: 978-1-61638-407-4
First Edition
11 12 13 14 15 — 9 8 7 6 5 4 3 2 1
Printed in the United States of America

Chapter 1

Oklahoma Territory, September 1907

*C*aroline Frankston's hands clinched into fists, her breath coming in short spurts. Through the parlor window, she watched life go on in a normal, orderly fashion, but here in this room her world lay fragmented like shards of broken glass. Each piece cut into her soul, causing pain that she no longer wanted to bear. The bleeding had to stop.

"If I don't leave this town, I'll never get married." Caroline Frankston spun around to face her mother. "Barton Creek has no men who interest me, so I would like to move to Oklahoma City and start a new life there."

Her mother's blue eyes flashed with anger. "You'll do no such thing. You have responsibilities here."

Caroline's jaw tightened. Mother's demands only caused more determination. "What responsibilities? Going to luncheons and meetings with you and sitting around listening to you decide what people should do?"

The rigid set of Mother's mouth warned Caroline to be careful with her next words. Now was the time to stand firm and not back down. "I know you want what's best for me, and right now a move seems to be it."

Mother remained silent, a vein in her neck throbbing in response to the tension in her jaw. A mixture of anger and disbelief sparked from her eyes. She stood tall, with her back ramrod straight. Mother wouldn't back down.

Envy for her brother's freedom gnawed at Caroline. Being male, Rob could pick and choose what he wanted to do, and he'd proved it with his law office and his marriage to Becky last year despite Mother's disapproval.

Without waiting for a response, Caroline headed for the door, but not without one last comment. "I'm sorry. I'll be twenty-seven soon, and if I don't do something now, I never will. I don't want to be stuck here as spinster with time on her hands and no purpose in life."

She darted from the room and up the stairs before her mother could react and spew forth a torrent of words to thwart Caroline's plan. Recently a college friend had written to her of the job openings at the new Carnegie library in Oklahoma City and invited her to come live with her in her town house with another roommate. Caroline had just told her mother she wanted to apply for the job and move to the city. This evening she would break the news to her father.

Standing in front of the mirror on her bureau, Caroline picked up a stylish blue hat and pinned it on her upswept hair. Although she did love the hat, it had been chosen by her mother, as had most of the clothes in Caroline's wardrobe. In Oklahoma City she could set her own standards and not be dictated to by her mother.

Some of Mother's ideas and beliefs about fashions and social protocol left Caroline with the feeling that no one could measure up to what the mayor's wife expected, not even her own daughter. Being the daughter of the mayor had its advantages, but now they hindered her and kept her from pursuing other avenues of interest.

She gathered up her reticule. Time had come for a visit with her sister-in-law to seek her advice. After all, Becky had once pursued a newspaper career without thought of marriage. She could tell Caroline what it was like to be a single, working-woman on her own.

But deep in her heart the real reason she wanted to see Becky lay hidden. Maybe Becky would have some insight into why her brother, Matt, had been so distant the past year. Of course Mother was delighted with that turn of events, but Caroline was deeply hurt and at a loss as to how to reach out to her old friend.

She glanced around the room that had been hers since her family's arrival in Barton Creek seventeen years ago. She'd miss it, but the idea of being on her own filled her with excitement. She raced down the stairs and headed for the front door to avoid another confrontation with her mother. When her voice called out from the parlor, Caroline pretended not to hear and closed the door behind her.

She walked toward town, her feet disturbing the fallen leaves and making them swirl about her feet. Late September should bring cooler air to match the changing of the colors in the trees, but not this year. Caroline wished she'd worn a lighter weight shirtwaist and a less heavy skirt, but Mother had insisted on storing all summer clothes away for the fall season. At the next corner she turned onto Main Street, thankful she lived such a short distance from town.

A few more motorcars dotted the streets, which were now completely bricked. As mayor, her father planned to replace the boardwalks where people now strolled in front of business establishments with real sidewalks. She walked past the post office, the jail, and several other stores and shops before reaching the newspaper offices.

The odor of printer's ink greeted her nose as Caroline stepped through the doorway of the Barton Creek newspaper building. The bell over the door jangled and caused everyone but Becky to look up to see who had come in. The staff on the paper had certainly grown since Mr. Lansdowne made the paper available seven days a week. Becky sat at her desk behind the railing separating the office space from the entryway, staring at whatever was in the typewriter before her.

One of the young men jumped up from his chair. "How can I help you, Miss Frankston?"

Caroline smiled and nodded toward Becky. "I'm here to see Mrs. Frankston."

Becky glanced up then. "Oh, my, I was so engrossed in my story that I didn't hear the bell." She strode over to the gate in the railing. "What brings you here today?"

"I wanted to talk with you if you have time, but I can see you're busy, so I'll come back later."

Becky pushed through the gate. "No, no, it's fine. I think I'm in need of a break about now." She turned to the young woman across the room. "Amy, would you tell Mr. Lansdowne I'm taking a break and will be back shortly? I'll stop at the bakery and bring back pastries. He'll like that."

"Of course, Rebecca. Have a nice visit." The young clerk returned to the business on her desk.

Caroline admired Becky's attire. She wore the plainest of skirts and shirtwaists but made them come alive with fashion even though the signs of her coming motherhood were evident. Caroline would have been called a "Plain Jane" if she wore the same. Something about her sister-in-law gave life to whatever she touched or wore, one trait Caroline sorely envied.

Becky linked arms with Caroline. "Now, let's head to Peterson's for tea and cookies."

When they stepped out onto the boardwalk, Becky breathed deeply. "Isn't it a beautiful day? Although it's too warm for me, I love this time of year."

"I like it too," Caroline responded, although at the moment all she could sense was the stench of horse droppings and the fine layer of dust and dirt over everything. She glanced at the woman beside her. "So, you're still going by Rebecca at the office?"

"Yes. That's my byline on all my articles, so they all call me Rebecca." Besides reporting on town events, Becky wrote a column for women in the *Barton Creek Chronicle* each week to inform them of the opportunities and advantages of voting for their government leaders.

Caroline laughed. "But you'll always be Becky to the rest of us."

Becky returned the laugh, but hers had a musical quality that had earned the friendship of most of the people here in her hometown. "I don't mind it at all now. Rob convinced me I could be both, and he was right." She glanced up toward the windows of her husband's law offices.

At least Becky and Rob had rediscovered the love they'd had for each other as youths, and now they were as happy as any married couple Caroline had seen. Mother hadn't been too pleased with her son marrying a Haynes, and even now that Ben Haynes headed one of the wealthiest ranches in the area, her attitude hadn't changed, especially since Becky chose to continue her job at the newspaper after learning a child was on the way. To Mother, Becky would always be a cowgirl.

When they had entered the bakery and ordered their tea and pastry, Caroline chose a table away from the window so they would have more privacy.

"So what is it that you want to talk with me about?" Becky unwrapped her pastry and pinched off a small piece.

Caroline stirred her tea and grinned. "I'm moving to Oklahoma City. My roommate at college, Madeline Barrows, has invited me to come live with her, and I have a good chance at a job at a library there."

Becky dropped her pastry, spreading crumbs in its wake. She grabbed a napkin and wiped the bits off the table. "You're doing what? Leaving Barton Creek? But what does your family say?"

"Mother is completely against it, and by now she's probably let Father know, and I don't know what he'll say. It really doesn't matter because my mind is made up."

"But what about Matt? Have you told him?"

Caroline dipped her head and concentrated on stirring her tea. "You know how much I care about Matt, but over the last few years his interest in me has dimmed. He's barely spoken to me since we ate together at the July Fourth celebration. I don't know what else to do."

Becky leaned forward. "I can't tell you much since I don't see him very often anymore. He's been quiet and withdrawn the Sundays we go out to the ranch for the family dinner. When we were younger, we enjoyed doing lots of things together, but that changed when I came home from college. And since I've married Rob, he's been much less open with me."

They sat in silence for a moment. Caroline's heart ached with the image of Matt sitting astride his great stallion and riding across the range. She bit her lip and leaned toward Becky. "I–I can't bear the thought of being a spinster, and there's no one here in Barton Creek except Matt I would consider as a husband. More opportunities to meet young men are available in the city. Many of my college friends stayed in the city, and I've been writing to several of them, and with Madeline's invitation, the time seems right. Although I care for Matt, I can't wait for him forever."

Becky blinked and shook her head. "I used to think my brother was working hard to establish himself before he took on the responsibilities of a wife and a family. But now that the ranch is doing so well, I don't understand is why he hasn't been more willing to call on you. I remember how you two were always together for every social event that came along before you went off to school. I guess I always thought you'd be his wife when he finally made up his mind it was time to marry."

"That's just it. I did too, but I've waited a long time for him to make up his mind." And they had been the longest years of her life. Now the time had come to look to the future and her life ahead before it passed her by completely. She turned to Becky and sat up straighter. "Now, tell me everything you know about going out on your own as a working woman!"

Matt removed his hat and wiped sweat from his brow with a bandanna. Fall may have been the season, but the air definitely spoke of summer. Late September usually brought cooler temperatures, but not this year. He stuffed the kerchief in his pocket and jammed the hat back on his head. Time to round up a few more strays.

He waved to Hank and headed toward the west pasture. The ranch hand rode up to join him. "You think some of the herd made their way out to Dawson land?"

"Yeah, they've done it before. Good thing those fences are around the oil rigs." Ever since the wells started producing, the noise of the pumps attracted whatever livestock meandered that way. He usually found around half a dozen or so head lined up at the fence staring at the work going on.

Hank tilted his hat back on his head. "I know that parcel of land wasn't any good for farming and such, but rigs sure are ugly despite the oil they're pumping."

"That's what worried Pa the most, but since it's away from everything and can't be seen from the house, he decided it was better to go ahead with Geoff's recommendations. So far that's been a good decision." Geoff Kensington had kept his word, and Barstow's Oil did everything Pa had requested. The first money from the oil deposits had surprised even Pa and Sam Morris. The two had put the money into a trust for the future after sending the original landowner his share.

"Your pa is a good businessman. I've admired him for many years. Remember how he took me in along with Jake and treated us like part of the family?"

"Yes, that's the way Pa was and still is." Matt loved his father even more for his treatment of other folks. If he hadn't believed in Jake, the young man would never have become a Christian and found out that the killing he'd been involved with in Texas was ruled self-defense. That cowboy might still be running from the law instead marrying Lucy and owning his own ranch.

Hank slowed his horse. "You know, I've been thinking. I'm not getting any younger, and the idea of settling down with a wife has its appeal. That young woman, Amy, who works with Becky agreed to let me be her escort for the church singing next week. You ought to ask Miss Caroline to it."

Matt cast a sideways glance at his partner. "You're a lucky man. Amy Garson is a pretty young woman."

Hank laughed and shook his head. "Matt Haynes, you're stalling me. What about Miss Caroline?"

Matt didn't respond, but his mind filled with the image of Caroline Frankston. He did love her at one time, but she had chosen a life far different from his. Just as he was about to ask her to be his wife, she'd announced she was going off to college. He remembered the day like it was yesterday. She'd been so excited when she showed him the brochures with all the information. She planned to major in fine arts and languages. Those were two things he knew nothing about.

"Matt, you hafta talk to her and let her know how you feel. I seen your eyes when we're in town and she's around. You can't look nowhere else."

"She's busy with her own life. Attending luncheons and meetings with her ma and doing all those things on committees and such. She has no time for me or for life on a ranch." Besides, the more he thought about it, the more he realized one Haynes married to a Frankston was almost one too many. Becky could handle the mayor's wife, but the idea of Charlotte Frankston as a mother-in-law didn't appeal to him at all. And if Caroline really cared, she wouldn't have run off to college when she did.

As though reading his mind, Hank offered his opinion. "It's that Mrs. Frankston, isn't it? She is rather formidable, but if you married Caroline and brought her out here to the ranch, you wouldn't have to deal with her mother that much."

Matt narrowed his eyes and worked his mouth. It wasn't anybody's business what he thought of Mrs. Frankston. He may be considered a coward for not facing up to her, but it was his decision to make.

"Matt, I think you're missing out on what life has for you if you let one woman ruin your feelings for another. If you really love Caroline, her mother wouldn't make any difference."

"That's easy for you to say. Have you forgotten how Mrs. Frankston treated Ma and Aunt Clara when everyone thought Jake was a murderer? Then look at how she hurt Emily Morris and Dove. That woman is rude and has no respect for anyone not of her own standing, but she's not the only reason, and it's best to keep your opinion to yourself."

"I understand, and I do remember those days, but I also remember Mrs. Anderson and how her heart changed. She was as mean as Mrs. Frankston toward Mrs. Morris and Dove until that prairie fire almost destroyed us all."

"True, but I don't see anything like that in the future to change Mrs. Frankston." Matt flicked his reins and spurred his horse. "Let's go hunt for strays. That's why we're out here."

His love life was nobody else's business but his. And as much as he was attracted to Caroline, he didn't care to saddle himself for the rest of his life with a cantankerous mother-in-law like Charlotte Frankston.

Chapter 2

*C*aroline sat at the dinner table with her heart pounding. The unreadable expression on her father's face didn't bode well for her. If he'd shown any emotion at all, she could prepare herself for his words. Her hands clinched in her lap as he gave thanks for the meal. When he ended the prayer, she unfolded her napkin, but her hands shook so much that she simply dropped it on her lap.

No one spoke until after Ruby served the meal. She left the room and Father turned his gaze upon Caroline. "Now, what is this Mother tells me about your desire to move to Oklahoma City?"

Even his voice gave no clue as to whether he may be angry with her. She swallowed hard to gain courage. Although she had rehearsed a dozen or more times what she would say, none of those words came to mind. "My friend Madeline Barrows lives there now and has written to me with an offer to come live with her."

Father nodded. "Ah, yes, I remember the Barrows. Her father is well known for his work with the statehood committee, and she has been active in the campaign also. I'm surprised she has not married."

"I believe she's been busy with her involvement in a number of charity causes." As well as the suffrage movement, but that information Caroline would keep to herself.

Father cut into his lamb roast. "And do you have any plans for providing for yourself while there?"

She cut her eyes to her mother, who sat with shoulders straight and lips pressed firmly together. "I'd like to apply for a job opening at the library where my language and fine arts background may be of use."

Father chewed for a few moments before answering. "I see." Then he spread butter on a piece of a roll.

Caroline's knees and hands both shook now. He didn't have to be so slow with expressing his feelings. She pleaded in silence for him to voice an opinion one way or the other. She'd seen him like this when pondering a decision with the town council, and it could be so exasperating to wait for his ruling.

In the meantime, Mother added nothing to the discussion. But then, she'd had her say with Father before dinner. Caroline couldn't tell if her silence meant she'd convinced Father to forbid her going or if Father had said he'd consider the move. Although the food on her plate grew cold, she couldn't eat any of it with her stomach churning as it did.

Finally he laid down his fork. "Caroline, I understand that you want to feel some independence and that you are unhappy with your life here. But that doesn't give you the wherewithal to pull up stakes and move away with no means of support guaranteed."

A cloak of gloom covered Caroline's heart. She wanted to stand firm, but her father's words held a truth she had to admit. Without the assurance she would have a position at the library, her decision did sound rash and impetuous. Still, her desire to be independent of her parents overrode her hesitancy.

"I understand that, but other opportunities are there if the library position doesn't work out. I just have to find them." At this point she might be willing to take the position of a nanny or a clerk in one of the department stores now dotting the city streets. Of course she knew little about either position, but she'd always been a fast learner. Father folded his napkin and laid it beside his plate. "I'll accept your decision, but I have a few stipulations before you follow through. If you can find gainful, safe, appropriate employment to support yourself, I have no objection to your living in Oklahoma City with Madeline. If you can't, then you must agree to stay here another year."

Fear flew out the window and hope took its place in Caroline's heart. "Thank you, Father. I'll write to Madeline and tell her the circumstances. Perhaps you and Mother could drive down to Oklahoma City with me and see the town house where Madeline lives." It would give her the opportunity to find out about employment opportunities as well.

Mother pressed her napkin against her lips then placed it on the table. "That is a good suggestion. I don't like the idea of your working to support yourself when your father and I can take care of you, but he seems to think it will be good for you to have a change, so I have agreed to this plan."

Caroline jumped up and ran to hug her father's neck. "I will find a wonderful job, you'll see, and I promise to come home every holiday."

Father harrumphed and adjusted his glasses. "It's not final, my child. Remember the conditions. After you have heard from Madeline again, we'll plan a trip down to the city."

Caroline straightened up and nodded. "Yes, I understand." She stepped to her mother's side and bent down to kiss her cheek. "I apologize for my behavior this afternoon. I won't be rude like that again."

"I accept your apology and will pray we are not making a mistake with our decision." She squeezed Caroline's hand.

Mother did understand, and God had answered her prayer.

Caroline's feet barely touched the steps as she raced upstairs. On her dressing table lay a letter already addressed to Madeline inquiring about the position at the city library.

When Caroline left, envy nestled in a tiny corner of Charlotte's heart at the vibrant spirit and independence of her child. She had feared that spirit had been squelched in the time Caroline waited for Matt to make some indication of his feelings, but today it had come out once again, and for that Charlotte was thankful. She loved her husband with all her heart, but that little corner still remembered the days of her own youth and the plans she'd once had for her life. Coming to this forsaken, barren land in Indian territory had not been a part of them.

She pushed those thoughts aside and reached over for her husband's hand. "I do hope we're doing the right thing for her. She has loved Matt Haynes for so long that I had begun to fear she'd let her life waste away waiting for him."

Maxwell grasped her hand in his. "I know it's difficult, but it's time to let our bird try her wings and fly on her own. Oklahoma City isn't so far away that she can't come home or that we can't go down for a visit."

Charlotte's lips trembled. Of course he was right. So many more opportunities were available there, and with statehood around the corner, the city would grow even more. Still, she would miss Caroline.

Like any mother, her main desire was to see her children happy and fulfilled in life. Somehow that had eluded Caroline up to this point, even though Charlotte had done her best to fill her daughter's days with social and civic events. Perhaps in Oklahoma City she would find whatever it took to bring meaning and purpose to her life.

Maxwell rose and came to Charlotte's side. Then he bent to kiss her cheek and whispered in her ear, "It will be all right. We'll go down and make sure all is well before we let our little bird flee the nest." His hand tightened on her shoulder before he strode away to study.

A deep sigh escaped Charlotte. If only he would really look at her and see her as the young woman she had been. That youthful girl still lived deep inside but never had much opportunity to come out and play in the world she had created for herself as wife of the mayor.

Her daughter's image entered her thoughts once again. Charlotte had seen the look in the girl's eyes whenever Matt was around. On more than one occasion she had noticed an answering one in Matt's, but his refusal to act on those feelings angered Charlotte. While she used to look down on him for being a cowboy, her time in Barton Creek had shown her the value of a ranching life. Now she disliked the young man simply because he had hurt her daughter. Caroline deserved someone who loved her and pursued her, not someone who dragged his feet all the way to the altar.

Then her thoughts turned to her son and unborn grandchild. A smile formed and became a full-blown grin. Despite her initial disapproval of Rebecca Haynes, Charlotte had to admit she had never seen her son happier than he was now. Rob would be a good father, just like his own had been. Her heart ached for Caroline to find such happiness. One part of Charlotte whispered to let her go and be on her own, but another part shouted to keep her here where Charlotte could make sure her daughter made the right decisions.

She pushed her chair from the table. No time to dwell on those thoughts tonight. Correspondence needed attention, as did planning the agenda for next week's meeting of the statehood celebration committee. With a satisfied sigh Charlotte rose and strode to her desk in the sitting room. Her appointment book lay open to tomorrow's date, marked with yet another luncheon to attend as the wife of the mayor. Soon all thoughts of her children disappeared, and ideas for how the town should celebrate Oklahoma's statehood filled the spaces in her mind.

Mellie Haynes noted the troubled look in her son's eyes at the supper table. Everything was going well with the ranch and the oil drilling, so something else must have caused his dark eyes to appear even darker. The only reason she could think of at the moment concerned Caroline Frankston. The girl loved him, and although Matt never indicated he felt the same, she had seen them together too many times in the past ten years to not know the feelings they kept suppressed.

Not one to pry, Mellie would wait until he came to her, if he ever considered such. Perhaps Ben had a better idea of what ran through Matt's mind, but then her husband wasn't one to betray confidences. Mellie sighed and wished Aunt Clara had not left Barton Creek last year. If anyone could get through to Matt, it would be the outspoken, feisty little woman who had helped Becky and Rob in their relationship.

A smile crossed Mellie's face as she imagined what Aunt Clara might have to say about the present situation. No doubt she'd give both Matt and Caroline her advice, just as she had Lucy, Dove, Becky, and the young men they loved.

Ben reached across the table and grasped her hand. "And what is causing your smile tonight? Are you thinking about Becky and your first grandchild?"

Heat rose in Mellie's face. "No, as a matter of fact, I am thinking about Aunt Clara. I miss her wisdom and our weekly visits." She may not have been telling the complete truth, but she truly did miss Ben's aunt.

Matt and Hank exchanged glances and then grins. Both had called the elderly woman meddlesome, so no doubt they didn't mind her absence. Mellie raised her eyebrows. "If you ask me, you two young men could stand a dose of her advice and wisdom. There's not a one of us she hasn't helped in one way or the other in the time she was here."

The three men nodded in agreement then turned their conversation back to ranching and oil. Ben finished the last bit of his potatoes then addressed Matt. "Geoff Kensington and I spoke the other day about how fast the oil business around these parts is growing. That new well at Tulsa, and the prospect of more down toward Guthrie and Oklahoma City, are going to bring in even more money and people to these parts."

Matt pushed back his plate and leaned on the table. "I'm glad you and Sam decided to let Geoff and Mr. Brewster take care of the drilling and transporting it out of here. They've been right pleased with the operation."

Ben scooted his chair back and stood. "And I'm glad they're taking care of it all. Sam and I are too busy with keeping the ranches working to worry about that oil. Mr. Brewster is a good man, and we trust him completely." He stretched his shoulders. "I have a few entries to make in the books. I'll see you two in my office when you're done here."

He winked at Mellie as he passed her chair and patted her shoulder. "Good supper as usual. If there's any of that pie left from dinner, I'll have it with coffee in about an hour."

Mellie smiled and squeezed his hand. "There's plenty. I'll have it ready for you then."

A few minutes later Matt and Hank followed Ben into his office, and she picked up the dishes to clear the table. Even with four people eating, the cleanup took far less time than she'd like. With the range cook taking care of the cowhands, she had less to do these days. At least Hank still came in to eat with the family like he'd always done. The kitchen had always been her haven, but now the only day she spent much time there was when all the family came for Sunday dinner.

With her chores finished and the coffee on the stove, Mellie wandered into the parlor and picked up her knitting. She pulled out several feet of yellow yarn and began working on the blanket for Becky and Rob's baby. Her first grandchild brought on a smile. Her niece Lucy had three, but her children were great-nephews and a great-niece. Not the same at all as Mellie's own daughter having a baby.

A hand touched her shoulder, and she flinched. Ben came around to sit beside her. "Sorry, didn't mean to startle you."

"I was daydreaming and didn't hear you come in." She held up the blanket. "Becky's favorite color. Imagine our little girl being a mother. I still see her as that thirteen-year-old girl who loved to ride horses and rope calves."

Ben chuckled. "So do I, but she's all grown up." He paused a moment then grasped her hands in his. "I'm still thinking about the worry I saw in your eyes at dinner. Want to tell me what has you so concerned?"

A deep sigh escaped and hung in the air as though punctuating her despair. "I don't think Matt will ever decide to marry Caroline. She's so in love with him, but though I see his interest, I don't see the same passion."

"I see. Mother hen worried about her chicks. To be honest, I expected him to marry Caroline long before now. I approached the subject in passing a time or two, but he's very tight-lipped and doesn't share his feelings. I have an idea that Charlotte

Frankston may have something to do with our son's reluctance to seriously date Caroline."

"And I would have to agree with you. It's not a good reason, but knowing our Matt, he would rather rope a wildcat than tangle with Charlotte and her snobbery. Even with Becky as Rob's wife, she hasn't warmed to us at all." She stood and slid her hand from his. "Let's let it be, Ben. We don't need to be meddling. God will take care of it." And she had to believe that, or she'd spend her time grieving for the two young people.

"I smell the coffee, and I have the pie ready. Let's have dessert." No matter what happened in the days ahead, she'd pray for Matt to make the right decisions about his future.

Chapter 3

*C*aroline's heart fluttered in her chest, and beads of perspiration dotted her forehead. She hadn't been this nervous since the spelling bee in eighth grade when she and Matt were the only two left in the competition. Downstairs, guests arrived to say their farewells before she boarded the train that would take her to Oklahoma City and new adventures in life. Several weeks of whirlwind activity had passed, and now she had only one more day at home before she rode away to become an independent, wage-earning young woman.

If Matt even spoke to her tonight, her resolve might melt, and if he asked her to stay, all plans would fly out the window. Having him declare his love outranked any job she may have waiting in Oklahoma City.

She licked her lips to make them shine and pinched her cheeks. Such effort would probably be wasted, but she did it anyway. Madeline, her friend and confidante from Oklahoma City, stepped into the room. "Caroline, you do look lovely. That dress is the exact same blue as your eyes."

"Thank you. I plan to pack it away tonight and take it with me when we leave tomorrow. I hope I will have occasion to wear it."

"Oh, you will; have no doubt about that. Once the young men discover your presence in our fair city, you'll be swamped with callers. I even have a few lined up for introductions."

Caroline turned away to hide the heat rising in her cheeks. In her two visits with her parents to her new home, she had seen several of the young men, and Mother had even commented on what excellent suitors they would be. Mother may mean well, but no one but Caroline Frankston would control who would or who wouldn't be calling on her. A sigh escaped her lips as she played with one of the curls lying against her neck.

Madeline's headshake reflected in the mirror. Caroline swirled around. "What's that supposed to mean?"

"Nothing. I heard the sigh. I figured you were thinking of Matt Haynes. He's a handsome cowboy with those black curls and piercing brown eyes. I would have flirted with him when he came into the Emporium this morning when we were shopping, but I know your feelings for him."

Madeline had turned a few heads in town with her golden-red hair and green eyes and no doubt would have attracted Matt's attention as well if she'd wanted. "Doesn't matter whether you do or don't. He hasn't given any indication he cares one way or the other about me."

Madeline grasped Caroline's arms. "Maybe not, but I've seen how you look at him, and the best thing for you is to do what you've decided to do. You'll see." She hugged Caroline. "It's going to be so much fun having you in Oklahoma City. We'll have a grand time."

A moment later she stepped away and grinned. "Now let's go down and dazzle your guests."

Caroline linked her arm with Madeline's, and together they headed for the curved staircase that would take them to the festivities.

Matt tugged at the collar of his shirt. Not that it was tight, but being dressed in a suit rather than jeans and a loose-fitting shirt never had been comfortable. At least Ma had let him wear a Western-style string tie rather than the fancy cravat favored by most of the gentlemen present.

His parents immediately found friends to greet and left Matt to fend for himself among the guests who had already arrived. He scanned the room for any sign of Caroline, but he found only prominent Barton Creek citizens milling about.

Mixed feelings about Caroline's departure divided his heart. One part longed to ask her to stay here, but the other didn't want to face rejection. He wanted what was best for her, but he had to admit he would miss her. Perhaps he'd taken her too much for granted, knowing she'd always be around when he finally decided what he wanted to do as far as marriage was concerned. They'd spent so much time together while in school that it never entered his mind that she might leave and go off to college. Now here she was, leaving again.

Rob clapped him on the back. "Hello, Matt. Good to see you tonight. Can you believe my sister has finally taken the step to go out on her own? I figured she'd stick around here until you and she married."

Heat rose in Matt's face, and his palms became moist. Rob may as well have been reading his mind. "Why would she do that? She's a right smart young woman, and I'm sure she'll do well with her new position at the Carnegie Library."

A grin twitched the corners of Rob's mouth. "All you have to do is ask her, and she'd tear up that train ticket to Oklahoma City."

At that moment all eyes turned toward the stairway. All the air sucked from Matt's lungs and his heart pounded. Caroline descended the steps with her hand lightly brushing the curved banister. He'd never seen her look more beautiful with her golden hair curled about her slender neck and wearing a dress as blue as a cloudless Oklahoma sky on a summer day.

Doubt again filled Matt, but he couldn't deprive Caroline of this chance to make something of her life. Being the wife of a rancher just didn't fit in with the way she had been brought up, with servants and plenty of money for whatever she wanted.

Caroline reached the bottom landing and appeared to float across the room, light as a feather.

"Good evening, Matt. How nice that you could come." She extended her hand toward him.

He grasped it in his, and a shock raced up his arm. His tongue became as thick as a slab of fresh-cut beef, and he could only stare. He glanced down and, seeing her hand still in his, pulled away. "You...uh...you look very nice tonight."

Her eyes opened wide, and he cringed. What a stupid thing to say. He had never been at such a loss around her before tonight.

She stepped back with a slight smile across her lips. "Thank you. Now I must see to my other guests."

A groan escaped, and Matt slapped his forehead. Rob chuckled beside him. Maybe it would be best to avoid being around Caroline the rest of the evening, or else he might forget all the resolve he'd mustered the past few days.

Becky joined her husband. "Matt, your eyes are bugging out of your head, but then Caroline is the belle of the ball, so to speak." She grasped his arm and stood on her tiptoes to whisper in his ear. "I hope you're not going to regret the decisions you've made these past few years, big brother. Love can overcome any obstacle. Remember that."

She then turned to Rob. "I see Ruth and Geoff over there, and I'd like to visit with them. If you'll excuse us, Matt, we'll leave you to mingle."

Charlotte observed the exchange between Matt and her daughter. She bit her lip and pushed back the idea that perhaps letting Caroline leave would be a mistake. Her child had no future with Matt Haynes, and besides, one Haynes in-law in the family was enough.

Ruby, their cook, had done an excellent job with the food for the party. The buffet table groaned under the weight of the pastries and delectable sweets the cook had prepared with help from the other two servant girls. Tonight would be one of the most memorable events in the social history of Barton Creek. Rebecca had already promised a grand reporting of the occasion in the Sunday edition of the *Chronicle*. At least that was one advantage of having a reporter for a daughter-in-law.

Charlotte made her way across the room, nodding and greeting guests as she passed by. Everyone on the guest list had responded with acceptance, which didn't surprise her in the least. Anytime the mayor issued an invitation to a nonpolitical event, Barton Creek citizens seized the opportunity to socialize in the mayor's home.

Times like this almost made up for all she'd left behind in St. Louis when she came west with Maxwell Frankston. He'd done quite well for himself and his family, but it still didn't measure up to the social life she'd had at home. Of course, after so many years she'd given up hope of ever going back and made do with what Barton Creek had to offer.

She stepped to her husband's side, and he grasped her hand. "Here you are, my love. I was just telling Dr. and Mrs. White how proud we are of the new clinic facilities. He can treat just about anything that comes along now since we were able to add the new surgery."

Dr. White nodded to Charlotte and circled his wife's waist with his arm. "The people of Barton Creek have been quite generous in their donations to the clinic. Old Doc Carter will be pleasantly surprised when he returns."

Charlotte's eyebrows rose at the news. "I didn't know he and Mrs. Carter would be coming back."

Anna White's smile lit up her face and her hazel eyes sparkled. "Oh, yes. I had a letter from Mrs. Carter this past week. She said they'd be winding up their trip back East and would be back in Barton Creek for Christmas. I think she just wants to be sure and be here when Becky's baby arrives."

Charlotte should have known Aunt Clara would want to be around to stick her nose into family affairs again. It had been her meddling that had finally brought Rob and Rebecca to declare their love for one another. "You're probably right about that. But what are you going to do for a place to live? Will your house be finished in time?"

"Oh, yes. Daniel has assured me it'll be ready for us to move in early December, if not before. The roof is already on, and they've begun with the inside walls."

Anna's description of her new home went on, but Charlotte's mind wandered elsewhere with the realization that Clara Haynes Carter would be returning to Barton Creek before year's end. Everyone may love the woman, but as far as Charlotte was concerned, the woman's meddling ways had caused more than one disturbance in the past. The two of them had a confrontation at their very first meeting ten years ago, and neither had ever forgotten it.

Charlotte smiled and touched Anna's arm. "Your home sounds delightful. I'll have to make it a point to visit after you move in. Now if you'll excuse me, I want to check on the buffet table."

She left her husband still conversing with the young couple

and strode toward the dining room, where she had seen Caroline headed with Madeline. When she found them, the two girls were giggling and filling their plates with pastries.

"Hello, Mother. You planned a wonderful menu for this evening. These pecan pastries are my favorite."

"Obviously; you have enough of them on your plate for two. Don't you think it would be wise to eat less and be assured you can still wear those new outfits we bought?"

Caroline's cheeks reddened. "It's a party, Mother. Just because you never indulge in eating sweets, I don't have to follow. Besides, Madeline and I won't have food like this when we're in the city. Right?"

"Yes. My cooking is very basic and what I've taught myself since I moved to the city. If we want to eat like this, we'd have to dine at the best restaurants in town, and I'm not sure our budgets would stand that very long." Madeline popped a miniature cream puff into her mouth and sighed. "This is delicious, but then everything I've tasted of Ruby's has been."

Charlotte shook her head and turned back to her guests in the other rooms. At least Caroline didn't appear to be crying over leaving Matt Haynes behind. This party had been one of the best ideas she'd ever had. From what she'd seen thus far, Matt would make no attempt to prevent Caroline's leaving.

Caroline rushed into the kitchen and shoved the food from her plate into the garbage bin. She didn't like wasting good food, but it was her mother's fault. If she hadn't made her critical remarks, then no more food would have gone onto the plate. Madeline happily ate all her choices, but Caroline's stomach churned and the food soured.

Ruby stood at the counter with her hands on her ample hips. "Miss Caroline, 'tis good food ye be throwing away."

"I'm sorry, Ruby. I know you worked hard, and it really is delicious, but my appetite seems to have left me."

"Has it now? And what might the cause for that be, child? 'Tis a man, I'm thinking." Ruby's carrot orange curls straggled from beneath her cap, and her blue eyes peered into Caroline's very soul. The good Irish lady had always been the one to see Caroline's distresses before anyone else.

Tears threatened, and Caroline blinked her eyes. "Matt has made no attempts to speak to me tonight except when I greeted him early on, and from all indications, he won't. He's completely ignoring me. I don't want to leave without his saying good-bye." Her heart ached with the admission he didn't care enough about her to ask her to stay.

Ruby wrapped her arms around Caroline's shoulders. "Sure and now what did ye think he would do? Ask ye to stay and not go to the city?"

"I don't know what I expected, but his completely avoiding me never entered my mind." She patted her cheeks to dry the tears. "I've never been able to figure him out. Sometimes he acts like he really cares, and then other times it's like tonight. What am I doing wrong?"

"Truth be told, little one, men are a worrisome lot. They don't let their emotions be seen like we women are apt to do. His eyes tell me he cares, but there's more—" Her lips clamped shut.

"What do you mean there's more?"

"'Tis not my place to be speaking out of turn." She turned Caroline toward the dining room door. "Best for ye to be getting back to your guests. I have work to do."

Caroline gazed at the cook for a moment more. Ruby knew something or had an opinion, but at the moment, a curtain shaded her eyes, and no more information or sympathy would be forthcoming. Caroline returned to the party, her heart even heavier than it had been earlier.

Matt eyed the clock on the mantel. Just a few more minutes, and he'd be able to say his farewells and get out of here. So far he'd managed to avoid Caroline, but one time when he had observed her from across the room, his resolve had almost disintegrated when her beauty had once again taken his breath away. This was early October, but she'd be back for Thanksgiving with her family, and surely she'd be home for the birth of Becky and Rob's baby.

He turned to leave but found himself face-to-face with Caroline instead. She glanced down at the white Stetson in his hands.

"Are you leaving so soon?"

The disappointment reflected in her eyes tore at his heart, but he inhaled deeply to strengthen his resistance. "Yes, I'm afraid I have to get back to the ranch and take care of some things so my parents can stay longer. I was going to look for you to say good-bye." That wasn't completely honest, but he couldn't bear to say the truth.

"I wish you didn't have to go. There's still plenty of food, and the music for the evening is just starting."

She smiled and melted his resolve. He breathed deeply to push back his reasons for leaving. Another half hour wouldn't hurt him. "So it is. I suppose I could stay awhile longer."

He laid his hat back down and tucked her hand on his arm. "Ruby did an outstanding job with the food, and I appreciate being invited."

"The party wouldn't be the same without you, Matthew

Haynes. You're the best friend I have, and having you here makes me very happy."

Her eyes sparkled as she stopped with him at the buffet table. He reached for the punch ladle. "Would you care for a cup of punch?" If she cared for him only as a friend, that was what he'd be.

"Yes, thank you. How are things at the ranch? I understand you are adding horses to your stock."

He poured a cup, handed it to her, and poured one for himself. "Jake is doing more of that. Pa is only acquiring extra horses to replace the ones that are getting too old for work on the range, but I do like working with the horses."

"I've always enjoyed riding, but Mother frowned upon my riding astride a horse in a split skirt, so I haven't since we were in school together."

He remembered those few rides they had taken together and how much fun they'd had. Now the days of their youth were lost in the adult world of reality. "Your schooling seems to have given you a great opportunity in Oklahoma City."

"Yes, my degree will certainly be an asset at the library. Many college students come there to do research."

Matt grinned and sipped the fruit-laced punch. "You always did like to help people."

Caroline's eyes opened wide. "You think so?"

"Of course. You always helped the younger students at school, and you make some of the best pies and cakes in town for the Fourth of July bake sale. And look at how you helped Becky form the women's group here in town last year." He gulped at the look of surprise and pleasure in Caroline's eyes. He should have told her these things before now. He swallowed more punch to let the cool liquid slide down his throat and quench not only his thirst but also the desire to take her in his arms and never let her go.

"Caroline, if I had—"

At that moment Mrs. Frankston appeared. "Matthew Haynes, I thought you had left already."

The disdain in her eyes and the ice in her voice said more about her feelings than the words. He refused to be intimidated by her presence in front of others. "No, I decided to spend a few moments with your daughter."

Mrs. Frankston gripped Caroline's arm. "My dear, you mustn't neglect your other guests." She pulled Caroline with her toward the parlor.

Caroline looked back at Matt with disappointment written on her face. He thumped his cup on the table. If he didn't get out of this house and away from Mrs. Frankston, he might say or do something that would not only make a scene in front of Caroline but also embarrass his parents. He strode toward the door, grabbed his hat again, and shoved it onto his head as he headed out.

Chapter 4

*M*att shaded his eyes against the sun and calculated the time of day. If his estimations were right, Caroline would be on her way to Oklahoma City now. Regret ate into his resolve to stay away from the station. As her friend, he could have at least gone to say good-bye, but he hated to admit how much her leaving bothered him.

Taking the early train on Saturday didn't make much sense after such a big going-away party, but if she had a job to begin on Monday, she did need to get settled in the city before then. Now that two trains a day made their way down through Guthrie to Oklahoma City, getting there was more convenient every day of the week.

Becky would give him a good scolding when she next saw him, but Matt didn't care at the moment. If he had gone to the station, he feared he would have asked Caroline to stay, but he had no right to keep her from following her plans.

A shadow entered his side vision, and Hank rode up beside him. "I don't think your parents were too happy with your decision to stay home from the station this morning."

"Don't suppose they were, but I had my reasons." And they were none of his family's business, especially Becky's.

"Figured you did. Unless I miss my guess, Miss Caroline played a part in those reasons." He held up his hand before Matt could retort. "But I ain't blamin' you. And I don't need to know the details. Your business is just that, your business."

At least someone understood and could keep his mouth shut instead of giving advice. He leaned on his saddle horn and pushed his hat back. "You planning on seeing Amy again?"

Hank laughed and moved on ahead of Matt. "Yes. She's agreed to let me call on her. Mrs. Claymore at the boarding even gave her approval in the absence of Amy's parents."

"Taking a chance, aren't you? Not knowing anything about her family or background?"

If Amy's mother was anything like Mrs. Frankston, Hank would be in for a difficult time continuing to see Amy.

"Not really. Seeing as how I have a life she knows little about, we're about even. If things go that far, I'll go out to their home and meet them."

"Hope it works out for you." As long as Hank had been working for the Haynes's ranch, his life before coming to Barton Creek was still a closed book to everyone except Pa. Pa had a habit of taking in strays, and one of them—Jake Starnes—even married into the family.

Hank slowed his horse and pulled the reins around to head home. "Come on back to the ranch. No sense in riding out here all alone and thinking about what you should have done."

How did Hank do that? He could get into Matt's head like no one else. In the past ten years the former ranch hand and now foreman had become more like a brother than a cowboy employed by Pa. "Tell Ma I'll be back in a while. I need a little more time to sort out my thoughts."

"Whatever you say, but I sure hope you're not going to drag around here. Your pa has cattle to get to auction, and we'll need every hand we can get to round them up and get them on the train and to the sale."

Matt nodded and waved at Hank but headed in the opposite

direction. Lots of work in the days ahead would take his mind off one Caroline Frankston.

Caroline leaned her head against the window frame of the train car. Matt hadn't even shown up to say good-bye. All these years she'd wasted waiting on him to ask her to marry him. If he didn't care that she was leaving Barton Creek, the marriage proposal would never come, and she'd best set her sights on something else for her future. Madeline continued to chat beside her, but Caroline didn't hear half of what her friend had to say. Too many images whirled through her mind in a cacophony of colors to concentrate on anything but her own mixture of joy and sorrow.

Her eyes misted over, and twinges of regret aimed straight for her heart. Leaving had been her only choice. She could have stayed and continued to wait for Matt to declare his intentions, but then that might never happen. No, leaving was best for everyone.

Something jabbed her arm, and she jerked her head around to find Madeline glaring, her arms crossed over her chest. "What was that for?"

"You haven't heard a word I've said since we lost sight of Barton Creek. I thought this was supposed to be an adventure for you, but instead you sit here moping like you'd lost your best friend."

Maybe she had. Matt was a good friend, but her decision may have cost that friendship. Caroline swallowed back the threatening tears and lifted the corners of her mouth into a smile she hoped looked sincere. "I'm sorry. Tell me again what you have planned for us."

Madeline let her breath out in a huff. "All right, but listen this time. Philip Marsden and Steve Burke are to meet us at the station and take us to our place. Steve offered to take us to dinner too. Since we were both too excited to eat much before we left, I think that's a swell idea. You should remember Steve and Philip. They both went to the University at Norman, and both are now working in Oklahoma City."

"I think I do, although that was awhile ago." Meeting two men so soon didn't really appeal to Caroline, but her friend had gone to the trouble, so the least to be done now was to go along.

Madeline continued without waiting for Caroline to respond. "Julia and her beau, Andy, will be there, so it'll be like a reunion of college friends. Some others like Charity Benson, Stuart Whittington, and Katherine have said they'd drop by to see you later in the evening. It'll be a lot of fun."

"Stop; you're running names by me faster than I can keep up. But why so many people tonight? I'd like to settle in before starting at the library on Monday after all the rush to get things done last week." With that many people in their town house, there'd be no place to be comfortable, and she did want to get a good night's sleep.

Madeline waved her hand in the air and laughed. "Oh, they won't stay long. They just want to meet you. When you were here before, your parents took up all our time in checking out the library, the church, and my home."

That was true. Mother had been quite fussy about the apartment, but in the end she approved. All Caroline now had to do was unpack her clothes and personal items into her new bedroom.

A smile creased her face. Seeing so many of her old friends from the university would be interesting, as they all had different careers. She'd enjoy seeing the changes in them after all these years. Of course she'd changed too. Maybe this time she'd be more open to the attentions of any young men she might meet. Anything to get Matt Haynes out of her mind and her heart would be better than moping around waiting for him to come around.

Charlotte opened the door to Caroline's bedroom and stepped inside. So empty without all the trappings her daughter enjoyed. Most of the pictures had been removed, and the dressing table was void of the jewelry box and perfume bottles and jars of facial cream.

She prayed Maxwell hadn't made a mistake in persuading her to let their daughter move to Oklahoma City. Even after checking out the apartment and where Caroline would work, Charlotte had reservations about the move. Madeline and Julia came from fine families, and Madeline's parents lived in Oklahoma City in a beautiful home. The Barrow family had been quite gracious in their hospitality when Charlotte and Maxwell had visited, so the girls did have someone close by to keep an eye on them.

Matt hadn't shown up at the station this morning. Caroline's disappointment had been hard to miss, but it was the best thing for her. The sooner she got that cowboy out of her system, the sooner she'd find another young man who really cared about her and would make a good home for her.

She sat down on Caroline's bed and picked up a lacy pillow, one of the few things left behind. Charlotte's fingers traced the rose design in the lace. She had this pillow made for Caroline when they redid her room when she was in first year of what they now called secondary school. Eight years ago her daughter had been a happy girl, eager to explore the offerings of the university in Norman.

No matter what objections Charlotte raised, Caroline had insisted she'd return to Barton Creek and marry Matt Haynes someday. That happy girl had grown into one who moped about the house waiting for Sundays and times she would see Matt in church or in town.

A knock on the doorframe sounded, and Charlotte looked up to see Maxwell standing there. He made his way to her side and knelt there on the floor.

"Charlotte, this was the best thing for our girl. She'll renew old acquaintances and meet new people there in Oklahoma City."

"I know, but it's so quiet and empty without the children."

Maxwell rubbed the back of her hand with his thumb. "And I brought you out here to this barren land thinking we could build a good life here. I was wrong. My dream was fulfilled, but yours has never materialized. I'm so sorry I chased away that fun-loving, happy young woman I married."

Her back stiffened. "Whatever do you mean, Maxwell? Of course I couldn't stay young and fun-loving, with the responsibilities of motherhood and being a mayor's wife." Her heart mourned the loss of the young woman she'd been, but to think that Maxwell missed her too sent daggers of guilt deep into her soul. She had done nothing to make his life easier as mayor of Barton Creek, and she had alienated many of the good women in town and on the ranches.

He stretched up and kissed her forehead and then her cheek. "I love you, Charlotte, and never forget that. You're a good woman down deep. I just wish the rest of Barton Creek could see it."

He stood then and walked from the room, leaving her to sit and ponder his words. Her fingers touched the cheek where his lips had rested. It'd been so long since the last time he'd kissed her on the lips, but he loved her despite what she'd become.

She'd been bitter for so many years that she'd lost her way. People needed her apologies, but she wasn't ready to give them. She had learned to live in the world she had created for herself, and for her it was a safe world she wasn't ready to leave.

Chapter 5

*C*aroline awakened and sat up in bed. Her head pounded with pain, and her mouth may as well have been filled with cotton. She massaged her temples with her fingers and wished she had not stayed up until the wee hours of the morning. She and her friends from college days had spent the last two evenings recalling events and pranks of those times. Not accustomed to such a loss of sleep, Caroline paid the price with a headache. Still, she had to get up and prepare for her first day as a library assistant.

Madeline popped her head around the door. "Oh, good, you're awake. I wasn't sure you'd hear the alarm clock, so I came to check."

Caroline moaned and dropped her head to her knees, now drawn up to her chest. Why did Madeline have to talk so loud? "I didn't hear it. The pounding in my head woke me up." She lifted her head just enough to peer at Madeline through the narrow slits of her eyelids. Never had such pain assaulted her, not even when she had broken her arm as a child.

"Oh my, I'll be right back." Madeline disappeared from the doorway then returned only moments later with a glass of water.

She sat on the side of the bed and handed Caroline the glass and a piece of folded paper. "Here is a packet of aspirin powder I got from my doctor for headaches. It'll send the pain scurrying in no time."

Caroline grasped the water glass with one hand and held the

powder packet in the other. She managed to slip the powder into her mouth then followed it with a long drink of water to dispel the bitter taste of the aspirin. She handed the glass back to Madeline. "Thank you. I hope it works." She shoved back the covers. "Now I have to get up and get dressed. I don't want to be late on my first day."

"Of course not, but you have plenty of time. It's only six-thirty, and the library doesn't open until nine. Rest a little longer, and I'll go fix breakfast for us. Julia is already up, and she'll be ready to eat too." Madeline left the room and closed the door.

Caroline reached over and turned on the lamp. If she lay back down, she'd go back to sleep until noon. Best to get up and get dressed. Already the pain had begun to ease, so she gathered up what she needed and headed for the bathroom she shared with her friends.

Julia greeted her in the hallway, her ebony hair perfectly groomed, her face shining and ready to meet the day. Her cheery "Good morning" brought forth a grimace. "I don't know that it's so good for me."

"We shouldn't have kept you up so late. We do it all the time, so it doesn't bother us anymore. You'll get used to it." She continued on to the kitchen.

One look at herself in the mirror and Caroline groaned. What a face to wear to meet her new employer and her co-workers. They'd think she'd been partying all night. Well, that was partly the truth, but it didn't have to be so evident that she'd missed her sleep. After splashing cold water over her eyes and cheeks, she dried her face then picked up her brush to tame her wild locks.

After a thorough brushing, her hair lay in smooth waves about her shoulders, and the pain had all but disappeared. The day looked a lot brighter than it had half an hour ago, and wonderful smells enticed her taste buds. She pinned her hair up and secured it with combs on the sides.

In the kitchen Julia and Madeline both sat at the table sipping coffee. Madeline grinned and reached for the pot to pour a mug of coffee for Caroline. "I must say you look better than when I saw you in bed."

"I feel better too. Thank you for the headache powder. I've never had to use anything before." She didn't depend on medication for any ailment; although this morning it had been a welcome relief, she didn't intend to make it a habit. "Last night was fun, even though the results this morning are not."

Julia reached for a muffin and grinned. "You certainly made a hit with Stuart and Philip."

"It's weird, but I barely remember them from the university. I know we were all involved in some of the same activities, but most of the boys are just a blur." Of course her mind had always been on Matt, so she had not made any effort to attract any of the young men. What a waste of four years of her social life. She counted on one hand the number of dates during those four years. It wasn't that she hadn't been asked, but the interest hadn't been there.

Madeline emptied her cup into the sink and rinsed it out. "And I wonder why that was? Really, Caroline, we hope you plan to participate socially more than you did then. Not many unmarried young men grace these parts, but we do have some very nice, eligible ones in our circle of friends."

That was the reason for her being here instead of Barton Creek, and she intended to make the most of her opportunities. Matt must be banished to the recesses of her memory and replaced with new ones. "I plan to do just that. In fact, Stuart asked to take me out to dinner this Friday, and I said I would be delighted to have dinner with him."

Julia and Madeline both squealed and hurried to her side to hug her. They both talked at once, and Caroline laughed at their enthusiasm. "My gracious, you sound like I just accepted a proposal of marriage." It was only one date after all.

Caroline grabbed a muffin and buttered it. She ate and listened to Madeline and Julia talk about all the things they had planned for the next few weeks. If they kept up a pace like that, Caroline would have to adjust her sleeping habits and outlook on life, but then that's what she looked forward to and wanted to accomplish in the months ahead. She wanted nothing left of her old way of life in Barton Creek.

Mellie washed the dishes and set them on the counter to dry. She had to bite her tongue this morning to keep from scolding Matt, but she had to remember he was not a child but a grown man. Still she had considered it poor manners not to go to the station Saturday to say good-bye to Caroline. The poor girl had searched all over for him, and the look of disappointment on her face was enough to make Mellie want to cry.

For so many years she had figured that both her children would marry a Frankston. Becky had done just that, but Matt seemed to be avoiding marriage much like he avoided rattlesnakes out on the range. Despite Charlotte's rudeness and unfriendly attitude, Mellie had to admire the courage it took to let her only daughter leave Barton Creek for life in Oklahoma City. Of course Mellie had let Becky go off to Boston, but she'd been there with family and to attend school. Caroline's departure was completely different.

Since her going-away party, Matt had nothing to say about Caroline or the fact that she was gone. Still, Mellie sensed a deep regret in her son, but he would be the last one to admit to any feelings for Caroline or anyone else. He made up for his apparent lack of emotion with an uncanny ability to solve problems on the ranch and take care of business. He'd been the first one to realize something was not right with a few head of cattle. His quick thinking had separated the sick animals from the rest of the herd and prevented an epidemic.

Mellie sighed and shook her head. Matt may be content to spend the rest of his days helping his pa manage the ranch, but she prayed every day for him to find a nice girl, marry, and start a home and family of his own. With the events of the past few weeks, the likelihood of that happening grew less the older he became. She'd have to look to Becky to provide any grandchildren in the near future, and she was already on the way with the first one.

The front door opened, and Mellie hurried into the living room to find Lucy with Amanda in her arms. "Oh my, what a nice surprise." She held out her hands to Amanda, and the child wrapped her arms around Mellie. She kissed the golden curls on the baby's head. Here she'd been bemoaning the fact she had no grandchildren yet, and here was her niece with Amanda, who may as well be a grandchild, as well as her brothers, Micah and Charley. God had blessed Lucy with the three little ones, and Mellie loved them as her own.

Mellie led Lucy to the kitchen. "I'm so glad you dropped by. I've been thinking about Matt and Caroline all morning. I saw how terribly disappointed she was when he didn't go to the station to tell her good-bye." She handed Amanda back to Lucy. "I'll make us some tea."

Lucy jiggled Amanda on her lap. "That will be nice. I saw Caroline's disappointment too. As long as they've known each other, I was sure they'd be married by now."

"I've been mulling it over in my mind and have come to the

conclusion that my son isn't interested in marriage to Caroline. I'm not sure if he'll ever want to settle down with a wife and family of his own." Mellie busied herself with filling the teapot with hot water from the back of the stove and steeping the tea.

"He will someday. He's only twenty-seven, so he isn't in any rush. Maybe he's afraid Caroline won't like ranch life after growing up in town and having things done for her. Jake told me that's one of the reasons he didn't want to fall in love with me, but then look how I turned out." A wide grin spread across Lucy's face.

"Oh, how well I remember that, and you did just fine. I believe Caroline would too if he gave her half a chance. It's so hard to have patience and wait for the Lord to work things out, especially when he puts all those miles between those two young people." Mellie poured two cups of tea and brought them to the table then reached for a plate of cookies.

Lucy handed Amanda a cookie. "The reason for my visit has to do with Aunt Hilda. Becky has asked her to move into town when the baby comes and be a nanny when Becky goes back to the newspaper."

Mellie bit her lip. Lucy's aunt from Boston had been in town a little over a year, but she had become well loved even though her husband had once tried to harm Lucy. Mellie had finally accepted the fact that the widow Hilda was nothing like her husband had been. If Becky had her mind set on continuing with the newspaper after the baby's arrival, Hilda would do well as a nanny. That was her choice, but Mellie would much rather see Becky stay at home and care for her family as the other Haynes women had done.

"That's good, I suppose, but what will you do?"

Lucy laughed. "With Charley and Micah in school, there's really not enough for two women to do around our place.

Without any children of her own, Hilda is excited to be helping Becky with the new baby." She hugged Amanda. "And this little girl loves Aunt Hilda, don't you, sweetie?"

The little girl grinned and tilted her head. "Love Aunt Hilda." Then she pointed to Mellie. "I love Aunt Mellie too."

Mellie's heart melted at the smile on Lucy's youngest child's face. She loved all three of the children, and having Becky's would only add to her joy. She leaned over and kissed Amanda's cheek. "And Aunt Mellie loves Amanda very much."

She straightened and then worried with the napkin by her cup. "Becky has done well, but of course I worry that Charlotte Frankston may be one reason that Matt holds back."

Lucy wiped cookie crumbs from Amanda's mouth and placed the teacup out of the child's reach. "That may well be, but if his love is strong enough, that shouldn't make a difference. She and Becky seem to get along all right."

"I think it's more like Charlotte tolerates Becky than anything else, and of course Becky won't let anything or anyone stand in the way of what she really wants. My daughter does have a way of ruffling feathers, but then she's usually able to smooth things over with her charm and wit. Matt, on the other hand, is the strong, silent type and is very sensitive to the attitudes of others."

Her son had grown from the rambunctious little boy who loved horses into a very serious businessman, determined to be as successful at ranching as his father. He still enjoyed a good time, as she had seen when he was with Hank and the other cowboys on the ranch, but it hadn't carried over to his personal life.

Mellie planted the palms of her hands on the table. "I just thought of something. Charlotte and I are going to be grandmothers to the same child. I think it's about time I made an effort to really get to know Becky's mother-in-law. Perhaps if I do, I can better understand her behavior."

Lucy laughed and hugged Amanda to her chest. "I think that's a marvelous idea—just the thing to soften her sharp edges. At least it's worth a try."

Yes, it was worth a try, and if she could become friends with Charlotte, the path may be smoother for their children. At the moment anything would be better than the misery she had seen in Matt's and Caroline's eyes on more than one occasion. She'd start with Becky and see what her daughter knew about her mother-in-law before she and the mayor settled in Barton Creek, but finding a time to do that would be the first hurdle to overcome.

Matt spotted Jake Starnes across a group of cattle he was herding and waved. "Jake, good morning." He rode up to Jake's side and pushed back the brim of his hat. "Looks like we have a good bunch to take down to Fort Worth."

"Yep, Ben's pretty sure they'll bring in a tidy sum, but I'm not going with him."

"What I heard. Looks like you're going out for more horses instead of cattle."

Jake shrugged his shoulders and gazed across at the cattle dotting the landscape. "I'll keep a finger in the cattle pie, but horses are more to my liking. Your pa, Sam, and you can handle the cattle business around here." He lifted a hand and pointed toward a group of steer being herded back toward the Haynes's ranch. "That bunch is going to Barstow's packing company in Chicago. He really likes our beef."

"Good, that's what I came over to check. Pa's sending two of our best to ride up there with the stock. I guess I'll be going down to Fort Worth with the others."

Matt rode beside Jake in silence for a ways. So many questions filled his mind, but none seemed the right one to start. After mulling over his choices for a few moments, he blurted out the one he hadn't intended to ask until much later.

"Jake, how did you know you loved Lucy enough to marry her?"

"Whoa now, that's a loaded question." He pulled on his reins, brought his horse to a stop, and grinned. "I think I fell in love with Lucinda Bishop the moment I saw her waiting at the depot in town."

"Yeah, but how did you know it was enough love for a lifetime?"

Jake leaned on the horn of his saddle and tilted his hat with his thumb. "I believe it was when I thought I'd never see her again. My heart hurt so bad, I thought it would bust wide open."

Matt had seen that kind of love between his parents. Even Becky had only adoring looks for Rob. Everyone must be in love but him, but then he did care about Caroline and always had.

Jake cleared his throat, and a knowing grin spread across his lips. "This about Caroline Frankston?"

"What if it is?"

"Then you have some explaining to do as to why you weren't at the station to say good-bye." He pulled his hat back down on his forehead and turned his horse to follow the herd.

Ma's eyes held that same accusation when she returned from the depot and again this morning at breakfast. He didn't need to explain to anyone but Caroline, but even then he didn't have the words she wanted to hear.

Then the question that always hid itself in the far recesses of his thoughts popped to the surface again. Would he have already asked Caroline to be his bride years ago if her name wasn't Frankston?

Chapter 6

*C*aroline smiled and handed a student the research book he requested. "This should give you all the information you need for your study."

The young man thanked her and hurried away to settle at one of the tables already stacked with other books and papers. She gazed about the room and marveled at the number of students busy with their studies. Only a week on the job, and Caroline had grown to love the library and those who used it.

Although the first few days had been spent reviewing the Dewey decimal system, she'd seen how many students came in every day. Excitement buzzed among the young men and women as they worked. With the fall semester well underway, many of them pored over materials for research projects. Caroline remembered those from her days as a student and welcomed the opportunity to assist them in the quest for information.

The watch pinned to her bodice reminded Caroline that Stuart would be along soon to take her to dinner. She ran her hands over her cinnamon-colored skirt to smooth out imaginary wrinkles. Not exactly date attire, but it did accentuate her narrow waist, and the braid trim on it and the jacket would give a more formal appearance. Besides, it would have to do since she worked later on Friday evenings and Stuart had insisted on picking her up here.

She retreated to the employees' room set aside for women and retrieved her purse. Just enough time for a quick touch-up for her hair. She gazed into the mirror and tucked in a few dangling strands of hair and pinned them, then pinched her cheeks to add a bit of color. Upon her return to the main room, she spotted Stuart by the front entrance and hurried toward him.

"Hello, Stuart, I hope I haven't kept you waiting long."

His grin warmed her heart. "Of course not. I just arrived." He reached for her hand and tucked it under his arm. "I've made reservations for seven, so we must hurry along."

Caroline waited for tingles, shocks, or even heat when he took her hand into his, but nothing happened. It could have been Rob or even Father beside her. A sigh escaped, and she shot Stuart a quick glance. His facial expression didn't change, so perhaps he hadn't heard. The spicy aroma of his aftershave penetrated her senses. Not an unpleasant smell, it reminded her again of how much attention young men in the city paid to their personal appearance.

She stole another quick glance at Stuart as they walked down the street. His clean-shaven face revealed a firm jaw and high cheekbones. A black felt hat covered his brown hair, and a sack coat fit with perfect precision over his broad shoulders.

No matter what happened the rest of the evening, she would try her best to concentrate on the man at her side and not on Matt Haynes. Even as she resolved to focus away from Matt, his face filled her thoughts. Friday night in Barton Creek meant he might be in town for the weekly dance and festivities at the town hall. Mother and her committee had planned it to give young couples an activity in town, and Matt usually showed up along with Hank and a few others from neighboring ranches.

A hand squeezed hers, and she jerked her gaze up to Stuart.

He grinned down at her, his eyes filled with amusement. "You're a million miles away, Caroline. Thinking of home?"

"No, I mean yes. Oh, I don't know. My thoughts just

rambled." She bit her lip. What a rude way to act on the first date with a nice young man. He'd never ask her out again. She must learn to be better company for young men or she would never find a husband.

"Then I'll have to do something to rectify that." The smile flashed again as they stopped in front of a restaurant Caroline had heard about from her parents. She hesitated a moment, thinking of her plain attire. Then she squared her shoulders and strolled through the leaded glass door he held open for her. After all, she was a Frankston, and such places as this restaurant were not foreign to her.

Stuart addressed the man at the reservation desk. "Reservations for two, Whittington."

The host nodded and led them to a table, where he held Caroline's chair for her. She smiled and murmured her thanks then settled into the seat. Sparkling crystal chandeliers reflected in the windows gave the room a warm glow. Maroon napkins, folded into a triangular shape, sat on silver charger plates accented by silver flatware on snowy white tablecloths. Sheer elegance in the surroundings followed through in the names of the foods on the menu.

Stuart ordered for them both. "I hope you don't mind my ordering for us. Everything they serve here is delicious, but in my years of dining experience, I've developed a few favorites."

"I don't mind at all, as it saves me from having to make a decision." Indeed, seeing all the choices had overwhelmed her at first. Although she preferred ordering for herself, this time she appreciated Stuart's initiative.

He nodded to the waiter, who promptly filled their wine glasses. Caroline swallowed hard. She had to refuse the drink, but she didn't want to embarrass Stuart either. "May I also have a glass of water?"

The waiter scurried away but returned moments later with a crystal pitcher of iced water and filled her glass. When he left, Caroline toyed with the glass and felt the heat rise in her cheeks. "Stuart, I'm sorry, but I prefer not to have any wine."

Again that amusement flashed in his eyes. "I understand, Caroline, and it's perfectly all right. I've developed a taste for it at mealtimes. Maybe you will after a while."

Caroline didn't think so, but there was no need to argue with him now. One thing she'd noticed the night of her arrival was that Madeline and Julie both had served and consumed wine. That was one habit she didn't intend to pick up. She'd seen what excessive drinking did to people, and she wanted no part of that.

Several people stopped by their table, and Stuart introduced her to them as the daughter of the mayor of Barton Creek, one of the fastest-growing towns in northern Oklahoma. Most had heard of the town and expressed delight on meeting her. She recognized a few of the names as those she had seen in the paper in connection with Oklahoma politics.

Caroline smoothed the napkin in her lap. "You must know a great number of people here in the city."

"As an attorney and the son of a state representative, I make it my business to know people. I have my eye set on politics like my father. He's certain that statehood is mere weeks away, and new positions in the government will open up. I've heard that your father was interested in a state legislative seat."

"That's true, although he hasn't talked much about it lately."

"I met your father at one of our committee meetings, but he may not remember me." He sipped from his glass and peered at her over the edge.

Heat filled her cheeks at his intense observation. "I'm sure he will. That's one of the things that has made him such a good mayor. Father meets people and remembers their names and some fact about them. The next time he sees that person, he calls him or her by name and then makes some comment about the fact he knows." Talking about him now caused a lump to form in her throat.

"And that's also why he'll be an asset in the state legislature. He'll work for the good of the people, and he'll be sure to know what they want." He leaned forward a bit and raised an eyebrow. "And what are your feelings concerning impending statehood?"

Caroline's eyes opened wide for a moment. No one had ever asked her opinion, and she'd certainly never offered one except around a few friends. She paused for a moment to gather her thoughts for an intelligent answer.

"Statehood will be the best thing for us. Being a part of what is already a grand republic will bring many advantages to our land. Men like my father and Sam Morris have forged ahead and made Oklahoma a great place to live, and she has a rich heritage of both Indians native to the land and people who traveled long distances to stake out a future here."

By the look on Stuart's face, he was as surprised as she by her answer. At that moment the server set the first course before them. Talk then turned to the food, and through the rest of the meal no more mention was made of Oklahoma's impending statehood. Becky had been more of an influence than Caroline realized. Being able to express her opinion and not be scorned filled her with courage. Being independent had its rewards.

Stuart placed his napkin beside his plate. "Caroline, this has been a most enjoyable evening." He hesitated then grinned. "Would you be so kind as to be my escort for the inaugural ball in Guthrie when we become the great state of Oklahoma?"

A small gasp escaped, and Caroline's hand pressed against her chest. "It will be an honor to attend the ball with you." All earlier thoughts of homesickness vanished, replaced by visions of ball gowns, elegant surroundings, and a handsome escort.

Matt sat on a bunk and laughed while Hank polished his boots. "You're really getting spiffed up for just a Friday night in town. Must want to impress Amy tonight."

"Maybe I do, but it sure beats sitting around here all the time, jawing with a bunch of cowhands." Hank laid aside the polishing cloth and pulled on his boots. He shook his head at Matt. "I don't understand why you don't ask a girl and have a good time. Caroline's gone, and it's time for you to socialize."

If anyone but Hank had scolded him, Matt would have put him down in a hurry. He and Hank had been friends and partners for too many years for Matt to consider the words as anything but pure concern. He wrinkled his nose as Hank splashed an amber liquid over his fresh-shaven face.

"What's that stuff you're using? Smells like Ma's spice cabinet."

Hank laughed and patted his cheeks. "It's some new shaving lotion I bought in town at the barber shop. Stings at first, but then it feels good on the skin, and the girls seem to like it." He tossed the bottle toward Matt. "Oughta try it yourself."

"No thanks. I'll just go with soap and water."

Hank picked up his hat and set it on his head. "You coming with me, or you gonna sit there all night?"

"Guess I'll come with you. Ma's been after me to get out more, so this will get her off my back." One night in town would not make a difference one way or the other with Ma, but at least he could say he made the effort. Besides, he needed something to get his mind off Caroline.

The ride into town was silent with only small talk about the cattle and shipping a group off to auction soon. Matt wanted to ask Pa about going with the herd down to Fort Worth, but if he did, Ma would read more into it than she should. But she'd be right. He figured if he went with the herd, he'd have an excuse to call on Caroline when they stopped in Oklahoma City. One part of his heart wanted her to be successful, but one little part held back and wished for her to come home to Barton Creek.

He lifted his head and breathed deeply of the crisp fall air. The temperatures had finally dropped from the eighties down to a pleasant daytime level and cool evenings. Just a few more weeks until November, and that usually brought on the first cold spell. Cooler weather also meant preparations for the winter ahead with getting enough feed for the livestock from the hayfields and moving them to winter pasture.

Music and rousing voices drew Matt's attention. Many horses lined Main Street in addition to a number of buggies and wagons. Singles as well as couples made their way to the town hall, the center of social life in Barton Creek. Men now outnumbered the women in town as the oil company hired young men to work the oil rigs out on the Dawson land. A few married couples had moved in as well, but Geoff Kensington preferred hiring single men who didn't have families to worry about.

Hank slapped Matt on the back. "I see Amy, so you're on your own. Have a good time. I'll see you back at the ranch."

Matt waved at Amy, who waited near the door of the town hall. Hank removed his hat and grasped Amy's arm before leading her into the building. A ripple of jealousy rolled across Matt's heart. Caroline had once looked at him with adoring eyes as Amy did at Hank. He shook off the feeling and headed for the music and gaiety.

Men and women lined the walls, and several couples made

their way to the dance floor. As the fiddles and bass swung into a rousing rendition of "Turkey in the Straw," Sheriff Claymore headed for Matt. The man had been sheriff as long as Matt could remember, and although he was close to seventy, he had the build and stamina of a much younger man. His wife ran the town boarding house, so he knew just about everything that went on in town. Claymore stood a head taller than most of the men and eye to eye with Matt. The lawman's shirt strained across his shoulders, and his badge glinted in the lamplight.

He stretched forth one hand and with the other clapped Matt on the shoulder. "Good to see you, Matt. Looks like we'll have a good crowd here tonight. I have two of my deputies over there watching the punch. Mrs. Frankston will have my head if anyone manages to put anything other than fruit juice in it."

Mrs. Frankston wouldn't tolerate drinking of any kind at these events. Her efforts to shut down the saloon had met with defeat, but she was determined to control what went on elsewhere.

"That's not a bad idea, Sheriff. No sense in letting this crowd get unruly. If they want to drink, let them go over to the saloon. I'm all for keeping it clean and peaceful here."

"Thought you would be." He glanced around the room. "You here with any particular young lady?"

"Nope. Just came to enjoy the music and the fun." Of course that didn't mean he wouldn't dance with a young lady or two if given the chance. Most were several years younger than he, but age didn't seem to matter at all at these socials. Still, none had the blue eyes and blonde beauty of Caroline. He held her image in his mind for a moment before the sheriff squeezed his shoulder.

"I imagine you'd like to have Miss Caroline here, but there's a mighty sweet young thing who'd like to have your attention for the evening. Catherine heard her talking about you with one of the other boarders at dinner the other night. Might ought to ask her to dance later on."

Matt only nodded as Claymore ambled away with a sly grin on his face. The girl he spoke about had to be the new school-teacher. Sweet young thing or not, no one would be matchmaking him with any woman he didn't choose for himself. He decided to have one dance then head on home. With his mind set, he strode to the refreshment table.

Chapter 7

Caroline opened one eye and peered at the clock on the table beside her bed. She blinked and looked again. That couldn't be right. She sat up straight and grabbed the clock. Sure enough, it was after ten in the morning. She'd already missed Sunday school and would never be able to get ready for church in time.

She pushed back the covers and jumped from the bed. She grabbed her robe and ran into the hall. "Julia, Madeline? Are you up yet? Why didn't you wake me?"

Muffled sounds came from behind each door, and Caroline realized neither girl had awakened. She'd assumed they would be up early this morning to attend church and had not set her own clock to awaken her early. She opened Madeline's door.

Her roommate still lay in bed buried beneath the quilt. "Why aren't you up and getting ready for church?"

Madeline pushed the cover down to her nose and peered at Caroline through narrowed eyes. "We decided to sleep in this morning since it was so late when we went to bed. Besides, I have a terrible headache. Just let me sleep." She plopped over and pulled the quilt back over her head.

Dismayed, Caroline strode into the kitchen and grimaced at the unwashed dishes in the sink and the leftovers on the table. Empty wine bottles poked out of the trash bin. They reminded her of her first taste of wine last night and how bitter it had been. She much preferred the new drink, Coca Cola, which she had for the first time this past week. At least she had put away the perishable items before she retired last night.

They had been up late, but she had gone to bed first. Madeline and Julia had stayed up because Andy and Steve were still there. No telling what time they had left. Having young men stay so late without a chaperone, even in these days, was more than Caroline could accept. She reached for the percolator and prepared it for her morning coffee. Living in the city certainly brought on unexpected changes.

If her mother knew the hours they had kept these days, she'd be calling for Caroline to come home immediately. Perhaps she could be an influence on her friends in some way. She didn't like missing church, but there was nothing she could do about it this morning.

She set about to tidy up the kitchen while the coffee perked. After throwing away the trash and food scraps, she wiped the tables and counters clean and put away the now clean dishes.

The aroma of fresh-perked coffee filled the air and caused Caroline's stomach to rumble with hunger. She grabbed a cup and filled it, then found a muffin in the bread box to ease her hunger. With food in hand, she wandered into the front parlor. A gasp escaped from her mouth at the sight that greeted her.

If she had thought the kitchen was bad, this was worse. Dirty dishes, empty glasses, and cups, napkins, and silverware covered the side tables as well as the floor. How could eight people have made such a mess? Such clutter and disorder soured Caroline's stomach. She set her coffee and muffin on the dining table and proceeded to pick up the trash and plates left behind. This wasn't the way she had envisioned spending her Sunday mornings, but at least it gave her something to do since she had missed church.

When she finished in the parlor, she checked the time on her watch. An hour and a half had passed since she arose. Surely her roommates knew it was closing in on noon. Caroline hurried back to Madeline's room and knocked on the door.

"Madeline, it's almost noon. Don't you want to get up now?" She eased the door open just as Madeline jumped from the bed.

"Oh, my, I didn't intend to sleep this long. Steve will be here at one. We're going out to Belle Isle Park for the afternoon." She stopped and pressed her fingers to her temples. "Oooh, I need one of my headache powders." She pushed past Caroline and headed for the bathroom.

Julia's door opened, and she poked her head out. "Don't be long, Madeline. I have to get ready for Andy. He'll be here with Steve." She retreated into her room and closed the door.

Caroline shook her head. It looked like she'd be spending the afternoon alone. She shrugged and headed for her own room. After making the bed, she plopped onto it and rested her chin in her palms. What did one do with oneself on a lonely Sunday afternoon in the city?

After Sunday dinner with the family, Becky grabbed Matt's hand. "Come with me. Ma and Lucy are taking care of the dishes, and Jake and Rob are with the boys, so I want a few minutes of your time."

Matt shook his head and let her lead him to the parlor. He eased into a chair and crossed his legs, one ankle resting on his knee. "All right, sis, what's so urgent that you drag me away from my cousins?"

She slapped at his arm then held out a sheet of paper. "You are incorrigible, big brother. I wanted to share some news from Caroline with you."

Caroline? His throat closed, and perspiration wet his palms.

He started to stand but kept his seat. He didn't really want to hear if she had already found someone new or was having fun in her new surroundings, but curiosity took over. "What does that have to do with me?"

She grinned and smoothed out the letter. "Oh, I just thought you might be interested. She loves her job at the library, and because of the students, she gets to help with research. Madeline and Julia keep her busy with all the things they have planned. She misses us here in Barton Creek, but it's nice to renew her old acquaintances from college days."

Matt swallowed hard to control his feelings and his voice before commenting. "It's unusual that so many of them would be unmarried at their age." He should have thought a little longer. That sounded rather stupid to him.

Becky simply laughed. "And you forget that you're their age and you're not married either? Not everyone gets married right out of high school or college these days. More women are finding careers for themselves first."

"Hmm. Didn't take you long to decide on marriage."

"Well, you don't find too many men like Rob around. He loves me enough to let me do what I love doing and take care of our home too."

Matt lifted his gaze. "The baby might change all that."

She reached over and knuckled his knee as she had done so often when they were children and she wanted his attention. "Don't try to change the subject. I want to know if you plan to go see Caroline. I can read between the lines, and I know she misses you."

From what he'd heard, Caroline didn't have that much time to miss him. Still he wanted to see for himself where she lived and what she was doing. "If you'll give me her address, I might decide to write to her."

Becky squealed. "I knew it. You do still care about her. I told Rob you did. I just wish you'd do something about it." She handed him the envelope. "Here, her return address is on it. Take it and write her a letter. You won't be sorry."

He didn't know about that, but he grasped the envelope then folded it and stuffed it into his shirt pocket. He stood and stretched. "Now, if that's all you wanted, I'm going to find my cousins. They can't play ball without me."

Micah and Charley had been crazy about the Oklahoma City Metropolitan baseball team last summer and pestered Jake to teach them how to catch. Neither Jake nor Matt knew much about the game of baseball, but they were willing to learn for the sake of Micah and Charley.

He found them in the backyard tossing a baseball back and forth. Micah spotted him and came running to jump into Matt's arms. "Hey, Matt, you come to throw balls to me?"

Matt hugged the boy then set him on the ground. "Sure. I bet you're really getting good now with all this practice." The mild October temperatures made for a perfect afternoon to spend time with the two boys. Jake and Lucy's boys were growing so fast that they'd be too big to worry about playing with him or Rob in a few years.

The rest of the afternoon passed in a blur of playing ball and then wrestling and rolling in the grass. All the time he played, the folded envelope in his pocket reminded him of what he needed to do, but he'd have to figure out the words to say that wouldn't raise Caroline's hopes until he figured out for himself exactly how he felt about her.

Charlotte stood at the window in her parlor. Maxwell had retired to his study to brush up on some proposals to be presented at the town council meeting in a few days. The days had grown so lonely without Caroline. A tear rolled down Charlotte's cheek, and she brushed it away with a finger.

This was the best thing for her daughter. According to her last letter, she'd already had a dinner date with the son of a member of the legislature of the Territory. Maxwell knew the man and had met him on several occasions when he was in Guthrie to see how the statehood committee was coming along.

Meanwhile Charlotte filled her time with meetings of the Mission Society and Altar Guild at church, the Civic Improvement Committee, and the committee for planning special events and celebrations for Barton Creek. But even with all the things she could find to do, loneliness set in when she came home. She had made friends with Marie Fleming, the banker's wife, and Anna White, the doctor's wife, but they were busy with their own families and didn't have the spare time for many leisurely visits.

She sighed and turned to find the baby blanket she had begun to crochet for her coming grandchild. This was Becky and Rob's Sunday to have dinner with her parents, so even Sunday dinner had been quiet.

The room had darkened, so she raised the wick in the oil lamp to give more light. In a few minutes her fingers flew with the crochet hook as she worked on the gift she planned to give Becky.

Maxwell entered the room and strode to her side. "I see you're getting something ready for the new baby."

She grinned and held up the multi-pastel afghan. "I thought I'd make it lots of different colors so it won't matter whether it's a boy or a girl."

Her husband sat beside her on the sofa. "It's very pretty. You should do more projects like this."

Her hands stopped their task, and she gazed at Maxwell. "I

hope Becky doesn't have a difficult time having the baby. Of course she's not blood kin to me, so she shouldn't have the same problems I had with Caroline and Rob, and…" She couldn't bear to bring up the sons they had lost.

Maxwell's arm encircled her shoulder. "She's a strong young woman, so things should go well for her."

His hand squeezed her arm, but he said nothing. He did remember the two babies who didn't live—one before Caroline, while they were in St. Louis, and then another before Rob. Rob would be the last, as she almost died, and the doctor had to end her ability to conceive. Maxwell's small gesture encouraged her with his love and concern. So many times she doubted his continuing love, but at times like this, once again he proved how much he cared.

"My dear, Becky has wonderful care under Dr. White, and I'm sure if there's a problem, he will be able to handle it with all the new equipment he has in the infirmary. With two nurses now, he's able to take care of more patients who need to stay there overnight."

She sighed and stuck the needle into the blanket then folded it so it wouldn't unravel. "I know, and for that I am most thankful." Charlotte reached over and grasped his hand. "I am so proud of you and all the wonderful improvements you have brought this town. When we first came here, I had my doubts, but we're growing in the right direction."

"Thank you, and I'm grateful to have had you by my side through it all." He paused a moment then said, "You miss Caroline more than you want to admit, don't you?"

"Yes, I do. I miss our late evening talks and reading together. Though I wish she were still here, I want what is best for her, and this seems to be it."

Maxwell kissed her cheek then stood and reached for her

hand. "Let's go upstairs. It's been a long day, and I'm ready for a good night's rest." He lowered the wick in the lamp then led her from the room.

In the entryway, he picked up a small lamp to light their way up the staircase. Charlotte bit her lip. Maxwell had always taken such good care of her, and she loved him so much. All these years she'd let her resentment about coming west fester and grow like a boil. In the seventeen years she had grown a sore that now demanded attention, but her heart wasn't ready to bear the pain of lancing the wound and letting out all the bitterness and heartache of those years.

Chapter 8

$\mathcal{C}$aroline changed from her work skirt and top to a heavier dark green brocade skirt and matching bodice trimmed in cream lace. Madeline and Julia had a special party planned for this evening to introduce Caroline to more of their friends. How those two young women loved to party. Of course, she had come to this place to meet more people, especially young men, and her friends hadn't disappointed her.

Guilt spread through her body with a chill that sent doubts to her heart because she hadn't attended church since arriving in the city. Caroline shook off the pangs. After all, she'd been busy settling in that first weekend, and last weekend she'd overslept. This Sunday would be different. She smoothed her hair and inserted another hairpin to corral a loose curl.

There was plenty of time to find a nice church to attend. None of the young people she had met thus far talked about church or religion or anything spiritual for that matter. Back home, church had been the center of social activities, but here that didn't seem necessary. Musicals, fine restaurants, and theaters provided plenty of entertainment.

With one last look in her mirror, Caroline deemed herself ready to meet guests. She reached the entryway just as the doorbell rang and the first guest arrived. An hour later the names and faces tumbled in her mind like rocks in a grinder. At least a few were not strangers, and she depended on them to provide conversation.

They had not planned a true meal but had hired a caterer to provide substantial refreshment. Caroline sampled a bit of beef in a pastry and nodded. Though not as good as what Ruby could prepare, the tidbit would satisfy the hunger of most of the people there.

"You ladies have done a wonderful job tonight."

Caroline whirled around to find Stuart Whittington standing by the table. "Oh, thank you, but we had it brought in by a caterer." Then she giggled. "Of course none of us really know the first thing about how to prepare food for a party. We can take care of basics, but nothing like this." Caroline had spent hours with Ruby learning the ins and outs of cooking, but food like this was beyond what she'd learned.

Stuart reached for a pastry and winked. "I'll never tell."

Caroline's knees almost buckled. So different from Matt, Stuart's clothing and grooming were impeccable. The only time she'd seen Matt anywhere near being dressed up was for church. She'd almost forgotten how well mannered and sophisticated college men could be.

Stuart added another pastry and a cookie to the array on his plate. "We'll keep your little secret and let everyone believe the three of you planned the menu and prepared the food." Then he glanced around the room. "This town house is much larger than it appears from the outside. Probably twenty or so people here, but it's not the least bit crowded."

"I think that's because of the open design. The dining room and parlor flow into each other, and only the kitchen is really set apart."

"Hmm, I suppose you're right." He set his plate on the sideboard and reached for her hand. "Caroline, would you do me the honor of dining with me again next Friday night?"

Her heart sank. As much as she'd like to go out with him

again, she couldn't. "I'm sorry, but I'm going to Barton Creek for the weekend. I promised Mother and Father I'd come home then." No need to tell him it was her birthday. He'd want an invitation, and she wasn't ready to introduce him to her family just yet.

"Then you must keep your promise to them. We can go out after you return. But don't forget, you said you'd attend the inauguration ceremonies and the ball with me when the time comes, and from what my father reports from the committee, it will be soon."

"Of course I won't forget that. My father is of the same opinion as yours. He can hardly wait for President Roosevelt to sign the papers. From what I've heard, Guthrie has big plans for the great occasion." All of her mother's letters had been full of news concerning the inaugural events. She and Father had their invitations and were ready to attend at a moment's notice. Mrs. Weems had been working on Mother's dress for weeks, as well as one for Caroline.

At that moment Madeline clapped her hands and called for everyone's attention. "We're going to play a few games and see how clever some of us are."

Caroline and Stuart moaned and groaned along with most of the other guests, although Caroline had prior information about a few of the games. She, Julia, and Madeline had spent time last evening coming up with ideas on how to stump their friends.

Madeline held up a silver spoon. "The first game is called Spoon Pictures. I'm going to send someone out of the room then take a picture of one of you with the spoon. The person will then come back into the room and look into the spoon and guess whose picture is there."

Stuart leaned close to Caroline and whispered, "Now that I would like to see."

"Oh, it's easy and fun." She held up her hand. "I'll be the first to go out and come back in to guess."

Madeline grinned then pointed to Philip. "You will be the one to take the pictures, and Caroline will be the one to guess whose picture you took." She handed the spoon to him, and Caroline left the room.

A few minutes later she was summoned to come back and guess. After studying the spoon a moment then gazing around the room, she pointed to a girl named Beth as the picture subject. As the guests exclaimed and wanted to know how it was done, Caroline grinned at Madeline and winked. "Anybody can do it. Julia, why don't you give it a try?"

Julia hopped up from her seat. "I'd love to. See you in a few minutes." She left the room and closed the door behind her. Caroline pointed to Stuart. "You take the picture this time and see if Julia can guess who it is."

Stuart grabbed the spoon and peered at each of the guests. He zeroed in on Philip and made a clicking sound with his tongue. "Now your picture is in the spoon. Let's see if Julia can see it." He grinned as if he'd played a great trick.

Caroline laughed and called for Julia to return. When Julia guessed correctly, everyone started talking at once and asking to have a turn. For the next half hour Caroline alternated taking pictures with a few others, but none of the players guessed the person in the spoon.

Finally Caroline held up the spoon. "It's time to reveal our secret. Julia, Madeline, and I aren't psychic, and we don't see things in spoons, but we do have a trick. When one of us comes back in, the other two sit exactly like the person whose picture was taken, and then the guess is easy."

A series of moans and groans and "no fair" comments coursed through the group, but then everyone began laughing at the trick played on them. Stuart sat beside Caroline and leaned over. "You had me going there for a minute; I was trying my best to see how you could see a picture in the spoon. That was fun."

"I'm glad you enjoyed it. Madeline has a few other games she found in a parlor game book, so don't be surprised if you're fooled again." She had looked over many of the games in the book herself, and all looked like they would be fun to do. Good food, good fun, and good fellowship brought on a peace Caroline hadn't felt in a long time. Yes, this move to the city had definitely been the best thing for her.

Matt followed Hank and Monk into the loading docks for the cattle and helped corral the animals into the proper spaces. They had managed to drive the herd from Barton Creek to the stockyards in Oklahoma City, where they would load the beef steer onto a train to take them on down to Fort Worth. His job with the cattle was finished for the moment, and he was ready for dinner.

Hank removed his hat and wiped his brow with his kerchief. "Sure would be nice if Oklahoma City had meat-packing companies here already. This would be the end of our trip instead having another four or five days on the road."

Matt reined in his horse beside Monk. "That would be nice, but that's at least a couple of years away." He frowned and rubbed his stomach. "I'm hungry as a bear after hibernation. Where are we going to eat?"

Hank pointed down the road. "There's a pretty good

restaurant that way. I've eaten there when we've come before. We can ride there and tie up our horses."

The cowboy led the way with Monk and Matt following. His first trip with the cattle to Fort Worth was easier than the ones he'd made in the past to Chicago with the cattle bought by Mr. Barstow. It only took the better part of the day to get them down from Barton Creek, and in another day they'd be in Fort Worth. The sale began on Monday, and Matt had confidence that this group would bring a good price.

Monk shook his head. "I had no idea so many folks in Oklahoma City had motorcars. They sure are noisy."

Hank laughed. "And smelly. Good thing we don't have more than half a dozen in Barton Creek. I'll take a horse any day over one of them contraptions."

Matt slowed his horse as they approached the restaurant. "I don't know about that. Been thinking of ordering one of them motorcars myself. Sure would be easier getting around town than a wagon or buggy." He swung down from the saddle and wrapped the reins around the hitching rail. "Now let's get us some grub."

During the meal Matt glanced at his watch several times. A Friday night, and no doubt Caroline would be busy, but he'd go by her place anyway. Pa had made reservations for them at a hotel for the night since the train wouldn't leave for Fort Worth until morning.

After they paid their checks, Matt went out to his horse. "I'll see you later this evening. I have some exploring I want to do."

Monk and Hank's laughter roared in the night air. "Wouldn't be planning to visit a certain Miss Frankston now, would you?" Hank slapped him on the back.

"And what if I am? No concern of yours." Matt hitched his leg over his saddle and tipped his hat. "Y'all have a nice evening."

Caroline's address burned in his memory. Fifteen anxious minutes later he climbed down from his horse and looped the reins through a hitching post. He walked down a few houses so that he stood across the street from the town house where Caroline lived. Lights shone through the downstairs windows, revealing a number of people inside. He observed for a few moments then moved back into the shadows when the door opened and a girl he recognized as Madeline stepped onto the stoop. Those who had been inside now spilled onto the street with laughter and loud talk. He noticed them pairing off and looked for Caroline. Then she was in the doorway in a dress as green as the emeralds he'd seen her mother wear. His heart skipped a beat, and his breath caught in his throat. She looked so beautiful, and her smile pierced his soul.

Then a young man appeared behind her and leaned close. Her laughter rang out with such a happy sound that he shivered. She walked down the few steps with the young man then stood facing him as he held her hands. Matt bit his lip hard to offset the pain that settled in his gut. She was having a good time and looked so happy. A moment later the young man squeezed her hands then walked away. Caroline remained on the stoop with her friends and bid their guests farewell.

With a heavy heart Matt moved through the shadows and back to his horse. He should never have come here. For years Caroline had waited patiently for him to declare himself, and now she had moved on to a new life. All the excuses he'd made now melted away like snow in the warmth of the sun and left only a cold emptiness in his heart.

A movement in the shadows across the street caught Caroline's eye just before she turned to go back into the house. A tall, lanky figure made his way down the street, avoiding the lights from the street lamps. Matt. He walked just like she remembered. She opened her mouth to call out but stopped. Matt was in Barton Creek, not Oklahoma City. Her mind played tricks on her.

She entered the house and turned again to see the figure, but it had disappeared into the night. Caroline swallowed the tears that threatened to fall and headed upstairs before Madeline or Julia could make a comment.

Matt's face swam before her eyes. She loved him so much that now she was seeing him when he wasn't there. No matter how much fun she had with Stuart and the others this evening, believing she had seen Matt brought up dozens of old memories. Instead of parlor games and good food, her head filled with images of him on horseback, strolling down the streets of Barton Creek, and sitting in the Haynes's family pew at church. She hugged her pillow and rocked back and forth on her bed. What was wrong with her? Why couldn't she put him out of her thoughts?

Next weekend would be a true test as to what her future may be. She'd give Matt another chance. That was the real reason she hadn't wanted Stuart to know about her birthday party. She wanted nothing or no one to distract her attention away from the cowboy who still owned her heart.

Chapter 9

*T*hrilled to be home for her birthday, Caroline descended the stairs to greet her father, waiting in the entry hall below. He smiled up at her with pride glowing from his blue-gray eyes. His usually ruffled white hair now lay neatly against his scalp, and his new dark gray sack suit showed nary a wrinkle. He held out his hand to assist her on the last step.

"You look beautiful as usual, my dear. I am so proud of you."

She leaned toward him and kissed his cheek. "Thank you, Father, but I do believe you're somewhat prejudiced in your thinking."

"Now, Caroline, you know that's not true…well, perhaps it is, but I mean it."

Mother stepped into the entryway, pulling on a pair of black leather gloves. "I went over to the town hall, and it looks magnificent." She twirled her fingers. "Turn around so I can see the full effect of Mrs. Weems's work."

Caroline pivoted around with satisfaction. The seamstress had outdone herself this time with the royal blue taffeta dress trimmed in ecru lace. The rounded neck of the bodice showed off her creamy white skin while still being modest in its depth. She would have preferred not to wear a corset, but the narrow waist of the garment demanded it. If she could get through the evening without losing her breath or fainting, then the suffering would be worth it.

Father held out the matching cape then draped it across her

shoulders. Ruby's skills in the kitchen were outdone by her skills with hair dressing. Caroline patted the curls cascading from the crown of her head and pulled on a tendril left dangling in front of her ear. She reached up to check the security of the blue silk flowers Ruby had pinned in place atop the curls. Assured that all was well, she placed a gloved hand on her father's arm.

Father retrieved his hat from the hall table and led Caroline outside with Mother following behind. They boarded the motorcar and settled into its leather seats. Caroline would rather have walked the three blocks or so, but Father did like showing off his car, so they would ride to the town hall tonight. The maroon Buick chugged down the brick-laid Main Street. Several people waved as they passed by, and Caroline returned the greeting. How nice to be home among familiar faces and friends.

She regretted the fact that Julia and Madeline had not been able to come and celebrate with her, but Madeline's mother had taken ill. Of course her friend had to go home, and Julia and her beau had already planned something special for the evening. Julia wasn't such a close friend that she'd want to change her plans.

The motorcar pulled up in front of the town hall, and Caroline gasped. She stepped down from the car and gazed up at the decorations. A huge banner wishing her birthday greetings hung above the double doors, and a garland of orange, gold, and yellow fall flowers outlined the framing. When they stepped inside, many guests had already arrived and turned to greet her. Tables were laden with food and adorned with her favorite yellow and bronze chrysanthemums. Mother must have searched for days to come up with this many beautiful flowers. One table held a large tiered birthday cake and punch bowls.

"Oh, Mother, it's beautiful. Thank you so much. I had no

idea you'd go to such great lengths for my birthday, especially since you just gave me a going-away party three weeks ago." Besides, turning twenty-seven really wasn't something to celebrate, especially since it brought her closer to being thirty and still without a husband.

"Your birthday is always special, my dear child." She reached for Caroline's cloak. "Now go and enjoy yourself. Practically everyone in town is here."

After handing over her outer garments and gloves, Caroline gazed about the room at the smiling faces. Only one she didn't see, and that was the one she most wanted to be here.

Geoff Kensington and his wife, Ruth, made their way toward her. Geoff bowed when he reached her. "It's good to have you home, Caroline. Happy birthday."

Ruth smiled and hugged Caroline. "I want to hear all about your adventures in Oklahoma City before the evening is over."

"And you shall. It's been a most delightful few weeks there."

Becky and Rob stepped up to greet her, and Becky leaned over to hug Caroline. "Oh, it's so good to have you home. I've missed our little chats over tea and cookies at the bakery."

"It's good to be home, and I've missed you too." She stepped back and surveyed Becky at arm's length. "You're certainly looking like a mother-to-be. How much longer until our new little Frankston arrives?"

"The middle of December, so that's about another six weeks or so. And before you ask, I feel wonderful." She grinned at Rob standing beside her. "And your brother has been the most attentive husband I could ever hope for."

Rob laughed and kissed Caroline on the cheek. "Have to make sure our little heir or heiress is taken care of properly." He wrapped his arm around Becky's waist. "This is the best thing that's happened to me since our wedding."

Geoff clapped Rob on the shoulder. "And for a while there we were all wondering if that was ever going to happen."

Caroline listened to the chatter, but her eyes continued to roam the room looking for Matt. He'd been invited, and his parents had come, as well as Jake and Lucy, but he was nowhere to be seen. Her spirits fell and the smile she pasted on her face tightened with disappointment.

Becky must have noticed because she whispered in Caroline's ear, "He'll be here. He and Jake were late getting back from Fort Worth, but Jake said Matt planned to come. So don't let your hopes down."

Relief flooded Caroline's soul. He'd be here, so she'd have to be patient. "Thank you, Becky."

The two couples left, and several others came to offer her greetings and best wishes. Although her back was to the door, the moment Matt entered the room, Caroline sensed his presence. She dared not turn around and look for fear he'd ignore her. Her heart beat like a hammer in her chest, but she managed to keep her eyes straight ahead and her voice smooth as she chatted with her guests.

Charlotte Frankston spotted Matt as soon as he walked through the door. She rushed to his side. "I wasn't really expecting to see you tonight. I thought you were on a cattle run to Fort Worth."

Matt narrowed his eyes. "Jake and I returned home on the late afternoon train. I was invited, or was that invitation a mistake?"

Heat rose in her cheeks. "Of course you were invited. I just didn't think you'd make it."

"Well, I did. I wouldn't miss a party for Caroline. After all, we've been friends since we were in grade school." He hung his hat on a peg by the door then nodded to her. "If you'll excuse me, I see my sister and Rob." He strode across the room to greet them.

Charlotte stared after Matt as he made his way to Becky and Rob. He would ruin everything. Madeline had kept her informed as to what Caroline was doing in the city, and Charlotte had been elated to learn her daughter was seeing a statesman's son. He would be a much better match than that cowboy Matt Haynes. Besides, he let Caroline go on believing there might be a chance for them to be together one day. Even if he had declared his intentions, she would have tried to change her daughter's mind. Caroline had better opportunities than to be a rancher's wife.

She had been disappointed that Caroline hadn't invited Stuart Whittington tonight, but she couldn't voice her disappointment, as her daughter had made no mention of him in any of her letters. Madeline's reports must be kept quiet. If Caroline learned her mother had been spying, no amount of apologies would make up for it. Becky laughed and hugged her brother. No, two Hayneses in the family would be too many, although she had to admit that Matt had grown handsomer as he matured. Still, he was a cowboy and not the sort of husband she wanted for Caroline. If he spoiled the evening for Caroline, Charlotte would be even angrier with him.

"Charlotte, may I speak with you a moment?"

The voice at her elbow startled her. She jerked her head back at the sight of Mellie Haynes standing so close. Guilt coursed its way through her veins, but Mellie had no way of knowing her thoughts about Matt. Proper etiquette required her to respond with a smile.

"Of course, Mellie. How can I help you?" No matter what the woman wanted, Charlotte would try to accommodate her simply in order to keep peace. If anything happened to ruin the evening, it wouldn't be her doing.

"Ben and I will be in town after church tomorrow to have dinner with Becky and Rob. I was hoping that you might be available for a visit later in the afternoon."

Charlotte swallowed her surprise at the suggestion. Mellie Haynes had made a few efforts to be friendly in the past, but Charlotte always had some excuse for not visiting with her. However, a talk with her might be interesting. "I will be free after Caroline returns to Oklahoma City. Would two o'clock be all right with you?"

"Yes, that will be fine. Thank you, Charlotte. We do have much to talk about." She smiled and turned back to the party.

Now what could Mellie want to talk about? Of course, it had to be Becky and the coming baby. After all, they both would be grandmothers for the first time. Then again, she may want to discuss Matt and Caroline. Well, that was one subject she didn't care to discuss with anyone, especially Mellie Haynes.

After Mrs. Frankston's greeting and obvious objection to his presence, Matt wanted to leave, but he wouldn't give her the satisfaction of running him off. He listened to his sister tell of some escapade at the news office and marveled at the sparkle in her eyes. When she looked up at Rob, her face filled with so much love that it squeezed Matt's heart like a rope around a lassoed calf's hooves.

The fact that his little sister would soon be a mama filled him with a strange new longing to be a father himself. Sure, he'd wanted to be married before this. But just when he'd felt like he could consider taking a bride, Caroline had up and gone off to college. Even though she didn't know his thoughts about marriage, he had still felt the sting of rejection.

After she had come home, he had seen a change in her. She was no longer the simple small-town girl he had known but a young woman with poise and polish. Her mother quickly involved Caroline in all the activities of the town and kept her so busy that it seemed she had no time for him anymore. No doubt about it, Charlotte Frankston had run Caroline's life for her.

He pondered his situation and made the decision to be happy for Caroline and let her know that he wished her great success in Oklahoma City.

The time had come to speak to the honoree of this party. He turned to seek her out and found himself at once gazing into her eyes. She looked genuinely happy to see him as he strode across the room to offer his greetings.

"Good evening, Caroline. You look lovely, but then you always do."

Her cheeks flushed crimson, but a smile formed on her lips. She held her hand out to him. "Thank you for coming, Matt. It's always good to see you."

His resolve to wish her happiness and success almost dissipated, but he set his jaw with determination. "Becky tells me you are having a good time in the city. You must enjoy your job at the library."

"Yes, I do like it. I have the opportunity to meet so many interesting people who come looking for books to read or to do research." Her gaze locked with his, and her lips quivered for a moment. "I heard you went down to Fort Worth to sell some cattle."

"That's right. We loaded them onto the train at Oklahoma City then rode with them down to Fort Worth. We just arrived back on the early train. I have to say, your city is much bigger and busier than I would have ever thought."

Her eyes opened wide. "You were in Oklahoma City?"

"Only for the evening. We stayed at a hotel near the depot." He wouldn't dare tell her he'd been close to her home and had seen her with another man. Jealousy reared its head, but he refused to let it settle in his soul. Caroline had her own life to live, and he had no business meddling in it. This was her choice, and he would honor it.

The small band struck up another tune. Seeing as how he stood in front of her, Matt couldn't find an excuse not to ask her for the dance. He held out his hand. "Would you do me the honor of this dance?"

Surprise filled her face, but she didn't hesitate to place her hand on his shoulder and rest her other one in his. Without a word he spun her onto the floor, thankful that this was one dance he knew how to do. Her waist was so small that he could probably circle it with his hands, and her curls bounced against her bare neck. The deep blue of her dress made the blue in her eyes even more intense and accented her beauty. He marveled at her gracefulness and hoped he wouldn't disgrace himself with his awkwardness.

"You are as graceful as ever, Caroline. You've always been light on your feet. I seem to remember a few times I stepped on your toes."

She grinned and tilted her head to the side. "Ah, I was just thinking about how much you've improved since those days. Have you been taking lessons?"

He noted the humor in her voice and relished the moment so much like old times. "Not really, but Becky has been a help."

This time Caroline laughed, and it was like music in his ears. He hadn't heard it for a long time. He swallowed hard. So much he truly wanted to say to her, but he held his tongue. He loved her, but he couldn't stand in the way of her happiness and success. On top of that, he wasn't quite ready to deal with Mrs. Frankston and her snobbery. Becky had no problem with her, but then his sister had no problems with anyone.

He finally decided to go back to a safe topic. "You said you are working with students and helping them with their research. That must be interesting."

She swirled effortlessly as they turned. "Yes, and I really enjoy it. Helping them keeps me busy, but it's fun, and I learn a few things myself."

"You always were one who loved school and learning, and I imagine your friendliness makes them feel at ease as well." She'd always made the highest marks in their class and was friendly to everyone, even Dove, a Cherokee Indian. That was what had attracted him to Caroline when they were younger.

"As I recall, you had a lot of friends yourself. You were always the one who was so quiet in class but loud and mischievous during recess. One couldn't help but notice you."

Heat rushed to Matt's face, but not all of it from what she said. His hand at her waist burned too, and his heart thumped so loudly in his chest that surely she must hear it.

Of one thing he was certain: this would be the only dance this evening with Caroline. Being so close to her again stirred emotions he didn't want to feel.

When the music ended, he smiled and thanked her before heading for the side door. Perhaps a breath of fresh air would cool those feelings arising in his chest.

Caroline raised her hand to her throat to stifle the cry threatening there. Her heart beat furiously as Matt strode away. The warmth of his hand in hers and on her back still permeated her being, and she longed for his continued presence. Stuart may be a senator's son and handsome in his own way, but he would never compare to the down-home goodness of Matt Haynes.

Then the memory from the past week entered her mind. He had been in Oklahoma City but said nothing about being near her home. Had she imagined the shadow to be Matt, or had he actually been there? She dare not ask him, for if he was there and had hurried off, she could only believe he hadn't wanted to see her.

Her hopes for his attention dashed, she blinked her eyes and turned away, not wanting to look for him any longer. Still she noticed that he danced once with his sister and once with his mother before turning to leave.

Caroline's insides quivered. Now that he was gone, she longed for the evening to be over. The sooner she returned to Oklahoma City, the sooner she could get Matt Haynes out of sight and out of mind.

Chapter 10

After seeing Caroline off at the train depot, Charlotte climbed aboard their car with Maxwell and headed home. Charlotte's heart had filled with joy at the success of the birthday party and the fun of having Caroline home, but now sadness replaced the joy. They were going home to an empty house and a long, lonely Sunday afternoon.

It being late October, the weather was pleasantly cool. Charlotte welcomed the warmth of her coat as they drove into the shed Maxwell had built for the automobile. He helped her step down from the seat and held her arm as they walked into the house.

They entered through the back porch, where the washtubs sat waiting for Monday morning's laundry. Wonderful aromas wafted from the kitchen, tempting Charlotte's taste buds. From the predominant smell of cinnamon and apples, Ruby must have prepared another pie. If this kept up, Charlotte wouldn't be able to wear the dress she'd ordered from Mrs. Weems for the statehood celebrations.

Maxwell removed his gloves and driving hat when he stepped into the kitchen and sniffed. "Hmm, it does smell delicious, Ruby. Is it apple pie?"

"No, sir, Mr. Frankston, it be a new dessert I wanted to try out. I found the recipe when I was down to Anderson's this week. I'll have a dish ready for ye with tea and coffee later this afternoon."

Charlotte smiled at her cook. "Thank you, Ruby. I'm sure it will be wonderful. We'll be in the parlor at four."

When she entered the foyer, she removed her coat and hat and placed them on the hall tree. Maxwell did the same behind her then grasped her elbow. "Come into the parlor with me. I have a little something I want to tell you about."

Her curiosity rose as she followed him. Usually Max went straight up to take a nap on Sunday afternoons, saving any talk they may have until later. Whatever he had to say must be important for him to delay his ritual.

Once they were seated on the sofa, Charlotte sat with hands folded in her lap waiting for him to tell her what was on his mind. Perhaps it was another trip to Oklahoma City to visit with Caroline.

He grasped both of her hands in his and gazed at her. She saw nothing but pure love and perhaps a little mischief shining from his blue eyes. She longed to reach up and smooth down the unruly hair made even more so by his driving cap, but she sat still.

"My dear Charlotte, with both children gaining independence, I say it's time for us to take a trip back to St. Louis to visit with your family."

A lump formed in Charlotte's throat, and she swallowed hard to keep it from filling her throat. At one time her heart had longed to return to her home in Missouri, but too many years had passed. If only Max had suggested such a trip when the children were still young, she might have been more excited. The eagerness that gleamed in her husband's eyes told her more than his words how much he loved her, and she didn't have any desire to see the flame extinguished.

Tears misted her eyes. "That's a wonderful idea, but when

would we go? You can't just go off and leave the running of the town to somebody else."

"But I can. Mr. Fleming is on the council and has been appointed as my temporary replacement and will fill in while we are gone."

Her heart skipped a beat. Such a plan had never entered her mind. "Shouldn't we wait a while before we make any plans like that?" Right now, simply knowing he'd plan such a trip for her was all she needed to reconfirm his love for her.

"We could, but it would be better to go before winter sets in." He pulled an envelope from his inside pocket. "Here are tickets for the train leaving for Kansas and Missouri on Tuesday, and they have no set return date, so you can stay as long or short a time as you'd like."

Seeing the Kansas and Missouri countryside in the fall of the year would be a wonderful treat. She quickly ran through the events and appointments she had set up for the next few weeks. None of them would suffer without her presence. Still, one thing concerned her. "What if the committee and President Roosevelt confirm our statehood while we're gone? I don't want to miss out on any of the inaugural activities. We've waited too long not to be involved in the celebration."

"I've been informed that it will be at least another three weeks, perhaps a month before that will happen, and we'll be back by then." His arm went about her shoulder, and he pressed her head to his chest.

"All right then. It will be good to see my sisters and brother and their families." She raised her head and reached up to touch his cheek with her fingers.

His hand grasped hers, and he pulled it to his lips. "My dear Charlotte, you have been a wonderful wife, mother, and companion to me even when you disliked living here so much.

I love you with all my heart, and I'm going to do everything I can to make our remaining years together happy ones. I know you're going to be a beautiful grandmother. Our children are fortunate to have you, and this trip is my gift to you for all these years." He then released her and leaned over to kiss her on the lips, not on her cheek, as was his usual habit. "I'll be upstairs when you've finished here."

Words danced in her head, but none would form in her throat as he left the room. Her fingers touched her lips where his had just been, and tears slid down her cheeks. How she longed for him to show such affection more often, but she must cherish this moment and remember it, for it may be many months before another such display would be forthcoming.

Then her eyes opened wide. If they were to leave on Tuesday, then she had much to do in order to be ready. A list of things to take care of formed in her mind. Charlotte straightened her back with determination to have everything ready for their departure.

Just as she started up the stairs, she remembered Mellie's request last night. She checked the clock and gasped. Mellie would be here in ten minutes. She hurried into the kitchen to make sure Ruby would have tea and some refreshment for her guest. This was one meeting she now wished she had declined.

Mellie hesitated at the Frankston's front door. She lifted her hand to grasp the brass knocker, but her fingers hovered over it. Finally she breathed deeply and grasped the cool metal in her hand and pounded against the plate behind it. This had to be done, and the sooner the better.

Ruby answered the door and smiled broadly, her red head

bobbing in welcome. "Mrs. Frankston said ye'd be coming." She held the door open wide for Mellie to enter.

Mellie stepped into the foyer then waited for Ruby to give instruction as to where to go. The housekeeper nodded toward the parlor. "If ye'll wait in the parlor, Mrs. Frankston will be joining ye in a moment." Again she smiled and then disappeared down the hall.

Mellie strolled into parlor and sat on the deep green velvet sofa. The carved roses in the wood reminded her of the fine Victorian furniture she'd seen at her sister's home in Boston. Charlotte did have good taste in decorating, and every inch of the room proved it. A vase filled with deep gold and bronze mums adorned a table near the window. Probably a bouquet from the party at the town hall last night.

Her stomach began to churn and roil as if in protest of her errand today. Mellie swallowed hard to keep bitterness from filling her mouth. If Aunt Clara were here, she'd know exactly what to say and how to say it, and even if it offended Charlotte, Clara would speak the truth. Well, she wasn't Clara, and it was up to Mellie to get to know Charlotte and try to understand her. A discussion of Caroline and Matt could wait until another time. Today would be about Charlotte only.

A movement at the door caught her eye, and she glanced up to see Charlotte entering. "Good afternoon, Mellie. I didn't mean to keep you waiting, but Mr. Frankston gave me some surprising news a while ago, and I'm still trying to absorb it."

"It hasn't been long, and I hope the news was good." From the look in Charlotte's eyes and the smile on her face, it must have been very good. Maybe this talk would go much better than she dreamed if Charlotte was in a good mood.

The mayor's wife sat across from Mellie in a Prince Albert chair that matched the sofa both in color and carving. "We're taking a trip back to St. Louis on Tuesday. I'll have a chance to see my sisters and brother. We haven't been there since my mother's death several years ago, and that was only for a few days."

"How wonderful for you. I'm glad Mr. Frankston can take the time away from his duties."

Charlotte's hands fluttered against her chest. "Mr. Fleming will be sitting in Mr. Frankston's place as the temporary mayor. He's been on the town council longer than anyone else in town. Mr. Frankston feels he is quite capable of running the town's business for a few weeks."

The banker would make a good substitute. At least the mayor planned to leave Barton Creek in capable hands. But that had nothing to do with her visit. She wanted to know about Charlotte and her background. If Mellie could know more about the woman, perhaps her behavior could be better understood.

Ruby appeared with a tea tray and set it on the marble-topped table in front of the sofa. Two rose-decorated porcelain cups sat on delicate plates alongside the teapot, and two plates held a dessert that smelled of apples and was topped with whipped cream. Ruby bowed slightly. "If the missus doesn't need me, I'll be taking a cup of tea and a plate of dessert up to His Honor."

"Thank you, Ruby, this will be fine. I'm sure Mr. Frankston will enjoy having it."

Ruby left the room and Charlotte poured the tea. The aroma of the concoction on the table filled Mellie's nose with cinnamon and nutmeg. If she hadn't just had coconut cake at Becky's, the sweet would be most tempting. Still she must be polite and at least eat a few bites. Charlotte handed Mellie a cup of tea.

"Thank you," Mellie murmured. She sipped her tea, unsure of just how to begin the conversation. Finally she settled on last night's doings. "What a lovely party that was for Caroline. You did a grand job, but then you always do. You must have learned such things from your mother when you were younger."

Charlotte nodded. "Thank you, I did learn a great deal from my mother."

"Did she entertain frequently?" Mellie asked.

"Oh, yes," Charlotte said. "My father was Judson Sinclair, an investment broker who moved to St. Louis when he realized the potential of the western expansion. He and Mother met at one of my grandparents' social events. My mother was one of four daughters of Henry Dawson, a banker in St. Louis."

The name had no familiar ring as Mellie thought back to the people Ben had mentioned when he traveled home to Boston from Kansas and Missouri before they married. "Living in Barton Creek is certainly different than living in St. Louis or Boston for that matter. I remember when we married and came out West, I was overwhelmed at all that was expected of me as a rancher's wife. Our place in Kansas wasn't near the size of what ours is now."

"That's right, I remember you once lived in Boston, and Becky went back there for her schooling. I would have liked that for Caroline, but she was insistent about staying here in the Territory." She set her cup on the tray and picked up the plate with the dessert. "You must try this. It's a new recipe Ruby cooked up this morning. I'm not sure what's in it, but it does look delicious."

Mellie reached for the second plate and spoon. She scooped up a bit and lifted it to her lips. A crunchy-looking crust of rolled oats covered the apples in a thick sauce that was still warm. The cold whipped cream perfectly complemented the apple crunch. Charlotte was right. This was as good as any apple dessert she had ever eaten. She'd have to see if Ruby would share her recipe.

Charlotte placed her spoon on her plate and smiled. "It is quite good. Ruby frequently finds new dishes to try out." She patted her lips with a napkin then laid it back in her lap. "How did you find Becky today?"

"Very well." Mellie placed her fork on her plate. "The baby doesn't seem to be slowing her down in the least."

Charlotte smiled. "That is reassuring to hear. Pregnancies can be so unpredictable." She looked away, then back at Mellie, mustering a smile. "I imagine you are looking forward to being a grandmother as much as I am."

"Indeed I am!" Mellie agreed, glad to hear that Charlotte looked forward to the baby. She couldn't imagine any woman not wanting a grandchild, but Charlotte was so cool, so unapproachable at times, she hadn't known for sure. "That is why I came. Since I was in town, I thought it would be nice to get better acquainted. After all, we shall both be grandmothers soon to a certain well-beloved child."

Charlotte smiled. "I expect we shall be arm-wrestling for the chance to hold the baby."

"You think so?" Mellie laughed at Charlotte's unexpected joke. "I've been knitting a blanket for the baby."

"And I've been crocheting one!" Charlotte confessed. "But I promise not to be hurt if your blanket is the first to swaddle the little one. Becky is your daughter, after all."

Mellie smiled, touched by Charlotte's gesture. "I'm sure the baby will need plenty of blankets, being born in December." They laughed together again, and a new, strange feeling of comradeship filled the room.

Charlotte shot a glance at Mellie, then looked away as she spoke, her hands twisting her napkin. "I do hope Becky has an easy time with her birthing of this baby."

"I pray that as well."

A heavy silence fell then Charlotte's words rushed forth.

"I'm glad she's not blood kin, as she might have inherited my problem…"

Mellie waited a moment then prodded gently. "Difficulty in delivery?"

Charlotte shook her head. "In carrying to term. Then in childbirth as well."

A piece of fruit lodged in Mellie's throat, threatening to choke her. She swallowed hard, drank a bit of tea, and stared at Charlotte. Dare she tell the woman that Becky may indeed have the same problems because of heredity? Charlotte deserved to know the truth. "I'm afraid she may have difficulty, although she does seem to be quite healthy and robust. I had a stillborn son before Matt and lost another baby after Becky. Becky's was a difficult birth, and the doctor warned me, but we wanted so much to have another child. After that last one, the doctor performed surgery and made sure I would have no more."

Charlotte's back stiffened, and a hand went to her throat. When she spoke, her voice could barely be heard. "The same thing happened to us. Caroline was a troublesome birth. The doctor said I'd have to be very careful if I conceived again. I did, twice, and but neither one made it to full term. When Rob was born, he was like a miracle, but I almost died. We decided then that our family was complete."

"Oh, Charlotte, we have more in common than I could ever have thought." Mellie reached across the table for Charlotte's hands. "No wonder you've been so unhappy all these years. Losing your babies then coming out here to this forsaken place when you've been accustomed to having so much more."

Charlotte said nothing, her face inscrutable. Mellie squeezed her hands. "The women of Barton Creek have all had their problems. Did you know Bea Anderson lost a son to a diphtheria epidemic before they came here? And the pastor's wife had two little ones die from an epidemic on the wagon train that brought them to the Territory before the land runs. So many of us know the misery of losing children."

"I...I had no idea. I'm so sorry for your losses, Mellie. It appears that God gave us women more than our share of grief in child bearing."

Charlotte desperately needed good women friends with whom she could talk and let out all these things that seemed to be troubling her, and Mellie determined at that moment to make it happen one way or another. She slipped her hands from Charlotte's and sat back.

"Every woman in this town has a story to tell. We can be your friends if you'll let us. We all have come from different backgrounds, but that's what makes our town so wonderful. All these years you've been holding yourself aloof when you could have had faithful friends to share your stories with."

Charlotte remained silent. She simply folded her hands and stared down at them.

Mellie continued. "But we're strong, and we can overcome any troubles He puts in our path. You're a fine Christian woman, Charlotte Frankston, and it's time you let the people of Barton Creek see the real lady you are." She stood. "Now, I must be getting back to my daughter's house. I'm sure Ben is more than ready to go home." She held out her hand, and Charlotte grasped it. "No need for you to get up. I'll see myself out, but you think about what I said. Let people get to know the real you under that front you put up."

Charlotte's face looked so stricken that Mellie worried that she'd overstepped her bounds. Still, the woman had to know she couldn't go on cutting people down and trying to make everyone do things her way. She needed to become a part of the community.

When the door closed behind Mellie, Charlotte slumped in her chair. Mellie did understand her feelings. All these years she could have had a friend in the rancher's wife. Now that her children were grown and gone, she saw for the first time how lacking she was in true friends.

Somehow, someway Charlotte had to find her way back to that girl she had been when Maxwell fell in love with her. Softening her heart would take a lot of work, but if she didn't seek the forgiveness of those she'd hurt for so many years, she'd never be truly happy in Barton Creek.

A tear dropped from her eye and landed on her hand in a perfect dot. Charlotte stared at it a moment. Perhaps this was the sign that the time for change had come. Then she remembered her packing and preparations for the trip. Apologizing or anything else would have to wait for another day. She had bigger plans to take care of for the next week or so.

Chapter 11

*C*harlotte leaned her forehead against the window pane of the Pullman car. With the weather so much cooler, the windows could remain closed. That prevented so much soot and smoke from entering the car and dusting everything with black. Tomorrow their train would arrive in St. Louis, and butterflies danced in Charlotte's stomach at the thought of seeing her sisters. Both delight and dismay filled her heart.

The countryside she watched as they traveled was very different from that they'd seen when they moved west. How much would her sisters have changed?

The last time she'd come this way, her heart had been full of grief for her mother, and she had noticed very little of the country. Then her time had been spent thinking about the funeral service and all that her sisters had to do. She should have been there to help them. When she'd seen her mother at the funeral home, Charlotte had gasped to see how her mother had aged. She had grabbed the edge of the casket to keep from fainting and mourned the years she had lost and not being able to say good-bye.

She shook herself and pushed the memory out of her mind. Although they kept in touch through letters, Charlotte prayed her sisters wouldn't see this visit as an intrusion on their holiday preparations. With Thanksgiving just weeks away, they would be busy with plans for dinners and festivities with their own families. Then she remembered the day's date and realized it was already Halloween.

Her mind wandered to the subject of her soon-to-be born grandchild. At this point she didn't care if it was a boy or girl; she only wanted it to be healthy. Sharing the baby with Mellie could prove to be fun as well. The grin tickling her lips became a full-blown smile.

Maxwell leaned across from his seat. "Happiness is splashing all over your face like the fountain of youth. You look positively radiant." He grasped her hands and squeezed them. "Care to share with me?"

"Oh, I have the most wonderful idea. I told you about Mellie's visit, and I've come to realize what a good friend she could be. I want to invite her for Thanksgiving dinner."

His eyebrows rose. "Just her?"

"And Ben too, of course. Then Becky and Rob won't have to travel to see her family. The doctor said she needs to stay close to town during the last month of her pregnancy."

This time Maxwell's eyes knit together in a frown. "And what about Matt?"

Charlotte's heart lurched. She'd forgotten about Matt. He would have to be included, but it might upset Caroline. Maybe this wasn't such a good idea after all. "I hadn't thought about that. Perhaps we should wait until Christmas after Rob and Becky's baby arrives." But then Christmas would be such a busy time, and Becky may not feel like a big party or family get-together. Why did things have to get so complicated?

"It's a good idea, dear, and if you want to have a family dinner, then I will help you, and we'll have a grand time."

Trust her husband to support her ideas, even when they didn't sound so good in retrospect. She sighed. Her elation at the idea cooled. "Perhaps it would be better to wait and see how things progress with Mellie before making any big plans with family."

Maxwell patted her hand. "Whatever you say." Then he leaned back and closed his eyes.

More towns dotted the landscape as well as more farms. Fields of wheat gave way to rolling hills and then the Ozark Mountains through Missouri. The trees still carried leaves of red, gold, and yellow even though October was near its end, but they made for beautiful scenery that she had missed in the wide, open lands of Oklahoma.

Charlotte closed her eyes and bit her lip. She had never truly made the effort to make Barton Creek her home. Always her thoughts had returned to her youth and all the privileges she had enjoyed. Growing up with servants, a beautiful home, and social events with prominent citizens and leaders had made her move to Barton Creek unbearable. Still, she realized, she had as many responsibilities and events as she would have had in St. Louis, only they lacked the cachet of big-city life.

A hand touched hers, and she opened her eyes to find Maxwell smiling at her. "What is it, Maxwell?"

"It's time for dinner. Shall we head for the dining car?"

Charlotte composed herself and shook off her comparisons of the past and present. "Yes, I'm ready for dinner." So far the food on the train had been quite good, much to Charlotte's surprise. Not gourmet, but it surpassed most of what she had to eat in Oklahoma restaurants.

He stood and gestured for her to go ahead of him. She smiled and made her way down the aisle, holding to the backs of seats as she passed them in order to keep her balance. The train from Oklahoma City to St. Louis didn't have a car with private quarters, so they had settled for the Pullman cars, which was another inconvenience that had turned out to be not as bad as she had feared. Just one more night and part of the morning and they'd be in St. Louis, where she could again enjoy life as she once knew it.

Caroline shelved the last of the books from her return cart and headed back to the front desk. The headache from this morning had returned during the day, and she blamed her lack of sleep. She'd had fun last night, but now she paid for it. One of Madeline's powders and a nice, comfortable bed sounded like the best thing for her this evening.

She didn't want to admit that her ill feeling might be due to anything other than late hours. Surely a little wine with dinner and later with dessert wouldn't make her feel this rotten. She sighed and returned the cart to the storage area and headed for the employees' room, where her coat and handbag waited for her.

Five minutes later she boarded the trolley that would take her within a block of her home. The cool air relieved the pain somewhat. It had been a welcome relief after the stuffy air of the library all day. At least tonight she would be home just as darkness settled on the city. On some nights the skies had already filled with stars by the time she reached home. She hated walking that dark block alone, but unless Stuart picked her up, she had no choice.

She had no desire to be on the dark streets on this Halloween night. Maybe Oklahoma City would be different from Barton Creek, but probably not. Mischief makers abounded in both cities and towns. Madeline and Julia planned to attend a party tonight at another friend's home, but Caroline had declined. With Stuart out of town, she didn't relish the idea of attending such an event unescorted.

He had told her after dinner last night that he would be in Tulsa until Sunday, so she could get a few good nights of sleep before he came to visit after his return. Stuart had been a wonderful escort and had taken her many enjoyable places. Still, her feelings for him didn't change. She liked being with him, and he was good company, but he simply didn't create a spark of caring for him other than a friend. Of course she should be satisfied with that, for she had heard of couples who fell in love after marriage.

Where had those thoughts of marriage come from? She'd only known Stuart a short time and shouldn't even be thinking along those lines. He would make some woman a wonderful husband, but she didn't see that in her future with him. She massaged her temples with her fingers. This headache gave her crazy ideas. Then guilt settled in her heart. Continuing to see Stuart would only lead him to think she could offer him more in her feelings and wasn't truly fair to him. She bit her lip. A decision would have to be made soon, but it could wait until after the inaugural ball.

The trolley halted at her destination, and she hurried to the exit door. Home, headache relief, and a soft bed beckoned. She walked at a brisk pace along the sidewalk just as the street lamps came on and provided pools of yellow light at the corner. Lights gleamed through the windows of the town house, which meant her roommates were still home.

She shoved the key into the lock then stepped into the foyer. There both Julia and Madeline pounced on her.

Madeline grabbed Caroline's handbag. "Hurry upstairs and change. You're going with us."

Caroline shook her head. "Oh, no, I can't. I have a terrible headache and need to sleep."

Julia shoved her from behind. "Take one of Madeline's

powders, and you'll be fine. Go on and change. The boys will be here soon."

"No. I don't want to go to a party without an escort and barge in with you and your dates."

Madeline shook her head. "We don't expect you to. Steve and Andy are bringing Philip with them, and we're all going together in Steve's parents' touring car. It has plenty of room, and it'll be a lot of fun." She pulled Caroline toward the stairs. "We'll get the headache stuff and then you'll feel a lot better."

Sleep would make Caroline feel better than anything else, but she allowed her friends to shove her into her bedroom. Madeline handed her the powder with instructions to hurry and change then meet them downstairs.

Caroline plopped on the bed, raised the medication to her lips, then reached for the glass of water Madeline had left and took a drink. She eyed her pillow with longing. Just a few minutes' nap would help so much. Her body jerked. No, if she closed her eyes, sleep would take her away, and she wouldn't wake up until morning.

With a sigh, she rose and unbuttoned her shirtwaist top. A few minutes later she met her friends in the parlor. The young men had already arrived.

Madeline grinned and hung onto Steve. "See, Philip, I told you she'd come with us. Let's go."

Philip offered Caroline his elbow. "I'm so glad you decided to join us. This will be a fun party."

She placed her hand on his arm, and they headed out to climb aboard Steve's big motorcar. Despite being cramped, Philip and Andy sat in the backseat with Caroline and Julia all but sitting on their laps. Never had Caroline been this close to a young man except when dancing, and this was nothing like that. The heat of Philip's leg burned through the layers of fabric in her skirt, and his arm rested across her shoulder.

Every time the car turned or stopped, she had to brace herself to keep from falling onto Philip's chest. It couldn't be much farther to where they were going, although she had no idea where that was. Madeline and Julia had failed to tell her the location of the party.

The automobile stopped, and Steve turned around to grin at them. "We're here, so untangle yourselves and hop out."

Heat burned in Caroline's cheeks at the implication in Steve's voice. Philip helped her step down, and she looked up to see where they were. A gasp escaped her lips. This was no one's home. It was one of those night places where people went to drink and do whatever else they did in those places. She should have stayed home, but now it was too late as Philip grabbed her hand and led her into the building.

Several hands shot up and waved at them. Caroline squinted, trying to see who they were in the dim light of the room. Conversation buzzed around the tables as they made their way through them. Caroline wanted to hide her face. This was not the kind of place she wished to be. Philip pulled out a chair for her, and two other couples Caroline recognized welcomed them.

One of the girls giggled. "We thought you were never going to get here. Beth said you'd probably back out, but knowing you, I had no doubts you'd make it."

Madeline settled herself and removed her wrap. Not until then had Caroline noticed how low-cut both Madeline's and Julia's gowns were. Caroline's hand went immediately to her chest. She clenched her teeth to keep her mouth from gaping as well as to keep from saying something to embarrass them.

Madeline linked her arms through Steve's. "We had to wait

on Caroline to change clothes when she got home from the library, so it took a little longer. But we're here now, so let the party begin."

Several bottles sat open on the table, and Caroline realized the others had already been drinking before she and her friends arrived. With no way to get home, she sat back and swallowed hard. Since she was here, she may as well try to make the best of things. Philip laughed at something Julia said then filled Caroline's wine glass before she could protest. She stared at the golden liquid. She didn't have to drink it.

Hours later as she slid between the covers of her bed, tears slipped down Caroline's cheeks. She'd pay for tonight with another headache tomorrow. Three glasses of the wine had been consumed before she'd even realized it. Her cheek pressed against the pillow, her tears creating a wet spot. "God, where were You tonight? Why did You let me do those things? Don't You care about me anymore?" The whispered words hung in the air.

A sob filled her throat. She hadn't been paying much attention to Him lately, so why would God be concerned about her now? The evening had been a mess, but her head hurt and her eyes drooped. No time to think about such things. She pulled the covers up to her chin and turned to her side and let sleep overtake her.

Chapter 12

*C*aroline stepped off the trolley and headed for the library. The week had started out busy yesterday with students and other patrons checking out books and requesting information for research. At least she'd have no more late nights for the week since she'd seen Stuart on Saturday for dinner after he returned a day early from his trip to Tulsa. They had no other plans until Friday, when he planned to take her to the theater. They hadn't stayed out late Saturday evening, but once again she'd indulged in a few glasses of wine with dinner and overslept on Sunday morning. Her roommates had said they didn't want to disturb her, even though they knew she wanted to attend church.

Another employee held the door open for her. "Good morning, Miss Frankston."

"Good morning to you, Jimmy." She smiled at the student who worked several hours during the week to help pay his schooling expenses. Today he wore a red shirt with white bands or stripes on the collar. "Something special this week? You're wearing your school colors."

Jimmy glanced down at the shirt under his coat then followed her through the door. "Yes, ma'am, we're playing a football game, and a lot of us wear red and white to honor the team."

"That's nice." She wished he wouldn't call her "ma'am" because it made her feel a lot older than her twenty-seven years. Even though she had mentioned it a few times, he still persisted in saying it. Of course to a nineteen-year-old, she would be considered old.

She headed to the ladies' employee room, where she removed her hat and coat and hung them on a peg where her handbag already hung. Jimmy and his red shirt came into her mind. Football was one thing about which she knew absolutely nothing. She'd heard Rob and his friends talking about it once, and it sounded like a rough game to be playing on the hard, packed ground. Boys may enjoy hitting and roughing each other up, but it didn't appeal to her at all.

She went out to the main room and checked for returned books then placed them on a cart so she could shelve them later. Cold weather had finally arrived, and every time the front door opened, a blast of chilly air swept in. However, as the room became more crowded with people, the air grew stale, and the fresh breeze actually came as a welcome relief.

At lunch two workers were allowed to eat at a time, and Caroline's turn came at eleven thirty. She retrieved the pail in which she had packed a lunch of bread, sausage from breakfast, fresh fruit, and cookies Ruby had sent to her. As she spread out her meal on a napkin, one of the other girls joined her.

"Hmm, your lunch looks good, Caroline. Do you mind if I sit here?" The young woman nodded toward a chair.

"Of course not. I'd appreciate the company." Josephine had proved to be a friendly companion. She didn't gossip and didn't ask too many personal questions.

Josephine spread her food on the table. "Can you believe it's November already and that it's finally turned cold?"

"No, the month I've been here has passed so quickly." So much had happened to make the time fly. Her friends had begun to think of her and Stuart as a couple, and that wasn't exactly a bad thing, but she hadn't intended to settle for one man in such a short time. Perhaps Philip would ask her out again. Josephine's voice broke into her musings.

Caroline set her attention back to the girl. "I'm sorry, what did you say?"

"I was just asking about that handsome man who has come by to see you a few times."

"Oh, that's Stuart Whittington. He's a lawyer like my father and brother." That caused a smile, and Caroline almost laughed. When she thought about it, the idea was rather boring. After all, she really did want someone different from her own family members.

Josephine gasped. "Is his father Representative Whittington?" Her eyes had opened wide, and she looked like an owl behind her glasses.

Caroline nodded. "Yes, he is. When I came to Oklahoma City I didn't dream I'd be seeing a lawyer, but Stuart is the first man I met and the first one to ask me out."

Josephine pushed strands of her dark hair off her face and sighed. "It would be nice to have someone look at me the way he looks at you."

"And how old are you? Nineteen? Don't you think there's plenty of time for you to find a young man?" Guilt pricked her conscience, and her heart fluttered. She was a fine one to give advice, since the man she loved didn't pay any attention to her. If she could be nineteen again, she might do things differently, but she wasn't and here she sat. Envy crept in at the fact of Josephine's youth and the years she had ahead of her.

"I don't know. Most of the time I'm never asked for a second date even if I ever have the first one." She leaned over and gazed at Caroline. "If I had a pretty face and curls like you, I might be asked out more, but with my glasses and unruly hair, I'm not much to look at."

Caroline had to admit Josephine was rather plain, and the thick glasses did make her eyes appear much larger, but the girl had such a sweet personality. Surely there must be some young man out there who would be interested in her. The cut and style of the girl's dress spoke of her lack of funds for new, more fashionable attire, but it didn't take away from her smile and friendliness. This was a young woman her mother would probably ignore or snub, but Caroline wanted none of that.

"Josephine, would you mind if I worked with your hair and helped you style it?"

The girl's hand went to her throat. At first she lowered her gaze then peered back up at Caroline. "You would do that for me?"

"Yes, I would. You're a nice girl, and there's a wonderful young man out there somewhere just waiting to meet you." Where she would find him Caroline didn't know, but at least she could start her on the road with a little more confidence.

"Please call me Jo, and I can't thank you enough for wanting to do this."

"All right, Jo it is, and don't thank me until you see how it turns out. Let's check out our work schedules this week and see if there is a time we can meet. I can come to your home or you can come to mine. I live with two other young women."

The stricken look in Jo's eyes gave the answer before she even spoke. "Oh, could I come to your place? I would love to see where you and your friends live."

Understanding dawned in Caroline. The girl didn't want her home to be seen. It couldn't be worse than some back in Barton Creek, but Caroline would respect Jo's wishes. "That will be fine. I can get my friends to help." She eyed Jo's figure and thought of the dresses in the closet at home. Perhaps there would be a way to offer Jo one without offending her. The pleasure of helping someone else sank deep into Caroline's heart, and she couldn't wait to get started.

Tears welled in Jo's eyes. "I've never had anyone to care about me like you have. Thank you."

Caroline smiled and gathered up her scraps and stuffed them back into her pail. "Remember, wait until after you see the results before you thank me too much." She stood and picked up her lunch things. "It's time we get back to work and let the other two come have their lunch. We can talk later."

At that moment Jimmy walked into the eating area. "It's about time you gals left. I'm starving." Mrs. Caskey, the head librarian, followed him and frowned at the girls.

"Spoken like a true college boy," Caroline teased. She snagged Jo's arm and walked out to the main room. A smile tickled the corner of her mouth. What kind of conversation would Jimmy and the prim and proper head librarian have? If she could be a fly on the wall, she'd like to hear that little exchange.

Matt spotted Jake headed toward him and slowed his horse to wait for his cousin to catch up. "What brings you out our way today?"

Jake grinned and pushed back the brim of his hat. "Got a proposition for you. Just received a wire from a friend up in Wyoming where we've bought a lot of our horses. For some reason a huge herd of them have come down to his land, and he's offered to corral some for us if we want to come up and get them."

"Isn't that a bit much for this time of year? Winter will have already set in up there."

Much as Matt loved horses, riding through snow and ice to get them wasn't his idea of a good trip. He still remembered the blizzard that had almost taken his father and Hank ten years ago.

"Not really. He'll have as many as we need set aside and ready for us in Laramie. All we have to do is get them from there to Denver. I plan to have several rail cars ready to load the horses onto and then bring them on to Barton Creek. Hawk and Eli have already agreed, and we thought you might want to go with us."

The idea didn't sound too bad, and getting away from home right now might be the best thing for him. Jake, Eli, and Hawk were three of the most experienced horsemen in these parts, and a trip with them would be an adventure as well as one to benefit their ranches. He'd heard tales of the beauty of the Rocky Mountains and the great lands of Wyoming, and even covered in snow they'd be a sight to see. "But what about the mountains? Can you get through them in the winter?"

"We won't really be in the mountains. From Laramie we head east and then down south to Denver on the east side of the mountains. It isn't as difficult that way."

"How long will it take?" As much as he wanted to be away for a while, he didn't want to miss out on the inaugural activities in case statehood came about.

"I've already been in touch with my friend and made arrangements for the rail cars, so we plan to leave in the morning. We should be back here by fifteenth of the month. You know I'm not about to miss Thanksgiving with my family."

Since there had been no progress reported from the statehood committee, Matt figured they'd be back in plenty of time. He could see nothing else to keep him in Barton Creek for the next ten days. "Sounds like a good deal to me. I'll tell Pa and meet up with you at the station in the morning for the Denver train."

Jake grinned, pulled his hat down low, and tugged at the reins on his horse. "Glad you're joining us. I think you'll learn a lot." He turned his horse and galloped away, calling over his shoulder, "See you tomorrow morning."

Matt gazed around at the cattle grazing nearby and waved to Hank. The day had become brighter with the expectations of the trip to Wyoming, a land he looked forward to seeing, even if it was cold.

Charlotte lounged in a bedroom at her sister's home, her fingers worrying the fabric of her silk skirt. Life had changed in St. Louis, and it wasn't the same place she remembered from her early days of marriage. So many more buildings, homes, automobiles, and people had turned the city into a place she barely recognized.

The city now had two baseball teams, and the Anheuser-Busch brewery had grown to be a leading supplier of their beverage across the country. St. Louis had hosted both a World's Fair and the Olympics. Her mind could barely take it all in. So many changes had turned the hometown she loved into a thriving, well-populated city.

Maxwell entered the room and slumped into the chair beside her. "I'm worn out. Your brother-in-law is one of the busiest doctors I've ever met, even more so than Dr. White or Doc Carter back in Barton Creek. I don't know how many patients he saw today, but it was plenty."

He leaned over and peered at her. "How did your day go?"

"Oh, we had a nice luncheon with a number of Marian's friends. Kathleen joined us, as did Aunt Chloe. All their talk revolved around the latest fashions, places to have dinner, and the upcoming holiday season. I suppose it was pleasant enough, but not of much interest to me."

They sat quietly a moment. Soon it would be time to go down to dinner with her sister and her family. Marian's son and daughter-in-law were to join them tonight, but they planned to leave their children in the care of a nanny. Charlotte vaguely remembered the days when her parents had done the same. Sometimes she and her sisters saw more of their nanny than they did their parents. She hoped Becky's child would fare better under the care of Lucy's Aunt Hilda.

The idea that her daughter-in-law planned to stay at the newspaper after the birth of her child didn't set well with Charlotte, but then Becky had a mind of her own, and Charlotte had learned she was unlikely to change it. Hilda Bishop came from a fine family in Boston, not like many of the uneducated, unrefined girls who usually sought such posts.

Thoughts of the baby sent a pang into her heart, and suddenly she said, "Maxwell, I'm ready to go home."

His brows bunched together as he peered at her. "Home? But this is your home."

No, St. Louis wasn't her home anymore. That realization had come without her even thinking about it. She grinned at her husband then moved to kneel at his side. "Barton Creek is home. Since coming here I've seen that I have memories of a place that no longer exists. Our son and his wife with their baby on the way are the ones I care about now. Our home is in Barton Creek with the people who have elected you as mayor for over ten years."

He reached down and pulled her to his lap then wrapped his arms around her. "My dear, I've waited a long time to hear you call Barton Creek home. If I'd known this would be the result, I would have brought you back a long time ago. The truth is that I was afraid I'd lose you to the world you had once known."

Tears misted Charlotte's eyes. "You'll never lose me to St. Louis or any other town. I love you, and my place is by your side wherever you are." And never had she meant it more than she did at this moment. A weight dropped from her shoulders, and suddenly she did feel just like that girl of so many years ago. She leaned back and smiled. "Let's go home. We have our own family waiting for us there."

Chapter 13

*B*en ran from the telegraph office and met Mellie outside the Mercantile. "It's close. We're going to be a state by the end of the week."

Mellie shifted her basket and placed a hand on her hip. "Ben Haynes, what are you jabbering about?"

"Got a wire from Guthrie, and President Roosevelt is about ready to sign the document to make us a state. With Murray and Harrell there, it won't be long."

Mellie's heart thumped, and she raised a hand to her mouth. "Oh, that's wonderful." She swirled around. "I have to find Charlotte. We have so much to do."

Charlotte and the mayor had just returned from St. Louis, and Mellie had seen her across the street at Mrs. Weems's dress shop earlier. Mellie headed down the street and met Charlotte coming out the door.

"What is all the commotion in the streets?"

Mellie patted her chest. "Statehood will be here soon. A wire just said that President Roosevelt would be signing the bill soon."

Charlotte's face lit up. "Oh, my, we have so much to do. I know Mr. Frankston already has the train car ordered for the people going to the inauguration from here, but we have to be sure everything is in place and ready for our celebration here as well."

Mellie had seen the extra coach car on the side tracks earlier in the week. All they had to do was connect it to the Guthrie train, and they'd be ready to go. The city that would be the new state capitol had been ready for weeks, but many arrangements must be made for the trip as well as the town festivities. "I'll go to the church and check with the preacher about our part. Pearl Jenkins needs to know too."

"I'll take care of her. She has all the plans we discussed at our last meeting, so she can be implementing some of them while we're in Guthrie." Charlotte fairly danced off the boardwalk. "This is so exciting. I must hurry and go to the Jenkinses'. Let's hope it's done tomorrow or the next day." She crossed the street and headed up the block toward the home where Pearl lived.

Mellie began a count of how many people from Barton Creek would be on the train. Mayor Frankston and Charlotte of course, Ben and Mellie, Lucy and Jake, the Flemings, the Andersons, Sam and Emily Morris, Eli and Alice Morris, Hawk, Geoff and Ruth Kensington, and Luke and Dove Anderson were all invited. According to her calculations, that made nineteen people from town going on the coach. All of them had been in Barton Creek from the days of the land run, except for the Kensingtons, but he was manager of the oil company here, and oil played a prominent role in launching Oklahoma into statehood.

Her fingers flew to her mouth. Becky and Rob were invited, but it was too close to Becky's birthing date for them to go. She turned and strode to the newspaper office, praying that Rob had talked some sense into her about not trying to attend. She stepped into the main room to find Becky typing furiously at her desk and the others scurrying around getting a special edition of the paper ready to print on a moment's notice. "Becky, can you stop a minute and talk with me?"

Becky swung her chair around. "Ma, what are you doing here? Oh, I guess you've heard the news."

"Yes, and you're not planning on going to the inauguration with us, are you?"

"Well, as much as I would like to cover the story for the *Chronicle*, I'm going to pass it on to Harry. He's been chomping at the bit ever since Mr. Lansdowne and I mentioned it to him. Of course Mr. Lansdowne plans to be there himself, but they'll be covering different aspects."

Mellie let out her breath in relief. At least her daughter was smart enough to know when to hand over responsibility. "I'm truly sorry you won't be able to attend with us, but you're wise to stay here."

"Oh, I'll be busy. I promised to help Aunt Hilda take care of Lucy's and Dove's children. Mrs. Weems will have Geoff and Ruth's, so we decided to have a statehood party for them. I think Catherine Claymore is planning to bake cookies and make punch for refreshments."

"That sounds like fun, but are you sure you're not overdoing it with the children?"

Becky's laughter rang across the room. "Too much for them or too much for me? Really, Ma, I'll be fine. Dr. White says I'm healthy as a horse. Even after you told him about your problems, he wasn't concerned. So you go and have a good time and don't worry about us. Rob is going to be with us, and he'll make sure I behave."

She sighed and went over to hug her daughter and kiss her cheek. "Well, as long as Rob is there and you behave yourself, you should be fine. But I know how you like to get down on the floor and play with your cousins. Promise me you won't do that."

Again Becky laughed and then patted her large stomach

under the full skirt she wore. "I don't think I'll have any problem with that promise. I can barely get out of a chair that isn't straight back."

Now a little more confident that Becky would be all right, Mellie kissed the top of her head. "I'll let you get back to work. I have lots to do out at the ranch, and I imagine your pa is tired of waiting on me."

At the door she turned back to face Becky. "Matt and Jake are supposed to be on the train from Denver tomorrow with new horses for us and the Morrises. If you see them, tell them to get on home right away."

Becky nodded and waved, so Mellie hurried back out to the street. Ben stood by their wagon, now loaded with supplies, and talked with Carl Anderson. When she approached them, Ben grinned and held out his hand toward her.

Mellie grasped her husband's hand and squeezed it. "I'm sorry I took so long. I was checking on Becky. She's not going to Guthrie with us, which I think is a wise decision."

"I knew our daughter had good common sense. Carl and I were just discussing our going on to Guthrie tomorrow."

"Tomorrow? Do you know something I don't?"

Carl Anderson shook his head. "No, no, Mellie, we just want to be sure to be there so we don't miss out on anything. We have a block of rooms reserved at the hotel under the mayor's name, and he thinks it a good idea to take the morning train tomorrow to Guthrie. He is certain the bill will be signed and the ceremonies and celebrations will be on Saturday."

Carl no longer wore the apron of a storekeeper. His business had grown into the largest north of Guthrie and carried everything they needed in the way of clothes, food, and household furnishings. Anything he didn't have in the store, he ordered from Sears Roebuck or Montgomery Ward catalogs. His gray sack suit gave evidence of his rise to prosperity in the town.

This news set her mind to swirling in circles with all that she had to do. "Oh my, does Charlotte Frankston know this?"

"Yes, we told her a few minutes ago, and she headed home." Carl nodded to Mellie and shook Ben's hand. "I don't suppose I'll be seeing you again until we board the train for Guthrie. I know you have much to take care of out at the ranch just like I do here at the store."

With that he pivoted and returned to the mercantile. Mellie sighed and allowed Ben to grasp her arm and assist her into the wagon. She rather missed the barrels of brooms, pickles, and other goods that once sat outside the store on the porch. Now everything was inside and much more organized than it had been only a few years ago.

When Ben climbed up beside her, she smiled at him with great pride in her heart. How wonderful it was for the families who had been here from the beginning to be together to watch history in the making, but then her mind returned to the things to be done before tomorrow morning.

"Ben, run the horses a bit faster. I'm anxious to get home and get started on packing for tomorrow. No telling how long we'll be in Guthrie."

He responded by flicking the reins on the team's backs and picked up their pace. They couldn't get home quick enough to suit Mellie.

Caroline opened the door to find Jo standing on the stoop. "Well, hello. I was beginning to wonder if you'd forgotten our meeting." She held the door open wide. "Come on in, and we'll go upstairs to my room. Julia will be here to help, but Madeline is going out with her beau."

Jo's shoulders hunched forward, and she let her chin droop. "Thank you, Miss Caroline."

"Hmm, the first thing I want you to do is to stand up straight." She tilted Jo's head with her fingers. "And always hold your head high."

"I'll try to remember that." After handing over her coat, hat, and gloves, she followed Caroline up the stairs, where Julia met them on the landing.

She grinned broadly and held out her hand. "Hello, I'm Julia, and I'm going to help Caroline." Julia wrapped her arm around Jo's shoulder and hugged her.

In her room Caroline gestured for Jo to have a seat at the dressing table. In a few minutes all the hairpins had been removed from Jo's hair, and it fell in loose waves to six or eight inches below her shoulders.

Caroline raked her fingers through the long strands in the back. "You have beautiful hair, Jo. It's soft and silky and has plenty of thickness. Let's see what we can do with it that you can do yourself later on."

She worked a hairbrush through the long, dark tresses and considered a style for the young woman. With Jo's youth, she could still get by with wearing it long and clipped in the back then fanned out between her shoulder blades. Caroline reached for a small frame over which to fashion the hair in front.

"I don't think I'm going to use the curling tongs since your hair has such a wonderful natural wave, and the texture is excellent. This smaller frame will give you just enough height and support for any hat you may want to wear." As she talked, she smoothed Jo's hair over the frame and secured it with hairpins.

The immediate result gave her face more room for the spectacles, which now didn't loom so large.

After a few more minutes Caroline grasped the long tail of hair in the back and secured it with a tortoise shell clip close to the neck then fanned out the strands in a silky fall. She stood back to admire her handiwork.

"There now, I think that's much better than the bun you had pinned up at your neck. You're much too young for such an old-fashioned style."

Jo peered at her reflection in the mirror then picked up the hand mirror and turned to see the back. A huge grin spread across her face. "I really like it, and it does make me look more my age."

Caroline laughed and patted Jo's shoulder. "Yes, and it really helps to see your beautiful brown eyes behind those spectacles. You're not quite so much the owl now."

Now Julia stepped up. "You have beautiful skin, and we don't want to ruin that. Will your mother object if I use just a small amount of color on your cheeks and lips?"

Jo frowned and shook her head. "I don't think she'll even notice. She never does."

Caroline sensed a story there but refrained from being nosy. She resolved to become a better friend and learn more about Jo and her family. In a few moments Julia's deft hands had brushed a hint of color to Jo's cheeks and added a touch of lip rouge to her mouth.

"Now that makes all the difference."

Caroline had to agree with Jo. Even with her glasses, the added color and the hair off her forehead gave Jo a different and attractive appearance.

A tear formed in the corner of Jo's eye, and Julia hurried to blot it away. "We don't want you to spoil the effect." Her smile softened the words as Jo blinked and swallowed hard.

"I don't know what to say. I hardly look like myself, and I do like it." She reached up to touch her hair then her cheeks.

Caroline spun around and headed for her wardrobe. She pulled out a dark yellow, almost gold-colored dress and handed it to Jo. "Try this on. I've worn it once, but the color was horrible on me. I looked like a jar of mustard. It will be perfect with your dark hair and eyes."

She and Julia helped Jo change from her plain black skirt and white blouse into the dress trimmed with cream and dark green cording about the waist and sleeves. When the dress floated down over Jo's hips, Caroline immediately saw that it would be a perfect fit because Jo's waist was slim with no need for a corset. She buttoned the closure in the back and stepped aside to see the full effect.

Jo gasped and placed her fingertips over her mouth. "It's beautiful, but I can't accept something like this. It's much too fancy for me."

Caroline and Julia both protested at once, and Caroline hugged Jo. "No, it's perfect. You can save it to wear for special occasions if you like, but the dress is yours. I would have worn it to work, but like I said, it's not my color."

"And it's way too long for me," Julia reassured her. "Caroline is at least four if not five inches taller than I, and Madeline is an inch taller than that, so neither of us could wear it."

Caroline nodded. "She's right, so please accept it as my gift to you. I'm so glad to see that someone can benefit from my fashion mistake."

They helped Jo remove the dress and Caroline folded it and found a box for it. Just as they started downstairs, someone knocked hard on the door.

"Who in the world is so anxious to see us?" Caroline hurried down the steps to the door and opened it. Stuart greeted her with a hug that almost knocked her off her feet.

"Great news. Oklahoma is a state—or will be when the president signs the bill."

Julia and Jo both squealed in delight, and Caroline stepped out of Stuart's embrace. "Oh my, that means the inauguration will be soon. When do you think it will happen?"

"By Saturday at least, and the inauguration will take place almost immediately. Everything is in place, so it can happen at a moment's notice. My father says that all the congressmen and other leaders are already convening in Guthrie awaiting the confirmation."

That meant her parents would be on their way to that town too. "This is so exciting. When do we leave?"

"I talked with my father, and he wants me there Friday evening. I plan to drive up. Would you like to come with me after work?"

Caroline blinked and calculated in her mind what she needed to do before then. "Yes, I would."

Jo jumped up and down behind her. "This is so exciting. You'll have to tell us all about it, Caroline."

Stuart grinned and grabbed Caroline's hand. "She will, but now we have a dinner date."

Caroline jerked her head back. "We do? I don't remember that."

"Because I'm telling you now. Get your coat, and we can go."

"But I'm not dressed or ready to go out or anything." Then she remembered Jo. "Besides, Jo is here." She turned to the girl and wrapped an arm around her shoulder.

"Oh, don't mind me. I can go home on the trolley. I do it all the time. You go with Mr. Whittington and have a good time."

Caroline wavered for a moment. As much as she wanted to

go out with Stuart, she hated for it to be so unplanned, and she worried about Jo going home alone. She glanced from her roommate to Jo and back again. With their smiles as encouragement, she shrugged. "All right, I'll go."

Jo reached over to hug Caroline. "Yes, go and have a grand time. Thank you for all you've done for me today. I'll never forget it."

Caroline peered over Jo's shoulder at Julia. She mouthed the words, "Don't forget the other clothes." She'd already given Julia a list of things to give Jo from some items Caroline no longer wore. Julia nodded in promise.

With that taken care of, Caroline grabbed her coat from its hook by the door and shoved her arms into it with Stuart's help. What a day this had turned out to be, and more excitement was to come.

Chapter 14

*C*aroline could hardly believe the day they had all looked forward to with such anticipation had finally arrived. November 16, 1907, would go down in history. Just a while ago, at 9:18 in the morning, Oklahoma officially became a state when President Roosevelt signed the bill. Guns, sirens, bells, and whistles all filled the air with a cacophony of sound.

The new governor of the state, Charles Haskell, was right here in this same hotel with his family and a few friends. The anticipation of all that would take place today swelled Caroline's heart to the bursting point with excitement.

Her mother entered, pulling on a pair of gloves. "Are you ready? We must get to our places at the library before the crowds grow too large. Your father just went down and will have a carriage for us."

"I'm ready. This is so exciting! I'm so glad Father was able to get us all rooms in the hotel and that the people of Barton Creek will be here." She sorted through the list of activities as they descended the stairs to the lobby. After the ceremony, a parade of dignitaries would go down the main street. Then the ball would be held tonight in the town hall. Stuart planned to meet her for the inauguration and marriage ceremony that would unite the Oklahoma Territory and the Indian Territory into one state.

Crowds of people swarmed through the lobby of the Royal Hotel. Charlotte followed her mother, who pushed and elbowed her way out to the street. Stuart stood with Father and waved to them. Caroline hurried to their side.

"We're going to have to walk down to the library. So many cars, carriages, and wagons are coming into town there will be no place to park. Better to leave the car where it is. We have reserved spaces, so we'll be fine." Father grasped Mother's hand and placed it on his arm. "Stay close to me so we won't be separated."

Stuart reached for Caroline's hand. "He's right. Even if we can't keep up with them, I can make sure you don't get lost." He secured her hand on his arm and turned to follow her parents.

Never had Caroline seen so many people or heard so much noise. All around them people shouted with happiness and called out to one another. Carrying on a decent conversation became almost impossible, so she walked beside Stuart and drank in all the excitement.

Matt had come with his family, but she hadn't seen him as yet. Just knowing she would before long sent currents of excitement through her veins. Then guilt crept in. Here she walked beside a handsome young man who paid attention to her and took her places, and her mind filled with thoughts of one who didn't care anymore. She had to forget Matt and concentrate on Stuart, who could offer the kind of life to which she was most accustomed.

They finally arrived at the library, where hordes of people milled about trying to find the best place to be for the ceremonies. Young men and boys climbed trees nearby in order to get a good view of the library steps. The sight of women in beautiful gowns and sparkling jewels almost took away her breath. They outshone the flowers and decorations that adorned the portico of Carnegie.

"Oh, Stuart, I can't believe we're here. Look at all the people from everywhere. Farmers, ranchers, businessmen, they're all here to celebrate, and everything is so well organized."

Stuart laughed. "This day has been planned down to the last detail for months. All that was missing was the time and date, and now we have those. This is a wonderful time to be a citizen of Oklahoma, and it's going to get even better."

"I'm so glad Father had the foresight months ago to secure a suite for us even though he didn't know the date either. He has a big celebration planned back in Barton Creek too. It'll be as grand as our July Fourth celebration, even with fireworks. I'm sorry I'm going to miss it, but I must stay in Oklahoma City."

He grinned and squeezed her hand. "And for that I am glad. You will plan to ride back with me to Oklahoma City, won't you?"

"That would be nice. I look forward to it, but now I'm more eager for the inauguration to start and for the ball tonight."

At that moment cheers went up and the crowds parted as Governor Haskell and his entourage made their way to the library steps. Shouts and hand waving met the man as he greeted the crowd. Shortly after noon, everyone stood in place. Caroline's pulse raced with the knowledge she stood as a witness to this great moment.

Stuart leaned over to whisper, "There must be at least five thousand people here if not more. Look, even the trees are full of spectators."

Caroline blinked her eyes in amazement. Young men and boys had climbed up into the branches of the trees. People were everywhere, and at this moment gratitude for her father's role in all the excitement filled her with love and sent tingles of wonder throughout her body.

A man stepped forward and introduced himself as Reverend Dobson, the pastor of the First Baptist Church of Guthrie. He announced that he was there to perform the marriage ceremony of the Oklahoma Territory to Indian Territory. Charles Jones stepped forward as the groom, and a Choctaw woman, Anna Bennett, stood beside him.

As Caroline listened to the vows, Emily Morris came to mind. She searched the crowd before her gaze landed on Mrs. Haynes and Mrs. Morris. The two women stood with their arms around each other's waists, and Mr. Morris had his arm around his wife's shoulder. Such a perfect symbol of what was taking place brought tears to Caroline's eyes. Mrs. Morris, as a Cherokee, had been shunned and ridiculed for so many years, but now she could stand as proud as anyone as a citizen of the grand state of Oklahoma.

Immediately following the ceremony, a justice of the peace formally inaugurated Charles Haskell as the first governor of the state of Oklahoma. He looked rather handsome in his Prince Albert attire rather than the usual sack suit worn by most of the other men.

Stuart beamed with pride during the inauguration speech. "Mark my words, Haskell is going to be an asset for this state, and he will accomplish great things for us."

Caroline only half-listened to the speech, but she nodded in agreement with Stuart. All the while she continued to gaze about the crowd, hoping to catch a glimpse of Matt. He had to be around somewhere, so he must be avoiding her. That thought cut her to the bone. No more thinking of Matt. She must focus her attention on Stuart and the festivities in front of her.

During the long parade of dignitaries and marching bands, Stuart turned to her and asked, "Will you have dinner with me tonight before the ball, or do you have something planned with your parents?"

She did plan to have dinner with her parents, but an idea

struck her. "Father has reservations for us, but I'm sure they'd be delighted if you'd join us."

"All right, I'd like to get to know them myself, and I'm sure they're more than curious about the young man interested in their daughter."

Yes, they would be, and they would probably read more into the relationship than there actually was, but it would be a step in the right direction for her. The sooner she could remove Matt from her thoughts, the sooner she'd be able to accept the attentions of another man.

Matt tugged at the stiff collar of his shirt. He'd rather be home on his horse out on the prairie than here at this ball. In fact, he'd prefer to be anywhere else but here, even in his hotel room alone. However, he would not dampen the spirits of his parents for this night. Their enthusiasm outranked his displeasure.

A memory from the inaugural ceremony stood out in his mind. He had purposely stood several rows behind Caroline and her family. She was with the same young man he'd seen on his visit to Oklahoma City. He'd leaned down to say something to her, and she had laughed and gazed back at him with a smile that gripped Matt's heart like a fist around the reins of a bucking bronco. She looked as happy at that moment as she had on the stoop of her home a few weeks ago.

When she had turned to gaze about the crowd, he had stepped behind two women wearing large hats with plumes and feathers to escape Caroline's notice. Although Matt had tried to harden his heart against Caroline, he couldn't. She had rejected him when she went off to college and again when she left for Oklahoma City. There would not be a third time, of that he was certain.

Even during the parade he'd managed to escape her notice, but here at the ball, he'd have no place to hide, and common courtesy deemed it necessary for him to have at least one dance with her. He turned toward the entrance just as Caroline and her family entered. His heart stopped a moment at the sight of her in a dress as purple as the iris growing in his mother's garden. Her blonde curls were secured to her head with a matching flower and plume ornament.

Matt swallowed hard and took a step forward before he realized she was on the arm of the same man he'd seen her with earlier. His name, Stuart Whittington, Matt had learned from his father before dinner. As a cowboy with no formal education, he could never compete with the well-educated son of a state representative.

He turned away and headed in the opposite direction to avoid contact with her. He would have to speak with her at some point in the evening, but not before he prepared himself to do so with no show of emotion. Although the room radiated with happiness and light provided by the electric globes, darkness filled Matt's heart and soul.

He joined the line of well-wishers filing by the governor and other members of the receiving party. After shaking hands and wishing the governor well, Matt retreated to a far corner behind one of the palm trees brought in for decoration. He glanced down at the program in his hands to see that twenty-two numbers were planned for the evening after the grand march. All around him people mingled and visited, with conversation flowing freely. He spotted Jake and Lucy at the refreshment table and headed their way. He would dance the one number with Caroline then make his excuses and head back to the hotel. The evening couldn't end soon enough for him.

Lucy looked beautiful as always in a deep red dress that Jake had ordered from New York City. Matt chuckled. Nothing was too good for Lucy, and Jake made sure she had the best and newest of everything. Lucy had come from a background of wealth and luxury, not much different from Mrs. Frankston. The difference lay in their attitude. Whereas Lucy embraced life on the frontier and loved everyone, Mrs. Frankston shunned those who were not like her and ignored the ranchers and others not of her class.

Remembering the cold, rude behavior of Mrs. Frankston toward his mother made him realize once again one of the reasons he shouldn't be thinking about Caroline as anything other than a childhood friend.

Lucy greeted him with a smile and a hug. "I'm glad to see that you didn't stay away tonight. We've hardly seen you all day."

"I'm sorry about that, but I was so caught up in all the activity that I didn't think to look for you and Jake." He shook his cousin's hand. It wasn't entirely the truth, but he had been busy avoiding Caroline.

At that moment the orchestra struck up the opening strains of the grand march. Governor Haskell and his wife took the lead. Lucy locked arms with Jake. "Doesn't Mrs. Haskell look gorgeous in that white lace and diamonds? I wouldn't be surprised if it didn't come straight from Paris."

Matt didn't know anything about that, but the women tonight were dressed with what he supposed would be called elegance. He nodded to Lucy and Jake. "I'm going over to join Ma and Pa for the grand march."

After making the trek around the room, Matt searched for Caroline. May as well get the dance over with, and then he could make his exit. He spotted her across the way with Stuart and another couple.

His mouth became as dry as the prairie during drought

when he approached her. "Miss Frankston." Was that squeak his voice? He cleared his throat. "May I have the honor of this dance with you?"

She glanced at Stuart then turned her full attention to Matt with a smile that dazzled him. "Yes, that would be quite nice. Will you excuse us, Stuart? Matt is an old friend from Barton Creek."

Her escort eyed him up and down, but of course he couldn't object to the request. Seeing Stuart's reaction caused Matt to swallow a chuckle.

A few moments later they spun about the dance floor. At first Matt counted in his head the way Becky had taught him, but after a few minutes, he had the steps and began to enjoy the music. He gazed down into Caroline's blue eyes and wanted to sweep her out of the room and back to Barton Creek.

Instead he simply smiled and said, "Living in the city seems to be agreeing with you."

"Yes, it's been quite good for me. Madeline and Julia have introduced me to many people, and of course a lot of our friends from college are there."

"I'm glad you're happy." He could say the words even though he didn't feel them. He wanted her to be miserable and come back to Barton Creek and to him. "Is that one of your new friends accompanying you tonight?"

"Yes, it is. Stuart Whittington is a lawyer and has great ambitions to follow in his father's footsteps as a statesman."

"I see, just like your father and Rob. That's a nice world, but I prefer the wide, open ranges rather than being crowded in the city. I'd never fit in here." This was her world. He had no place in it, and she would never fit into his.

Caroline gazed up at him. "Maybe so, but the city does have its attractions. Don't you ever get lonely out on the ranch?"

"Not with all the work that has to be done. Besides, there's Hank and Monk." That didn't mean he didn't get lonely and wish for a family of his own sometimes, but she didn't need to know about that.

"But cows and a few cowboys can't make up for friends and family." Her eyes searched his, and he knew what she was probing for. But she had Stuart now. What would she want with a boring cowboy like him?

He turned away, pretending to concentrate on his steps, and breathed in relief when the music ended.

When Matt led her back to Stuart, Caroline wanted to grab his hand and have another dance. Instead she smiled and thanked him, but the imprint of his hand on her back burned as though he had branded her like one of his calves.

Stuart swirled her around to the music, but it wasn't the same. She peered over his shoulder and sought Matt's familiar face. She spotted him speaking to his parents, then he headed for the exit. A lump formed in her throat. His dancing with her had been merely a polite gesture from a friend. Like a splash of water on dying embers, his departure drowned the last hopes of his caring for her.

Stuart's fingers lifted her chin. "Where is that sparkle I saw earlier as we came into the room? What could be causing the sadness I see there now?"

This was not the way to treat someone who spent time with her and cared about her. She smiled again and hoped it reached her eyes this time. "I was thinking ahead to when this is all over. It's back to work at the library and the same old routine."

"It doesn't have to be the same old routine."

The true meaning behind his words closed Caroline's throat

with fear, yet she had to recognize the fact that Stuart was here and now, and he cared about her future. Once again she resolved to forget Matt and concentrate on what Stuart had to offer.

Chapter 15

aroline spent a restless night fighting the love that had grown in her heart for the past eleven years. The first time she'd seen Matt in church in the early days of Barton Creek, she had liked him. By the time they were sixteen, she knew he was the only boy she'd ever love. Until this year her dreams always included marriage to Matt, but now those dreams lay dashed on the rocks of rejection.

Images of Stuart and his attentions to her swam in her memory, trying to drown all thoughts of Matt. By morning she had reaffirmed her decision to forget Matt and concentrate on all that Stuart had to offer.

The Whittingtons had not mentioned going to church this morning, but her parents planned to attend. When she had inquired about when Stuart wanted to return to Oklahoma City, she realized she wouldn't have time to go with her parents. Mama hadn't approved but gave in because Caroline had no real choice.

Now as they drove back to Oklahoma City, she almost regretted her choice. Going to church with her parents would have brought her comfort. "Stuart, is there a reason you had to be back in the city so early and not attend church?"

"Yes, there was, but it's to be a surprise. You'll see later. Besides, my parents checked out early, so I had to be out of the room by eleven myself."

His answer about a surprise intrigued her, but she asked no more about it. Stuart was a young man determined to succeed.

He'd already told her he hadn't married because he hadn't found a girl who could share in his ambitions to be in politics. With her father serving as mayor and planning to run for the state legislature in the near future, she hoped she would fit what he wanted. Of course they were only dating now, and no serious talk about long-term relations had ever occurred.

When they reached the city, Stuart turned in a different direction than the one to her town house. "I have a surprise for you. I went down this morning and arranged for the hotel kitchen to prepare us a picnic basket since I figured we'd get back here around noon. Looks like I was right, so we're headed to the park."

"A picnic! How wonderful. The weather is perfect for it. I can't believe you actually thought of something like this." Most men she knew were clueless when it came to things like picnics and how to impress a lady. Every day Stuart revealed more about himself and his caring ways.

She smiled and glanced up at a sunny sky filled with snowy white clouds. This was a day to enjoy living in the present, not thinking about the past, and that was exactly what she planned to do.

Stuart parked the car, helped her down, and then grabbed the basket from the back of the car, where he had stowed it with their luggage. "I see an empty table over there. Let's go."

Caroline started to dust off the bench at the table, but Stuart beat her to it with a cloth that swished all the dirt to the ground. "There, now you can sit and not soil your riding duster."

No matter that the coat was already soiled with road dust, but she appreciated the gesture and sat down. He opened the wicker basket and removed a white cloth to spread over the table.

"Now, that's not usual picnic fare, is it? How did you get it?"

"Oh, a few coins and bills exchanging hands here and there will get you just about anything you might want to buy.

Tablecloths and napkins are no exception." With that he produced two large white linen napkins and handed one to her.

Caroline spread it across her lap and leaned over to peer into the food basket. Stuart began pulling out all types of containers as well as two plates and some cutlery. This must have set him back more than a few coins or bills, but she truly appreciated the gesture. Besides, Stuart, like her father, didn't concern himself with cost.

Around them, other couples as well as families took advantage of the mild weather and enjoyed the park too. Many of them displayed their pleasure at Oklahoma's statehood with songs and games. It reminded her of the festivities of yesterday and created a longing to be in Barton Creek for the celebration tomorrow. She wished to have gone home with her parents, but that would have meant somebody would have to bring her the seventy miles back to the city afterward, and she hadn't requested having Monday off.

An image of Matt having a good time at the observance in her hometown formed, but she erased it from her mind. He must stay in the past. Her future lay here in the city with the people she had come to know.

She bit into a piece of cold ham Stuart had brought. Fresh fruit, thick slices of bread, and coconut cake rounded out the meal. She swallowed the bite of ham. "This is really lovely, and I adore coconut cake."

"A little bird told me you did. That's why I picked it." He grinned at her, and his light brown hair looked even lighter than usual and set off his eyes, which were as brown as her father's coffee without cream. Just a hint of a cleft in his chin softened the strength of his square jaw.

"Hmm, I wonder if that little bird was named Lucy?"

"I'll never tell."

They ate in silence for a few moments. Caroline truly appreciated Stuart's thoughtfulness and consideration. A small sigh escaped her lips, and she bit her lip. Had Stuart heard?

"What's on your mind this lovely afternoon, Caroline Frankston?"

Heat rose in her cheeks. "Nothing really, except how nice a day it is and how good this picnic has been."

He reached for her hand. "And it doesn't have to end. I know you must report to the library tomorrow, but I'm hoping we can spend more time together this evening. I can take you home so you can rest and change then come back to take you to dinner. I promise not to keep you out too late."

Caroline bit down on the corner of her lip and stared at the smooth hands grasping hers. So different from the calloused, rough hands of a working cowboy. No, she couldn't go there. She glanced up at Stuart, who sat waiting expectantly across from her.

"I think that would be lovely. Madeline and Julia won't be in until later this evening since they planned to stay in Guthrie with Madeline's parents for the day."

He grinned from ear to ear like a child with his hand in the candy jar. "Perfect. Let's get this cleaned up so you can rest awhile and unpack from yesterday." He began gathering up the remains of their picnic and placing it back in the basket.

Caroline shook out the cloth then folded it and placed it with the napkins to cover the leftover food. Now she had something to anticipate for the evening rather than the lonely hours in a quiet town house.

When they arrived at her home, he escorted her to the door and deposited her baggage inside. "I look forward to this evening."

"So do I." She smiled then closed the door when he bounded down the steps. As soon as she heard the motorcar start up and drive away, she raced up to her room to change into a clean ensemble. Her Bible lay on the table beside her bed. Caroline sat down. It had been so long since she'd been to church, read her Bible, or prayed, and her conscience pricked because she hadn't accompanied her parents to church this morning. Next Sunday she'd get up and attend.

Her face bunched into a frown. Next Sunday was the one just before Thanksgiving. Where had the days gone? She'd been in town six weeks already, and everything about her life and usual routines had changed. The idea of going back to Barton Creek didn't appeal to her at the moment, but if she didn't, her parents would be terribly disappointed.

With a sigh, Caroline removed her clothing and grabbed her robe. She'd clean up first then try to rest. Thanksgiving wouldn't happen for another week and a half. She didn't have to think about it until then.

When Matt stepped off the train late Sunday afternoon, Becky grabbed him around the waist, or as much as her protruding stomach would allow. He grinned and grasped her arms to push her back. "Hey, little sister, are you sure you're not carrying two or three babies in there?"

Her cheeks reddened before she slapped his arm. "Now don't you go criticizing my size. I'm just fine. Dr. White says so, and he should know." She hooked her hand on his elbow. "Now come on down to the house so we can hear all about yesterday. We got enough on the wire news to put out a special edition of the *Chronicle*, but I want to know details."

Ma's laughter rang out. "Now that I can give you, but I doubt Matt can tell you anything at all. I don't think he was paying much attention to any of the goings on."

Now the heat rose in Matt's cheeks. Ma had noticed his preoccupation during the inauguration and his early departure from the ball. By the look on Becky's face, she'd have a mile-long list of questions to ask him what Ma meant.

He said nothing but followed his family to Becky's. As they neared the house, Micah and Charley bounded down the steps and ran into Jake and Lucy's arms. Those two boys had certainly missed their ma and pa. On the porch, Aunt Hilda held Amanda, who stretched her arms out toward Lucy and called out, "Mama, Mama."

A deep longing stirred inside Matt. If he hadn't wasted so much time, he might have had a little one running out to meet him. Caroline could have been the mother. That wouldn't happen now, but it was time for him to think seriously about finding a girl and settling down.

Once all the greetings and hugs were finished, they followed Becky into her house, where Aunt Hilda had dinner waiting for them.

While they were eating, Ma and Lucy gave their account of the inauguration, parade, and ball. Becky fairly bounced on her chair as she took it all in. No doubt some of this conversation would appear in one of the news articles this week. He glanced at her round belly then away quickly, not wanting to think about the love that put the baby there. At the moment he doubted he'd ever find that kind of love. He'd had it in his hands but had let it slip through. He wouldn't make that mistake again.

On Monday evening Matt joined his parents and all but a few of the ranch hands to ride into town for Barton Creek's celebration of the statehood of Oklahoma.

When they arrived, everyone had gathered for the singing, band playing, and dancing, all arranged by the ladies committee. Matt grinned at the decorations used from the July Fourth festivities. Oklahoma didn't have its own state flag as yet, but it would probably carry the same colors as the United States flag did. The band played the same patriotic marches and songs that swelled Matt's heart with pride every time he heard them.

After numerous speeches and a report from the mayor, the stage cleared and the band struck up songs for a hoedown.

Becky waddled up to him, her hand on her back. "Ma said you danced with Caroline at the ball but left right after that. Why?"

The words to tell her to mind her own business sat on the tip of his tongue, but he didn't say them. "Because I wanted to leave. Caroline was with Stuart Whittington and seemed quite happy with him, so I saw no reason to stay." He cringed inwardly at revealing more than he had intended.

"Well, you shouldn't let that stop you. You've known Caroline longer than this Stuart guy, and you should let her know how you feel."

"That's not going to happen. She's moved on in her life in the city, and I respect her for that. She deserves to be happy." He turned away to forestall any more questions and caught a glimpse of Susannah Beall, one of the new schoolteachers. She'd be a perfect distraction.

"Good-bye, little sister. I want to dance." He strode over to where Susannah stood at the refreshment table. "Miss Beall, would you care to share a dance with me?"

Her eyes opened wide, and her red-gold curls shook as she nodded her head. "Oh, yes, I'd like that very much."

At the edge of the space, he encircled her waist with his hand and grasped the other one in his. He swung her out onto the floor to the tune of "Turkey in the Straw." Although she knew the steps and was light on her feet, she had none of the grace and poise of Caroline. He ground his teeth and tossed the memory aside. The pretty girl in his arms at the moment deserved his full attention.

"Miss Beall, I do believe you are the prettiest dancer here." Where had those words come from? That's not what he meant to say at all.

Her expression indicated she was as startled as he at the words, but she responded lightly. "Why, thank you, kind sir."

"My pleasure indeed," he teased.

He should have enjoyed the banter, but instead his heart felt heavier than the silver-studded saddle he used for special events. With his shoulders squared and a smile pasted on his face, he was determined to enjoy this day and look to the future.

At the end of the first dance, he escorted Susannah back to the refreshment table. "Would you like a cup of punch?" At her nod, he filled a cup.

When he handed her the sparkling fruit juice, she smiled over the rim as she raised the cup to her lips. Her gesture brought back the memory of Caroline the night of her going away party. He blinked and brought his attention back to Miss Beall.

He gazed at those eyes trying to decide what color they might be. Neither green nor blue, he couldn't come up with anything that would adequately describe them. He returned the smile as the band struck up the tune "Oh, Susannah." They both laughed, and he held out his arms. "Well, I suppose there's no way we can sit this one out."

As they turned and dipped on the dance floor, Matt loosened up and realized he was having a good time. When the music stopped, they were both out of breath and laughing. Before he had time to think he said, "Do you ride horses?"

Her eyes sparkled with merriment. "Oh, yes. I grew up around them. I had to leave mine at home when I came here to teach, but when I go home Thanksgiving, I plan to get Rascal and bring him back with me."

"How about taking a turn on one of ours? I can bring one into town, and we can take a ride. I can show you some of the country around here and maybe ride out to our ranch."

"I think I would like that very much."

"It's settled then. I'll meet you at the boarding house on Saturday."

Her face lit up with an enthusiasm. "Why don't I ask Mrs. Claymore to fix us a picnic lunch, or I can do it. Then we can eat out in the country. That is, if the weather cooperates."

"That's a fine idea. If it rains or is too cold, we can always go another day." At that moment he glanced over Susannah's shoulder and spotted Hawk standing to the side. His face looked like one of those thunderclouds on a spring day. Something must be terribly wrong for him to look so fierce.

"It's been fun, but I need to speak with a friend of mine for a few minutes. I'll be back." Matt grinned, tipped his hat, and turned to go find Hawk, but the man had disappeared. Must not have been as bad as he thought. Matt shrugged and headed to where Lucy and Jake talked with Ruth and Geoff Kensington. He'd been planning to check with Geoff about that new well they were digging, and now was as good a time as any. He could find Hawk later.

Matt said nothing about his plans all week but on Saturday said he was going into town. He picked up Becky's horse at the livery and headed to the boarding house to pick up Susannah. Mrs. Claymore stood on the porch with her hands across her chest to greet him.

"I understand you're taking Miss Beall for a ride in the country."

Her stern look spoke of her disapproval, but he smiled just the same. "That's right. Since her own horse isn't here, I borrowed Becky's for her. I thought she'd enjoy being out in the fresh air after being cooped up in a classroom all week."

"That's all you'd better enjoy. I like this girl, and I don't want to see her hurt."

Matt gulped. He'd had no intentions other than just a pleasant ride. What could be wrong with Mrs. Claymore? Thankfully, Susannah stepped out onto the porch at that moment.

"Hello, Matt. I didn't realize you'd arrived until I glimpsed you here with Mrs. Claymore."

She wore a divided skirt much like Becky usually wore, and her boots were well worn rather than shiny and new. Evidently Susannah did know about horses. He held out his hand to assist her down the steps. "I haven't been here but a minute or so. You look ready for our ride. I brought Star Bright. She's Becky's and a good mount."

In no time they were on the open road, then Matt veered off the road and out across the land. Susannah sat easily in the saddle, her posture in tune with the horse. Matt kept the horses at a slow trot to allow conversation.

"Tell me about your teaching, Miss Beall. I remember the hard times I gave my teacher."

Her laughter rang out, and she shook her head. "Please call me Susannah, and I just bet you did give your teachers a rough go. I have a few like you in the sixth and seventh graders in my class. They take great delight in tormenting the girls whenever they can get away with it and then roughhousing and wrestling all over the place during recess."

Matt had to chuckle at the description. "I had a few scrapes and bruises in my time doing just that." It was about that age when he and a few others discovered girls and did everything to attract their attention while at the same time pretending to hate them.

"I think I've wanted to be a teacher all my life, well, at least since the fourth grade. I loved the lessons and helping the teacher do all kinds of things."

Matt imagined what she'd been like as a young girl, and it was a nice picture. Her light brown hair done up in pigtails with her brownish-green eyes sparkling when she helped the teacher made a right pleasant image.

They rode for a few minutes in silence before Matt had an idea. "Susannah, Star Bright likes to run. Wanna race to that stand of trees in the distance? It's the leading edge of our property."

"Sure, why not." She dug her heels into Star Bright's flanks and whipped her reins. "Come on, girl, show us what you can do." She raced off, startling Matt with her quickness.

Matt jerked back then grabbed his own reins and dug in. "Come on, let's catch them." He pounded after Susannah, trying to catch up, but he should have known that would never work. Star Bright was in racing mode, and she refused to be caught.

He pulled up beside Susannah and panted. "That was a quick start."

She leaned over and patted Star Bright's neck. "I heard about her reputation as a racer, so I decided to see for myself."

Whatever else he thought, he had to admit that Miss Susannah Beall had spunk and was as good a horsewoman as his sister. Maybe she was worth getting to know better. He resolved to ask her out again at the end of their ride.

Chapter 16

*M*onday afternoon of Thanksgiving week, Charlotte checked her list once more to make sure she hadn't left off anything for her Thanksgiving dinner preparations. Becky and Rob would join them, and Caroline would be home on the afternoon train Wednesday evening. Becky would miss the Hayneses' dinner since Dr. White had decided the trip out to the ranch would not be good for her. Charlotte had certainly agreed with that decision.

Her plans to include the Hayneses for dinner had not materialized. Despite her desire to make amends for all the years of less than friendly behavior, she couldn't bring herself to take the first steps toward reconciliation. She laid the pen across the paper and closed her eyes.

This was one situation for which she hadn't prayed like she should, mainly because she was afraid of what the Lord would tell her to do. She did need advice, but Mellie had already given hers. Charlotte sighed and pushed away from her desk. She had to visit with her pastor. He would help her.

She walked into the kitchen to find Ruby. "I'm going into town for a little while, but I'll be back before Mr. Frankston comes home."

"Yes, ma'am. 'Tis a might cold today, so I'll have a spot of tea waiting for your return. 'Twill warm you up good and proper." Ruby smiled and continued to chop vegetables for the evening meal.

"Thank you, Ruby. I'll welcome that."

Charlotte retrieved her coat, hat, and gloves from the hall tree and donned them before opening the front door. A blast of cold air caused her to close the top button of her coat. She made sure her hat sat securely on her head before starting her journey to town.

On her way to the church she passed the bakery. She'd make a stop on the way home to buy a few pastries to enjoy with her tea later.

When she was only a block from church, she realized that only a few women had smiled or greeted her, and none had stopped to speak. Marie Fleming and Hannah Perkins were the only two women who ever did that, and they were the only two who had ever visited in her home for anything other than special occasions. That was one of the things she needed to change, but Charlotte feared the townspeople's rejection more than their present lack of friendship.

She reached the church steps and stopped before squaring her shoulders and opening the door. Such a nice, quiet place the church was in the middle of the afternoon. With no sun to sparkle through the colors of the stained glass windows, the interior turned gloomy, as though to match Charlotte's mood.

At that moment, Pastor Weaver stepped through the door leading to his office behind the choir loft. "Ah, Charlotte Frankston, what brings you to our church this cold afternoon?"

"I...I need to speak with you about a situation." Her nerves on edge, Charlotte's courage threatened to take flight like birds disturbed in the trees.

He beckoned to her and smiled in such a way that she couldn't help but go to him. "We can visit in my office."

When she was seated across from him, her mind raced, and the words chased each other like a dog after a cat. He sat silently, waiting for her to begin. Charlotte cleared her throat and grasped her hands in her lap. To save herself agony, she decided to make her situation as plain as possible.

"As you know, I am not the most popular woman in town. I may have many positions of leadership, but most come about only because of my being the wife of the mayor."

She stopped, but he said nothing and nodded for her to continue. "I have not sought to make friends; therefore, I have very few. I want to rectify that, but I don't know what to do. I'm afraid the women of Barton Creek have been scorned for so long that they no longer trust me."

Again she stopped and waited. This time he reached for his Bible. "Am I to understand that you want to make amends and seek the forgiveness of these ladies?"

Charlotte gulped. Seeking forgiveness had not entered her mind. Smiling, being friendly, and speaking to the women should be enough. "Yes, I do want to make amends, but what do I do about it?"

"My dear friend, you know exactly what you need to do. You don't need me to tell you. Have you prayed and asked God for guidance?"

Another deep swallow filled her throat. "Not really. I wasn't sure what to say or what to ask for." If she told him the truth, he'd know she hadn't prayed at all, and that would be embarrassing.

He placed his hands on the Bible and gazed at her with eyes that spoke of his caring for her and her dilemma. "Let's pray about it now."

She bowed her head and let his words flow over her. "Our Father God, our dear sister Charlotte has a problem. You have the answers for her, and I pray for her ears, her eyes, and her heart to be open to the message You want her to receive. Give her the strength she needs to take the first steps, and I pray the women of our town will open their hearts to Charlotte and embrace her offers of friendship. In Your name we pray. Amen."

A great peace fell over Charlotte like the warmth of a quilt on a freezing night. Pastor Weaver stood. "Now, I believe you will figure out what you need to do and how to go about doing it. It will be good to see you putting your faith in practice and stepping out to seek the forgiveness of those you have hurt."

Her heart raced with the idea of forgiveness. Then Emily Morris's face swam into her vision. How could she ever make up for all the unkind words she'd said about Emily and Dove? But she had to try.

"Thank you, Pastor. It may take a few days for me to figure it all out, but I will, and I'll pray for God to lead me." And that was a promise she intended to keep.

Outside the air didn't feel quite as cold as it had before. Maybe that was so because her heart had grown warm and looked forward to the days ahead. As she walked down the street, the cinnamon and sugar aroma from the bakery once again called to her. She stepped inside the store and inhaled the fragrance of fresh baked rolls and bread. A few of those muffins would be most delightful with the tea Ruby promised to have waiting. What a wonderful week of Thanksgiving this would be.

Caroline strolled into the employees' room to retrieve her coat and hat. Just a few more days and she'd be on her way home for the holiday weekend. With the library closed on Thursday and Friday, she looked forward to the extra days off.

Jo rushed into the room wearing a huge smile. The new hairstyle had proved to be one the girl could handle herself, and the two skirts and several shirtwaists gave her more self-confidence in her appearance. "Caroline, I can't thank you enough for what you've done for me. Jimmy and I went to dinner the other night, and now he's asked me out again. He's the first one to ever do that."

"That's wonderful, Jo. I'm so happy for you. Jimmy seems like a very nice young man."

"Oh, he is. He graduates from the university at Norman next spring and plans to stay here in the city and go into business with his father."

"Now that sounds like a young man with a plan for his life." Caroline had never seen Jo so animated and happy. It turned her into a very different young woman, and the warmth of accomplishment flowed through Caroline. Helping gave her a feeling like she hadn't experienced before, and she liked it. If only her mother could learn the same lesson.

She said her good-byes and hurried to the front, waving at Mrs. Caskey as she left. When she opened the door, she jumped back in surprise. "Stuart, what are you doing here?"

Stuart smiled, removed his hat, and bowed. "I'm here to escort Miss Caroline Frankston to her home." He gestured behind him. "I have the car with the curtains down and a good blanket, so you'll be nice and snug. Much better than riding the trolley."

Once again Stuart impressed her with his thoughtfulness. "I'd like that very much." She followed him to the car and gasped as he stopped by a new Pierce Arrow automobile.

"Stuart, this is a brand-new car. When did you get this?" She reached out to touch the shiny surface, smooth as a piece of glass.

Stuart grinned, and his chest swelled with pride. "Picked it up last night and thought it would be a nice surprise for today." He stepped over to the car and demonstrated the side curtains he'd obtained to protect passengers from the elements. "Now we can ride in warmth and comfort."

He grasped her hand in his and assisted her up into the front seat. He then joined her and slid beneath the steering wheel. The car started smoothly and chugged from its space. "It's not as noisy as some of the other ones on the streets."

Stuart steered the car around a group of pedestrians crossing the street. "It's the new engine. It purrs like a satisfied kitten after a bowl of cream."

"Yes, that's a good way to describe it, but how do you know about cats and purring?"

He laughed and reached over to pull her closer. "Mother loves cats, and we have had our share."

Caroline hesitated as his arm tugged at her shoulder, but she decided to move closer to him. It would help with the cold. Even with the blanket, the frigid air managed to chill her to the bone. She settled next to him and appreciated the extra warmth.

He swerved to miss a dog and yanked his arm from her shoulder. "I'd better use two hands to guide this thing or we might end up over the curb, but I much prefer the other." He cast a sideways glance at her that revealed the sparkle in his eyes.

It had been nice to be in his embrace, but now she was just fine and preferred he paid attention to his driving. When they reached her town house, he pulled up to the curb and stopped. Rather than stepping down, he turned to her and grasped her hands.

"Caroline, you are a wonderful young woman. I've come to admire you more than you can imagine." At that moment he leaned over, moved his hands to her shoulders, and brought his face to hers. He planted his lips on hers with a firm kiss.

At first, Caroline didn't move, frozen in place until she blinked and pushed him away. "Stuart, what are you doing?"

Before he could answer she scooted to her side of the seat and unfastened the curtains.

He grasped her shoulder. "Please wait, Caroline. I thought our relationship had developed enough that a kiss would not be out of order."

"Well, it was." She fumbled with the door handle and hopped down before he had time to stop her. He raced around from his side and grabbed her hand. A scowl appeared for a moment then quickly dissipated into a smile, and he held up his hands as if in defense. "I'm sorry. Guess I read the signs wrong. Please don't be angry."

She looked steadily into his face. "I'm not so much angry as I am surprised and disappointed."

"I'm sorry to have offended you. Give me another chance, please. Will you keep our next date after you get back from Thanksgiving?"

His eyes pleaded with her, and his smile beguiled her to the point she found herself saying yes without thinking it through.

"Wonderful. I'll see you then." He grinned broadly and bounded back to his car.

She unlocked her front door, then closed it and leaned against it. Her heart thumped, and she raised her fingers to her lips. One thing she'd always dreamed about was her first kiss, and she had always hoped Matt would claim it. He'd had his chances but had never done anything. She sighed and headed up the stairs, glad her roommates were not yet home.

The truth must be faced. Matt no longer cared about her, if he ever had, and Stuart was here and did. If she didn't seize this opportunity, she may never have another one with such promise for the future. Still, despite her resolve, she wanted to see Matt one more time, and that time would come with the holiday. If the opportunity arose, perhaps it was time to let him know what she felt.

Matt stepped into the newspaper office to catch Becky before she left for the day. Her eyes opened wide with surprise when she turned to find him in the building. "Hello, big brother. What brings you into town?"

"I had to send a wire for Pa, so I thought I'd stop in to see how you're doing and maybe treat you and Rob to supper at the diner."

She lunged at him and wrapped her arms around his waist. "Oh, I'd love that. I was just thinking about what we'd have at home. Most likely leftovers, so I'm sure Rob will be more than happy to eat at the diner."

He waited while she gathered her belongings. Every time he saw Becky, he marveled at the changes in his little sister. She'd always been rather stubborn and let people know what she thought, but now that was tempered with her marriage and a career where she could express her opinion in the newspaper. Her impending motherhood had helped soften her as well.

She grabbed his arm. "I know you're on your horse, but I like to walk, so you'll have to let him tag along behind us."

"Anything you say, but doesn't the walk tire you out?" He eyed her bulging middle. It looked like she had expanded even more since last week.

She patted her stomach. "Oh, no, I've been sitting all day, and little scamp and I need the exercise. Besides, you know how much I enjoy cold weather."

That was true. She'd always been one to love the outdoors and enjoyed the winter months even more than he did summer.

That one time fighting the blizzard had turned him into a warm weather lover.

As they walked, Becky talked constantly. Well, that was one thing that hadn't changed and never would. He listened with only half an ear until he heard Caroline's name. He jerked to attention. "What did you say?"

"I said Caroline will be home on the Wednesday evening train from Oklahoma City. She's going to help me pick out some items for the baby from the catalog."

He had forgotten Caroline would be home for the holiday. He'd already asked Susannah to attend the special services on Wednesday evening at the church. Since the train arrived later, maybe Caroline wouldn't be able to attend. If that was so, then he could possibly go the whole time without seeing her. Susannah planned to leave on the early train to Denver on Thursday to go to her home just a little west of Barton Creek.

Since he wouldn't be coming into town to see Susannah, he could make up reasons to stay at the ranch the entire time. With that resolved, he turned his attention back to his sister and her prattle.

Chapter 17

Caroline awakened in her bed and stretched. How good it felt to be sleeping in the room she'd had since she was young girl. She reached for a pillow and hugged it to her chest as daylight peeked through the curtains at the window.

Last night she had spent the evening talking with her mother and telling her about Oklahoma City and how everyone was so glad they were now a state. Her mother had inquired about Stuart, but Caroline had chosen to share only a small portion of what had happened with him. Her fingers touched her lips as she remembered the kiss. That she didn't want to share with anyone just yet.

She pulled her stockings over her feet and slipped them into soft shoes before padding across the floor to the wardrobe. After she finished dressing, she made her way downstairs, where delicious smells wafted from the kitchen. Cinnamon rolls, and homemade ones at that. Ruby must have started them last night.

Her father glanced up from his paper. "Happy Thanksgiving, princess. Did you sleep well?"

She settled into the chair on his left and reached for her napkin. "Yes, very well. It's nice to be home again."

Her mother swept in with a swish of her skirts and stopped to kiss Caroline's forehead as she had done every morning when Caroline had been a child. Some things never changed. "Good morning, Mother."

Ruby entered bearing eggs, bacon, and her cinnamon rolls on

a tray. She deposited them on the table, and Caroline breathed deeply. "I love the smell of your rolls, Ruby. Thank you for making them for me."

Ruby's face beamed and tinged pink. "'Tis a pleasure it is to be baking for ye again. And 'tis nice to have ye home for the holiday."

She pushed through the door to the kitchen, and Caroline bowed her head as her father bowed his. Saying grace was another habit she'd dropped in recent days. It seemed every meal was eaten in such a hurry or at a restaurant and she had no time for it. Hearing her father's rich baritone voice now as he thanked God for the food stirred guilt in her soul. Well, she'd be in church this Sunday, and then she'd catch up on spiritual matters.

Her mother began discussing the meal for the day and what time it would be served. Caroline let her mind wander back to Oklahoma City. Stuart would be enjoying a meal with his parents, who had come home for the holidays from their place in Washington. Caroline had only met them twice, and Mrs. Whittington had reminded her of Mother in her manner of speech and knowledge of proper etiquette. Of course as a senator's wife, she had to know those things, and she had seemed genuinely interested in Caroline.

Life with Stuart would be much like the one she had growing up, but in a larger city and with more people. One thing she vowed to do was to treat all people equally. Through her time with Jo she had learned how wonderful it was to help others. To see her friend so happy filled Caroline's heart with a longing to improve the lives of others. As the wife of a young lawyer with great ambitions, she could do a great deal of charitable work.

She imagined the girls she could help. Perhaps she could offer a charm school or school of etiquette. No, that would only attract girls with money to spend for such learning. Maybe a charitable group would be interested in having a program like that for impoverished young women.

Her mother's voice interrupted her reverie, and Caroline blinked. "I'm sorry, Mother. What did you say?"

"I said not to forget that Rob and Becky will be here at two, and we plan to eat soon after."

"Yes, I remember." Caroline looked forward to spending the holiday with her family. "I'll be so glad to see Becky and Rob." And she would, since she hadn't seen them since her birthday weeks ago. The only drawback was the fact that seeing Becky brought on thoughts of Matt, but she resolved to keep those buried for the time being.

Later that morning she returned to her room to rest and found one of her favorite novels, *Jane Eyre*, on the table by her window. For the next few hours she lost herself in the world of Jane and Mr. Rochester.

Only a noise from downstairs brought her back to the present. She marked her place before rushing down to greet Becky. Her sister-in-law had removed her coat and handed it to Father when Caroline rushed to her.

Becky's protruding belly kept them from hugging except at the shoulders, and they both laughed. "Well, I can see that my little niece or nephew is already coming between us."

"Just wait until it gets here, and you'll be one of the first to spoil him or her."

Mother joined them and kissed Rob. "I'm so glad you decided to stay in town and not try to ride out to the ranch. Becky doesn't need that kind of jolting around."

Becky hid her grin and hooked her arm with Caroline's. "Let's go into the parlor and talk until Ruby calls us."

Caroline settled on the sofa while Becky chose a straight-back chair and eased onto it. "If I sat on that sofa, I'd need two of you to pull me up." She giggled and patted her stomach. "I never realized how much weight I would gain or how big I would get. I guess I never really paid much attention to Lucy or Dove when they were waiting for their babies." She leaned against the upholstered back of the chair. "Now tell me all about Stuart and the latest news from Oklahoma City."

Matt pushed back from the table, full of Ma's turkey and stuffing as well as pumpkin pie. He laughed at his nephews as they fought to keep awake. Lucy gathered up Amanda then herded the two boys off to a back room for a nap, promising to be back in a few minutes to help Ma with cleaning up.

Instead of following his pa and Jake into the living room, Matt picked up plates and glasses and took them to the kitchen. Without Becky around, Ma had much more to do herself, and she had cooked most of the dinner. Of course Lucy would be back, but she had her hands full with the children.

Ma opened her eyes wide and lifted her eyebrows. "You don't have to do this. Lucy will be here soon as the children are down."

"I know, but you've already done so much. Seems wrong you should have to clean up the mess as well."

Her laughter filled the room, and she reached over and hugged him. "I've been doing this since before you were born, so don't worry about too much for me to do. Go on and join Pa and Jake. I'm sure they're talking about cattle or horses or oil. Take your pick. Lucy and I will take care of this."

Matt kissed her cheek. "OK, if you say so, and that was one of the best Thanksgiving meals we've had."

Ma's cheeks turned pink, and she shooed him away with her

drying towel. He sauntered back to the dining area, but sitting with Pa and Jake didn't appeal to him at the moment, so he headed out to the stables. He entered the building and breathed deeply of the musty air. Soiled hay and manure greeted him, and he coughed. Matt frowned. For some reason cleaning up had been forgotten this morning. The stalls needed mucking now. He retrieved a wheelbarrow from the storage room and then grabbed a pitchfork from a hook by the door.

Monk walked through the door. "Matt, what're you doin' here? Hank and the boys forgot about their chores this morning, so's I come to do it." He reached for another fork.

"The two of us should get it done in no time. Take the horses out to the corral, and I'll keep picking up hay."

Monk led the animals outside then rejoined Matt in the barn. "I done fussed at Hank. All us knows it ain't healthy for the horses to stand around in manure."

"It's OK this time. I need to work off Ma's meal anyway."

Monk laughed and tossed soiled hay onto the wheelbarrow. "I knows what you mean. Cookie fixed up a fine meal hisself along with the turkey your Ma prepared. She even baked extra pie for us."

"Sounds like Ma. Lucy brought over some fresh bread and rolls she'd made." Then he chuckled and leaned on his pitchfork. "Remember Lucy's first Thanksgiving and killing that turkey? I thought she was going to cry her eyes out when that axe came down on that tom's neck."

"Oh, yeah, I remembers all right. Seem to remember her ruining a few things learning how to cook."

"She's learned good because those rolls were the best I've eaten. Even Ma said so."

They worked in silence for a while but images of Susannah and Caroline kept Matt from concentrating on what he was supposed to be doing. He tossed a fork full of manure toward the wheelbarrow, but it landed on Monk instead.

The old man yelped, and Matt jerked around to find him brushing the foul-smelling mess from his shirt.

Matt stifled a laugh. "I'm sorry. I didn't do that on purpose."

"Didn't figure you did, but your mind's certainly somewhere else. Could it be that gal Miss Caroline, or is it that there Susannah?"

Had he been that obvious? "Both, I guess. Susannah is a wonderful girl, but she's not Caroline." As if that could make a difference now. Caroline was out of his reach, but Susannah was available, so why wasn't he happy?

Monk pulled off his gloves and leaned against the stall. "Seems to me you oughta quit chasing the devil around the stump and ask that Caroline to marry you. And iffen you don't and you lose her, don't come runnin' to me for sympathy."

Laughter sounded from the doorway. Hank stood there with his arms crossed over his chest. "That's what I've been telling him, but he won't listen, and now he's seeing Miss Susannah."

"Hang it all, why can't you two leave it alone?"

Monk picked up the pitchfork and hung it on the hook. "Cause we're tired of that hang-dog look on your face every time she's in town."

"Monk's right. Look, Amy and Susannah have become good friends, and Amy wanted me to invite the two of you to the play at that new theater in town. Won't Susannah be back for school on Monday?"

"Yes. Her pa is bringing her back with her horse so we can go riding again. She prefers her own saddle and mount." When he had told her good-bye on Wednesday, Susannah had been excited about seeing her family, but she was also excited about bringing her mare back to Barton Creek.

"What about the play? You think she'll want to go?"

"I'll ask her when she gets back." The more he had an opportunity to be with her, the less he'd think about Caroline. Hawk's face from the night of the statehood celebration filled his head. He'd never had a chance to talk with Hawk about what was wrong that night. He shook it off. The matter couldn't have been important, or Hawk would have said something.

With Hank's help, the chore was finished quickly. Matt sniffed the air and grinned. "Well, it does smell some better in here now."

After the horses were secure, Matt headed back to the house. "I'll let you know what Susannah says."

Hank waved and ambled out to the bunkhouse with Monk. Matt stopped and stared out across the ranch. If he was going to continue to see Susannah, he had to make more effort to forget Caroline.

Mellie stared out the window to watch her son as he exited the barn. His mood the past week had improved, but she feared he still had hopes of reuniting with Caroline. He'd gone riding with Susannah Beall, but Mellie still worried that he wasn't over Caroline.

Lucy came up beside her. "I can see you're still concerned about Matt. I am too. When we were at the inaugural ball and they danced, I could see how much she cares for him, and I know he loves her. What I don't understand is why they're so careful to make sure they don't let each other know."

"If I had the answer to that, then I think everyone would be happy." Lucy started to interject, but Mellie held up her hand. "I know what you're thinking. You think it's Charlotte's fault. Yes, Charlotte has been rude to many people, but she and I had a long talk a month ago. For the first time I saw the real her, not just the front she puts up. Losing Caroline has made her lonely and perhaps shown her that she needs more true friends. I think she truly wants to change."

Lucy nodded thoughtfully. "I would say that's impossible, but I know from past experience that God can perform miracles. I do believe it would go a long way toward resolving the issues between Caroline and Matt. Jake has told me more than once how Matt resents Charlotte for the way she treated us and especially for her attitude toward Dove and Emily Morris."

"I believe that's all going to change. With her trip to St. Louis and preparations for the inauguration and Thanksgiving, she probably didn't have the time or energy to deal with the townspeople. I have a feeling she will make her move soon." And Mellie prayed that she was right.

Thanksgiving evening, Charlotte brushed her hair at her dressing table. Although the celebrations had gone well, she still felt guilty for not following up on her idea to invite the Hayneses to dinner. And her heart told her that the time was getting ripe for her to do something about the townspeople. No more delays or excuses.

Maxwell walked up behind her and placed his hands on her shoulders. "It still looks like spun gold, my sweet." He bent over and kissed the top of her head.

She grasped his hand in hers. "Oh, Maxwell, I've been thinking. How am I ever going to make up for all the trouble I've caused over the years? I told Mellie Haynes I would try, but it's so hard to think about doing."

Maxwell patted her hand then stepped away and picked up a Bible from the table. "If those ladies are the Christians I believe they are, they will do as this good book tells them and forgive you."

Her hand gripped the brush in her lap, and fear squeezed her heart until it became lead in her chest. If the women didn't want to forgive her, they wouldn't want to be friends and let her make amends. She laid the brush on the dressing table and leaned her head on her palms. Tears threatened to squeeze their way from under her eyelids.

Maxwell grasped her arm and led her to his chair, where he sat down and pulled her onto his lap. He hugged her close and kissed her temple. "I think we need to pray about this."

His arms gave her the security and assurance of his love she needed at the moment, and she relaxed as he prayed.

"Heavenly Father, we come to You to seek forgiveness first from You for all the hurts we've caused in the past years by snubbing or talking rudely to the women of Barton Creek. We seek forgiveness for our neglect of looking to You first instead of acting on our own beliefs and feelings. We pray others will be as willing to forgive us as You are. In Your name we pray, amen."

Once again, as with Pastor Weaver, peace flowed through like the balm of Gilead. That peace would give her the courage to do what she must do to be in God's will for her life.

Maxwell eased her up from his lap and stood. "We're in this together, my love, and whatever happens, we'll face it together." He kissed her again, stirring up the embers of her love for him. With him and God on her side, she could face whatever came in the days ahead.

Chapter 18

fter Maxwell and Caroline both left the breakfast table to wash and dress, Charlotte sat there while Ruby cleared the table. Her mind swirled with images of the women in Barton Creek. So many of them she had shunned or ignored, thinking they were not of the same social class as she was. Yet after prayer time last night, she saw them in a new light. She'd told Caroline she was going out to run errands that morning, but in truth she planned a visit to Mellie Haynes. Mellie would help her decide what the next step should be. With that decision made, Charlotte let Ruby know she was going out then retrieved her coat.

Her first stop was the livery, where she asked Jonah to get a buggy ready for her to ride out to the Hayneses' ranch. After settling that, she headed for the newspaper office. At the door she stopped a moment. She still didn't understand why Becky wanted to continue to work with the baby's birth so near, but Charlotte determined not to be one who criticized but one who helped. Putting this new persona into practice may be difficult at first, but she resolved to do her best.

When she entered, she found Becky speaking with another young woman. Charlotte searched her memory and realized the girl was Molly Lansdowne. At that moment Becky noticed Charlotte's presence.

"Good morning, Mother Frankston. What brings you in today?" She hurried over to where Charlotte stood.

"Is that Molly Lansdowne? She's changed some since last year."

"Yes, Molly is in her second year of college and is studying journalism and English. She likes to write almost as much as I do. I'm helping her get ready to take my place when she's home for break between semesters."

"Oh, that will be nice for you and her father." That answered one question, and she hadn't even had to ask it.

"It will, but do you need something?"

Charlotte shook her head and grinned at her daughter-in-law. "No, I'm fine, but I do want you to know that I'm riding out to pay your mother a visit. She came to me a few weeks ago and we had a long talk. I can see now what she tried to tell me then, and I want her to know. Your mother is a fine woman, and I hope we can become good friends."

Becky's mouth dropped open before she reached over to hug Charlotte. "This is the best news I've heard since I found out about the baby." She stepped back with a smile on her face that brought sunshine to Charlotte's heart.

"I've really admired the way you haven't nosed into our life. I know you haven't approved of my continuing to work here, but you haven't criticized or told me I should quit and stay home to wait for the baby. I truly appreciate that."

Charlotte swallowed the lump rising in her throat and thanked the Lord she had kept silent because her feelings had been exactly what Becky said. Becky was a free spirit with such enthusiasm for life, and now Charlotte was grateful she hadn't tried to rein it in like a contrary horse.

"You're welcome, but now I must get to the stables. Jonah is fixing the rig for me, and I want to be on my way out to the ranch." She hugged Becky again before turning and walking away.

Jonah had buttoned on the side coverings for the one-seated

buggy he'd prepared for her, and those helped ward off the wind that blew from the north. He'd also wrapped a blanket around Charlotte's legs and lap to keep her warm. Jonah had been a blessing to Barton Creek in more ways than one. His longevity in the town had helped in knowing everyone's likes and dislikes when it came to boarding their horses and vehicles. Maxwell had built a building out back of their house for the motorcar, but Jonah still handled all their other transportation needs. His livery had been expanded twice, and now all but a very few people of Barton Creek depended on him to take care of getting them from one place to another.

His wife was another one she'd ignored. A faithful member of the church, Dorothy had served on the Altar Guild and deserved an apology too. Charlotte's lack of sensitivity had certainly created a long list of women she had hurt in one way or another. Making it up to them would not be as easy as she first thought.

By the time Charlotte arrived at the ranch, she had the beginnings of an idea as to how to let others know of her sincerity in making amends. She prayed Mellie would be willing to help her with the plan.

Mellie greeted her at the door with surprise written on her face, but a smile welcomed Charlotte. "Come in out of the cold." She stepped back to allow Charlotte to step inside.

Logs blazed in the great stone fireplace of the large living room. Furnishings of sofas, chairs, and tables made of light stained wood and leather upholstery, oil lamps placed about, and books on the tables lent a cozy, friendly atmosphere to the room. Bright colored pillows and a crocheted throw all added to the warmth. Although she'd been in the house twice since the tornado ten years ago, this was the first time Charlotte had really looked at it, but she hoped it wouldn't be the last.

Mellie took her coat and nodded toward the sofa. "Have a seat, and I'll hang your coat. Would you like tea or coffee?"

"Tea would be wonderful." Charlotte sat down on the sofa and ran her hands over the leather. So soft and smooth, and so different from what she had thought it would be. She glanced around at the other furnishings and saw the great oak dining table with ten chairs around it. It attested to the number of people in the Haynes family, and knowing Mellie, she probably had extra chairs and leaves to make even more room.

Mellie appeared in a doorway with a tray filled with a teapot, cups, and a plate of cookies. She set it down on the large oak table in front of the sofa. "I prefer tea myself, so I always have a kettle of hot water on my stove. These are cookies from the batch I baked for Lucy's children. Micah and Charley aren't fond of pumpkin pie."

She proceeded to pour tea into two porcelain cups decorated with roses and trimmed in gold leaf that were as pretty and dainty as any Charlotte had ever seen. With all the men in her household, Mellie probably didn't use them very often. She handed one to Charlotte. "Would you like sugar or lemon or milk with your tea?"

"I prefer just a bit of sugar." After that was added, Mellie offered her a cookie that had nuts and chunks of chocolate in them. Charlotte bit into one. "These are delicious. I've never had anything like them before."

"They're Lucy's recipe. They had a bumper crop of pecans this year from the two trees Jake planted when they married. They're a wonderful addition to the cookie along with chunks of chocolate from the bars we get at Anderson's."

Charlotte nodded and sipped her tea. The words she wanted to say wouldn't come, and her hand shook when she lifted the cup to her mouth. It clattered back onto the saucer. "I'm sorry, but I guess I'm nervous because I don't know how to begin what I want to say."

"Then take your time. It'll come to you, and I'm in no hurry."

Charlotte breathed deeply to steady her nerves. "I want to make amends and apologize to those I've hurt all these years, but I'm not sure how to go about doing it. You're one of the wisest women I know, so I decided to come to you for help."

"I see." Mellie sat silently for a moment then set her cup back on the tray. "I don't know about the wise part, but maybe you need to think about the ones you've hurt the most and start there."

Charlotte's eyes misted. Mellie's words contained no anger, no judgment, no bitterness, just good advice. Dove Anderson and Emily Morris came to her mind immediately, as well as Bea Anderson. Bea had been a good friend until her son married Dove and allowed a Cherokee half-breed to be part of the family. "But what can I say to make them know I'm sincere and really do want to be friends?"

"Sunday morning at church would be a good place to start. Take them aside and tell them. Knowing their hearts, I'm sure they will accept your apology, but first you will need to pray for God to give you the exact words you need to say."

Of course, prayer would have to be part of the picture. Only God's mercy could give her the courage to take those first steps. Now was the time to reveal the plan that occurred to her during the drive out.

"Mellie, I'd like to have a luncheon and invite those I've mistreated in the past. Dove, Emily, Bea, Lucy, Mrs. Weems, Ruth, Marie, and Hannah. Do you think they'd come?"

Mellie's laugh rang out in the large room. "If for nothing else than curiosity they'll come. I think it's a grand idea, and I'll be glad to back you up and make sure they know the reason."

"Thank you. I thought I could count on your support, but it's nice to know for sure." Charlotte picked up her cup. "Now let's talk about our soon-to-come grandbaby."

Since her mother had gone out for the morning, Caroline decided to see if Becky might have time for a visit. But when she opened the front door and a blast of cold air hit her in the face, she closed the door and removed her coat. Visiting Becky could wait. They'd been together just yesterday and would see each other again on Sunday.

Delicious aromas drifted in from the kitchen and drew her there to see what Ruby might have ready to eat. Caroline recognized the delicious odor as vegetable soup, and Ruby made some of the best around.

When Caroline entered the room, the cook stood at the counter by the sink mixing up something in a bowl. "Hmm, it smells delightful in here. It must be your homemade soup." She picked up a towel and lifted the lid of a pot on the stove. Potatoes, beans, and tomatoes swam in a rich broth bubbling around the edges.

"And I'm fixin' cornbread to go with it. 'Tis a cold day out, it is, and one perfect for a bowl of my soup. 'Twill take off the chill."

"And taste wonderful at the same time." Caroline dipped her hand into the big cookie tin Ruby always kept on the counter. "I see the teakettle is steaming. Do you have tea brewed? A hot cup would go well with these cinnamon cookies."

Ruby planted her hands on her hips. "Now don't you go ruinin' your appetite with my cookies. I know how you like them." She bustled over to the stove and picked up the kettle. In a few moments she had a cup of tea ready and set it on the table.

Caroline sat silently and nibbled her cookie. The tea soothed her insides, and here in the kitchen with Ruby she found a peace she hadn't achieved in the past few months. Ruby sat down across from Caroline and peered at her with those deep blue-green eyes. Red curls streaked with a hint of gray peeked from under the cap she wore.

"Miss Caroline, something 'tis troublin' you. I haven't seen the old spark of joy and excitement in your eyes for a long time. Do you want to tell me about it?"

Ruby had been in the family as long as they'd been in Barton Creek. Her husband had been killed in an accident shortly after moving here, and when Mother learned what a good cook she was, Ruby was hired on the spot and came to live with them when the house was built. Anything Caroline told Ruby would be kept in strictest confidence. She'd done so many times before, and this time would be no different.

"I'm thinking about my future and what I want to do."

"Are ye happy in the city?"

"Yes and no. I like working at the library, even though Mother thinks it's beneath my dignity to be working. I can't believe she actually has let me do it this long."

"And would the other part have anything to do with Master Matt Haynes?"

How many times had she sat here and poured her heart out to this sweet Irish lady? Always one to listen and never to judge, Ruby knew all of Caroline's secrets regarding Matt. "He doesn't care about me anymore. When we were in school together, I always imagined myself married to him one day, but since I returned from college, he's avoided me like the plague. Looks like all those cooking lessons you gave me won't be used for a husband anytime soon."

"Seems I remember ye being with him a few times at different events."

"But it wasn't the same." And it had changed when she'd returned from college, especially since Mother started keeping her so busy with town activities. Rob and Becky had been able to renew their love even though Mother objected, so why couldn't she? A new thought popped into her mind.

Her eyes opened wide, and she gasped. "Ruby, Mother doesn't like Matt. Do you think that might be the reason for his behavior?"

Ruby said nothing but bit her lip and frowned. Finally she leaned on the table and shook her head. "Miss Caroline, I love your ma, and I don't like to speak ill of her, but she's been anything but kind to the Haynes family. I don't think she really accepted Becky as Rob's wife until she found out the wee bairn was on its way."

Caroline had to agree. She'd heard enough complaints all during their courtship and wedding to know where her mother stood on that issue. If Matt avoided her because of Mother, she couldn't do much about it. Mother was here to stay. "If that's the case, there's absolutely no hope for Matt and me."

Ruby reached across the table and grasped her hands. "Child, there's always hope. If two people are meant to be together, God will make it happen somehow." She leaned back in her chair. "But I've heard talk of a young man in the city smitten with ye."

Nothing escaped the cook's keen observances. "Stuart Whittington has expressed interest in me, and he's really a nice man. He takes me places, and we have a good time together. I think he may be getting more serious about me."

"And how do ye feel about that?"

"I don't know." And if truth were told, she didn't. One part of her heart still clung to the hope of Matt loving her, but the practical side of her recognized the good that could come from marriage to Stuart. She didn't love him yet, but she enjoyed being with him, and he was usually courteous except for that one slip the other night.

"If ye don't know, then 'tis time to seek the Lord and find out what He wants for ye."

That was one thing Caroline hadn't done. In fact, she hadn't even thought of praying about it. Prayer had once been as natural to her as breathing, but in the last eight weeks she had hardly been to church and hadn't sought God's guidance in any way. He'd probably given up on her by now. She pushed back from the table. "Thank you, Ruby. You've given me something to think about."

As she left, Ruby reminded her, "Don't forget to come back down in a while to have soup. Your pa's coming home for lunch, and your ma should be back from her errands."

"I won't forget." How could she with the aroma filling the house? She glanced at the telephone in the hallway. Someday they'd have long distance and she could call Stuart, but with only local service, she'd have to wait until she returned to the city to talk with him. Since things weren't likely to change with Matt, her going with Stuart should make her mother very happy. Now if only it would make Caroline as happy.

Chapter 19

On Sunday Matt lagged behind his parents and Hank on the way to church. He wanted to arrive late enough that he wouldn't have to speak to Caroline. He had no words that would not give away his feelings, and he wouldn't stand in the way of her happiness in Oklahoma City.

When he arrived at the church, the Frankston motorcar was already parked. Everyone had made his or her way inside, so Matt slipped in and sat at the very back. He immediately spotted Caroline seated with her parents, and his heart squeezed with regret.

He joined in the singing, but when the preacher began his sermon, Matt's mind filled with memories of good times with Caroline.

Dozens of past events they'd attended together played through his thoughts. No other girl drew his attention, and she had seemed to have eyes for no one but him in those days.

One particular ice cream social stood out even now. They were both sixteen and so sure everything was perfect and nothing bad could happen. The people in town had banded together to have a fund-raiser to help out the farmers affected by the drought. Then the Fowler boys had spoiled it all. Zeb attacked Dove, and Bart stole the money they had raised.

Such a commotion went on, and Luke Anderson and Martin Fleming had gone with Jake to hunt down the men. Then Mrs. Frankston had verbally attacked Dove and her mother because of their Indian heritage and accused Mrs. Morris's sons of stealing the money. He'd never heard such vicious words in his life, and at that moment his feelings against the woman deepened.

The exchange had given Matt a whole new perspective of the evil nature of some men and women. After that, his relationship with Caroline took a turn and led him to seek her company less frequently. He still cared about her, but he couldn't get past his dislike of her mother.

When the last amen sounded, Matt scooted out the door and to the side to wait for Becky and Rob. Ma had prepared dinner last night and dropped it off at Becky's before church so they would all be together afterward.

Soon the voices of others filled the air as they filed out of church. He peeked around the corner to see if Caroline had come outside. She hadn't, but her mother stood with a group of women near the steps. He gasped and almost choked when he realized the women with her were Dove, Mrs. Morris, Mrs. Anderson, and his own ma. What was that hateful woman saying to them now?

He wished to draw closer to hear, but then he'd risk seeing Caroline and having to speak to her. The look on the ladies' faces told him something serious was being discussed. He'd find out later from Ma, but with Mrs. Frankston involved, it couldn't be good.

His horse had been tethered out of sight, so he made his way to him and swung up into the saddle. He didn't intend to wait around to see the results of the confrontation he'd witnessed. Pa would help Ma with whatever was said.

Becky's house was only a few blocks from the church, and that's where he headed. A good dinner and talk with Rob, Jake, and Pa would make for a fine afternoon. He hoped they'd be able to erase the fact that Caroline was headed to Oklahoma City on the train this afternoon.

Caroline stepped through the doors of the church just in time to see Matt riding off toward his sister's house. She had known the moment he entered the church just before singing began. She had turned her head slightly to confirm her suspicions, but he wasn't seated with his parents as usual. Her first thought was that perhaps she'd been mistaken, but seeing him now affirmed her earlier sense of his presence.

Becky stood beside her and placed a hand on Caroline's arm. "I'm so sorry he left like that." She peered into Caroline's face. "You still love him, don't you?"

"My heart says yes, but my common sense tells me there's no reason to keep up my hopes."

"I don't know what to say other than my brother is blind not to see what he's losing."

"Maybe so, but his complete avoidance of me these past few days is a good indication that he must truly be through with me, even as a friend." She blinked her eyes to clear them of the mist forming. "Is it true that he's been seeing Susannah?" Her breath caught in her throat, waiting the answer.

"Yes, but it only just started. They danced at the inauguration celebration in town and went riding together last Saturday."

Caroline's heart cracked a little more and then broke completely. All hopes of talking with Matt and how she felt vanished. This was the end. She'd go back to the city and pursue a deeper relationship with Stuart. Love would come eventually if she tried hard enough.

Becky gave her a side hug. "I'm so sorry. I truly would like to have you as a sister-in-law. I know you already are since I'm married to Rob, but you know what I mean." She waved at Rob. "I must be going. Please don't stop writing." She hugged Caroline again then headed off to meet Rob.

At the sound of women's voices, she turned to see her mother in a huddle with Dove and three others. What was her mother doing now? Hadn't she already done enough to hurt Dove and Mrs. Morris? She hurried over in hopes of smoothing over any hurt feelings.

Instead of angry words, she heard a bit of laughter. Caroline stopped in her tracks. All five women were smiling, and her mother even hugged Mrs. Haynes. What was going on now? She stepped closer to hear her mother speak.

"Then it's all settled. We'll have the luncheon at my house next week. I plan to ask Marie Fleming and Hannah Perkins and also Ruth and her mother." She leaned over and grasped Mrs. Morris's hand. "Emily, thank you for being so understanding. You are a far better Christian than I have been, but I certainly hope to make up for that in the coming weeks."

Caroline joined the women. "What's this about a luncheon?"

Her mother grinned like a child with a new toy. "I just invited these ladies to our house for a luncheon in a few weeks. I want to start making amends for all the hurt I have caused for so many in Barton Creek."

Caroline blinked her eyes and bit her tongue to keep her mouth from gaping open. "That's wonderful, Mother, but what brought this on?" Believing her mother could change so drastically took some doing, but the looks on the faces of the others helped confirm her mother's sincerity.

"I'll tell you all about it later, but it's time to get home for dinner so you won't miss your train." She turned back to the women. "I've enjoyed talking with you, and thank you for agreeing to come to my house." She headed back to the motorcar where Father waited.

Caroline nodded at the other ladies. "I don't know what just happened, but it will be interesting to find out."

Mrs. Haynes reached over and embraced Caroline. "It's going to be so much better now. Your mother has worked through some hard things, and I believe she will be happier for it."

Such a sudden turn of events created questions Caroline would ask at dinner today. "Thank you, Mrs. Haynes." She hurried away to join her parents.

Mellie's heart swelled with pride and gratitude that Charlotte had followed through with her plans. Those prayers offered up for two nights had been answered in a wonderful way. She smiled at the other ladies. "Wasn't that wonderful of Charlotte?"

Emily shook her head and frowned. "I don't understand why now after all these years of ignoring us she suddenly wants to be friends. She must have some other reason or motive for inviting us to her home."

Bea shrugged her shoulders. "I don't care what reason it is, but I know if you can forgive me for the way I acted, I have to forgive Charlotte for her actions in the past and look to a future as friends."

Three women stared at Mellie as if she had all the answers. This time she did. "Ladies, I can assure you Charlotte means what she said. We talked for the first time a month ago, and I could see something was stirring inside her. On Friday she came and asked my advice. We prayed about what she should do, and today is the result. God has worked a miracle in her heart, and we've just seen it with our own eyes."

Ben stepped to her side. "If you ladies have solved the problems of the world, some hungry men are waiting for you."

Mellie laughed and grasped her husband's arm. "We are, and if the rest are like you, they've been ready for dinner since the preacher started his sermon."

She walked beside Ben to their buggy. He patted her hand and asked, "What was that all about? I was sure Charlotte was having her say against Emily and Dove again, but all of you were smiling, so it couldn't have been bad."

"It wasn't, and I'll tell you all about it at dinner so I can share with Becky and Lucy too. No sense in repeating it twice." She imagined the surprise that would fill her daughter since Becky had been praying for this same miracle.

Skepticism grew as Matt listened to his ma, Becky, and Lucy discuss Mrs. Frankston. That circle of ladies this morning was not on the receiving end of her anger and rudeness but an apology. The idea that Mrs. Frankston could apologize to anyone was more than his brain could process at the moment.

"But Ma, do you really think she can change after all these years?"

"Yes, I do. We prayed about it Friday when she came to see me, and she prayed with her husband the night before, so if the ladies of Barton Creek are the Christian women I believe they are, they will forgive her and accept her into their circle of friends."

That was a lot more than he wanted to do at the moment. "Have you forgotten how horrible she was when we all thought Jake had killed that man down in Texas? She even told you that Rob couldn't be friends with Becky anymore, and she was rude to Lucy whenever we went into town."

"That's all in the past. I would hope we'd come a long way in the ten years since then."

That still didn't convince Matt. "It's hard to forget about her treatment of Dove Anderson and Mrs. Morris. Dove and her mother were the brunt of many of Mrs. Frankston's cruel remarks for years, as well as Hawk and Eli. She was the first to accuse them of stealing at that fund-raiser, and she's never approved of me either." In his shock, the words just poured out of him, and he went on. "Seems a rancher isn't good enough for her daughter, either, although Pa and you probably have as much if not more money than she does."

Lucy leaned over and grasped his arm. "Matt, money doesn't make any difference in how a person should be treated. I think that's what Mrs. Frankston has learned, and now she wants to make up for all the hurt she's caused."

He pushed back his chair. "I'll believe it when I see it and hear it with my own eyes and ears. Even then it will be hard for me to forget all that has happened." Matt strode from the room and out to the front porch. He slumped into one of the wicker chairs. Why did this have to happen now? Caroline had already found someone else to love. It was too late for him.

Jake eased into the chair across from him. "Hey, Lucy told me what happened in there."

Matt turned his head to peer at his cousin, whose expression held no judgment and no curiosity, only sincerity. "I find it hard to believe that a woman like Mrs. Frankston can change so quickly."

"But if she indeed does make the effort and is successful, can you find it in your heart to forgive her?"

A good question, and one he didn't have an answer for at the moment.

Jake leaned forward. "Look, if God could forgive all the

things I did before I became a Christian, He can certainly forgive Charlotte for all she's done, because even good Christian people sin and disappoint God. That means we have to forgive too. If we don't, we're no better than she is, and we put ourselves up as better than God. We expect to be forgiven for our mistakes, and that means we must forgive others for theirs."

Matt listened with sorrow in his heart for all the years wasted. "I know what I have to do, but I'll wait and see what happens. I'm not going to do anything I might be sorry for later."

"You'll never be sorry for doing what God wants you to do."

"I know that, but what can I do about Caroline? She's already found someone in Oklahoma City. I met him at the inauguration, and he's some senator's son. Much better suited for the life Caroline deserves, but…" His words trailed off, and he shrugged.

"If you still love her, it's not too late to let her know."

That was easy for Jake to say. He hadn't seen how Stuart held Caroline or how she looked up at him all smiles and happiness. Besides, he had Susannah now. "I appreciate what you're saying, but let's wait and see what happens at this luncheon deal. Then I'll think about what I have to do."

"OK, I think that's fair. Your mother will be pleased to know that at least you're thinking about it." He stood but didn't move toward the yard where his boys now played with their uncle Rob. "Just don't wait too long to go after what you really want in life. I almost did." He turned on his heel and jumped off the porch to grab Charley.

Watching them playing in the yard reminded Matt of all he had hoped would happen in his own life. Now here he sat at age twenty-seven, still single and no sons in sight. He sighed and leaned back in his chair. He had some heavy-duty talking with the Lord to do.

Chapter 20

*C*aroline yawned as she made her way to the kitchen. Although she had gone to bed early last night, the trip home and back had swayed her from her regular routine, making her more tired than she had realized. Both roommates had come in after she had gone to bed, but now their voices floated her way from the kitchen.

"Good morning. I didn't hear you come in last night." She went straight to the coffeepot warming on the back of the stove and poured a cup.

Madeline picked up a muffin. "There's plenty to eat this morning. Mother packed a basket of food for us to enjoy this week."

Caroline laughed and pointed to another basket on the counter. "So did Ruby. She said I was getting too thin, so she sent back homemade cinnamon rolls, fresh baked bread, a pie, a few dozen cookies, and I put several jars of her homemade soup in the icebox."

Julia smacked her lips and jumped up to search for a cinnamon roll. "I know how Ruby cooks, and one of her sweet rolls this morning is the best treat I can think of for breakfast." She pulled out one of the rolls and bit into it. "Hmm, heavenly. I love your cook."

Caroline retrieved one herself and sat across from Madeline, whose face now beamed brighter than the sun coming through the kitchen window. "OK, let's have it. You look like the cat that ate the canary and couldn't hide the satisfaction."

Madeline giggled and held out her left hand. A shiny ring adorned her third finger. The sapphire blue stone set in a gold band didn't register with Caroline or Julia for a moment. Then Julia squealed and jumped up to hug Madeline. "Steve finally asked you to marry him. You're engaged!"

Caroline almost choked on the bite of roll in her mouth. "Engaged? When did this happen?" She grabbed for Madeline's hand to see the ring more clearly.

"Yesterday when we were at my folks' house. He'd already asked Papa for permission, and he proposed right after dinner." Madeline's cheeks flushed pink, and the love in her eyes sparkled.

Caroline hugged her friend. "I'm so happy for you. The ring is beautiful."

Madeline held out her hand under the light to let the true beauty of the blue stone shine forth. "It belonged to Steve's grandmother, and she gave it to him last year before she died. She told him to give it to the girl he decided to marry as a token of his love and commitment to her. And I'm so glad he chose me."

Julia giggled and plopped back in her chair. "I'm really happy for you."

"The wedding will be on Valentine's Day, and I want you two to stand with me. It's going to be here at the church where I grew up, and then we'll have a big party afterward at a hotel. I'm going to choose my dress this week, and we'll pick out something for both of you to wear."

She rambled on about flowers and food, but Caroline stared at the ring. How would she respond if Stuart proposed to her?

Julia peered over the edge of her cup. "And when might we

be hearing news about you and Stuart? I've heard from Andy that he adores you, so…?"

The question hung in the air without an answer for a few moments. Caroline's cheeks filled with heat. Julia had voiced Caroline's thoughts. Her breath caught and her chest ached. "I'm…I'm not sure we've progressed that far yet."

Madeline laughed and reached for another muffin. "You may not think so, but Steve is of the same opinion as Andy, and I agree with them both."

Stuart had already taken too much for granted by trying to kiss her, but if his motives were true, she should consider her future with him. She glanced at the watch on her shirtwaist.

"Oh, my, if I don't get out of here I'll miss the trolley and be late for work." She hugged Madeline once again. "I'm really happy for you. It's going to be fun to plan your wedding and be a part of it. You can tell me more this evening."

Caroline grabbed her coat and hat from the hook by the door and raced to the trolley stop with only minutes to spare. On the ride she had time to think more about Stuart. All the reasons he'd be a good choice ran through her mind once more, and she couldn't come up with any reason not to accept his proposal if indeed one came about.

Then she remembered her mother and all that had happened yesterday. She'd never seen her mother as happy as she was when she rode home from church. Mother had apologized to Dove and Emily Morris and now was planning to have them as well as other women over for lunch. That was one miracle that had come completely out of nowhere. If it worked and made her mother happy, then whatever happened with Caroline shouldn't make a difference.

She stepped off the trolley and headed toward the library and another day of stacking books, shelving them, and helping patrons find what they needed. For now this job satisfied her desire to be of service to the community, but so much more lay out there that needed to be done.

The day ran very smoothly as far as Caroline was concerned, and at the end of it, she entered the employees' room to retrieve her coat. Jo followed right behind her.

The young woman now fairly blossomed with enthusiasm. "I'm so glad to have this chance to talk with you, Caroline. The things you've done for me have been an absolute answer to prayer. I can't begin to thank you. Jimmy and I have more dates planned, and he came by my house to meet my parents. Where I live didn't matter at all to him. He said before his family moved to the city, he lived on a farm, and it wasn't much different from where I lived, just more land. God sure knows how to make things just right."

Caroline wasn't sure what God had to do with it. She'd done all the work to help Jo with her appearance, and Jo had done the rest with Jimmy. "Whenever you need any other help, let me know. And if you need a dress for a special occasion or such, I have plenty and would love to lend you one to wear."

Jo almost bounced with the joy that filled her, and her face glowed with the same light Caroline had seen in Lucy and Dove on many occasions. "I'm glad you're so happy, Jo. Your life seems to be running smoothly right now."

"Yes, isn't God good? He takes care of every provision for us, and His love never fails us."

"How can you be so sure of that?" It seemed to Caroline that God had been failing her a lot lately.

"I'm as sure of it as I am of breathing. No matter what happens, God is in control. When I let Him be the guide in my life, He will always take me to the best place for me. Sometimes the way isn't easy or pleasant, but if I stay faithful, He will get me there."

Caroline bit her lip and considered the words just spoken. She hadn't been faithful at all the past two months. Since coming to the city she had attended church here only once, the Sunday before Thanksgiving. No time had been set aside for prayer, and her Bible still lay on the table. She couldn't even remember the last time she'd opened it.

"I guess that explains why you're always so happy these days. God has given you what you wanted." She shoved her arms into the sleeves of her coat and reached up for her hat. Jo's words sat in her mind like birds perched on a wire, and she hoped they'd fly away and leave her alone.

Jo shook her head. "You misunderstand. It isn't that He gave me what I want, but that He gave me what is best for me. I can be happy the rest of my life knowing that." She peered up at Caroline. "I thought you knew the power of prayer and the importance of being in God's will. I remember you saying you are a Christian."

Heat rose in Charlotte's face. That's what she had said the first day when Jo asked the question. "I know, but I don't think God is very pleased with me right now, and one thing I really wanted to happen didn't and most likely won't." She hurried out of the room before Jo could comment further.

Guilt pressed down on her soul, and her footsteps dragged as she trudged toward the trolley stop for the ride home. She hadn't prayed about anything for so long that at the moment, any prayer offered would most likely bounce back unanswered. Things might have been different if she'd included God in the equation of her life months ago, but now it was too late.

Matt rode up beside Hawk. "You about ready to call it a day? The sun's going down, and I'm hungry."

The big, half-Cherokee cowboy turned away and gazed westward. "Yep, I'm through. Thanks for your help."

Several times today Matt had spoken to Hawk, and like now he'd never looked Matt in the eye. Although Hawk as a habit didn't talk much when rounding up strays and filling feed troughs, the past few weeks he'd been very distant with Matt and avoided looking at him directly.

The only thing Matt could figure was that it might have something to do with Caroline. Just before they parted ways, Matt called out to Hawk. "Wait up a minute. I need to ask you something."

Hawk stopped and waited, but the frown on his face didn't bode well for Matt. "What do you have to say now that you couldn't have said earlier? I thought you were anxious to get home."

"I am, but I want to know what's eating at you. At first I thought it was my imagination, but you did it again when I mentioned going home. I thought we were good friends and you could speak your mind with me." Hawk was four years older than Matt, but he'd always allowed Matt to tag along when he was younger and wanted to know all about horses. Hawk had even been the one to teach Matt how to handle a handgun.

Hawk didn't move and simply stared hard at Matt as though deciding whether or not to talk to him. Hawk had not married, and that had always puzzled Matt. He'd heard many of the young women in town speak of Hawk with admiration, and any one of them would have been happy to have him pay attention to her. "Look, I saw you at the statehood celebration, and you had an expression on your face that made me wonder if you were angry or something was wrong somewhere. When I went to find you, you had disappeared."

Still Hawk said nothing, and Matt pulled on his reins to head home. If the man didn't want to talk, he wasn't going to waste time waiting for a response. It'd be dark soon, and he wanted to be home in time for supper.

He hadn't gone far when Hawk called his name. Matt stopped and turned in his saddle.

"You want to know what's wrong? Why are you courting Susannah instead of marrying Caroline?"

Matt's body tingled with the shock that roared through his body. That was the last question on earth he'd expected to hear. What business was it of Hawk's anyway? He weighed his answer with care before delivering it. "Caroline Frankston has found another man in Oklahoma City. She's happy with him, and that's what I want for her. We've both wasted too many years on something that wasn't meant to be."

"I always figured you and she would someday marry, but then I guess she's not the type who'd make a good rancher's wife. She's never lived anywhere but in that fancy house in town."

To his surprise, Matt found himself defending Caroline. "I'm not so sure about that. Lucy sure didn't know anything about living on a ranch when she first came. Look at her now. She's one of the best around these parts." He wasn't likely to ever forget her bumbling ways those first months after she arrived to live with them and how hard she worked to fit in as part of the family.

"Caroline's different. She's a lot older than Lucy was and more set in her ways." Hawk narrowed his eyes for a moment. "Did you know Mrs. Frankston has apologized to Ma and Dove?"

"Yes, my ma told me all about it." It was still hard for him to believe that she'd actually wanted people to forgive her. If she'd done it years ago, he might be with Caroline now.

"I pray she means it. If Ma or Dove is hurt again, I might do that old lady in." He hesitated then pushed up the brim of his hat. "You plan on seeing Susannah again? I noticed she brought a horse back with her, and I sure would like to get a closer look. He's a fine-looking specimen."

"Yes, Hank and I are taking Amy and Susannah to see that new melodrama at the theater in town later this week. I'm sure she'd love for you to look over Rascal." Darkness began to settle in, and Matt pulled on his reins. "I have to get home. We can talk later." Then once again that expression he'd seen a few weeks ago filled Hawk's face. Matt shook his head. Whatever bothered him, Hawk wasn't willing to share just yet.

When he arrived home, Ma met him at the back door. "It took you long enough. We've already eaten, but your dinner is on the stove keeping warm."

"Thank you. And before you ask, Hawk and I were talking and the time got away. I'm sorry to be late."

Mellie skewed her mouth. "You and Hawk? I suppose you were talking about the horses brought back from Wyoming."

"Yes and no. Actually, he's interested in taking a look at Susannah's horse." His stomach growled in protest against the long wait between meals. He went to the sink to wash up.

Ma fixed his plate and set it on the table, all the while muttering and shaking her head. He tilted his head to listen more closely. It sounded like she said, "You foolish boy. He's more interested in Susannah than her horse."

Matt stopped in his tracks. Had he heard her right? Could Hawk be interested in Susannah? He began putting two and two together and came up with the conclusion that Hawk might be attracted to someone like Susannah, whose sunny nature would balance his seriousness and who enjoyed horses as much as he did. How could he have been so blind to something right in front of him?

When he sat down, Ma sat across from him. "I know you still care about Caroline. I see it in your eyes whenever she's around." She reached over and grasped his hand to squeeze it. "I know Charlotte has apologized to you and explicitly encouraged you to pursue Caroline. So will you try to see Caroline when she's home for Christmas?"

"Too late for that. She's already found someone else in the city, and if she's happy, that's all that matters."

"No, it isn't, and by the way, I don't think you're being fair to Susannah. You should not be seeing her if you heart is not in it."

His mother must have said all she wanted because she stood from the table and adjusted her apron. "You may be making the mistake of your life by not pursuing Caroline. And you need to leave Susannah to someone who can love her with all his heart, soul, and mind. True love can conquer all fears and doubts, but you didn't give it a chance." She disappeared into the kitchen, and a few moments later he heard the water and the clink of silverware and plates.

Ma was right, but the truth ate at him like a field mouse gnawing a piece of wood. He'd let his feelings toward Mrs. Frankston block the way to declaring his love for Caroline, and he wasn't being fair to Susannah. He'd have to do something about that.

Chapter 21

harlotte opened the door and greeted Mellie. "Thank you for coming into town today. I hope I didn't inconvenience you, but I really wanted your input on the luncheon plans."

Mellie handed over her hat and coat. "We usually come to town on Saturday for supplies, so it's not a problem."

After hanging the coat and hat on the hall tree, Charlotte gestured toward the dining room. "Ruby is going to meet with us to plan the menu."

When they were seated at the table, Ruby entered bearing a tray with a teapot and cups. "I prepared tea for while we work." She set them on the table then sat down.

This luncheon meant more to Charlotte than she had let Ruby know, and the cook had questioned the need for a third party. But she needed Mellie to make sure the menu wasn't too fancy or pretentious for the ladies invited.

"Now, the invitations have been delivered, and I've heard back from all but one or two, so I think we're all set to decide on the menu." Charlotte pulled a sheet of paper toward her and picked up her pen. "I'll read a list of things that I've thought of, but I need to know if the recipes will be appropriate. I want this luncheon to be friendly and simple but elegant too."

Mellie laughed. "As long as it isn't stew and cornbread, I'll be happy. That's about all I've been cooking during these cold days. They're Ben and Matt's favorite."

Ruby nodded, her red curls dancing with the motion. "I've prepared plenty of that in my time. Good and hearty for this time of year."

"Well, now tell me what you think. Clam chowder to start or cream of tomato soup or corn chowder, roasted chicken or beef, endive, Waldorf or ambrosia salad, bread and butter pickles, asparagus, baked acorn squash, popovers, biscuits, yeast rolls, gingerbread or Lady Baltimore cake or fruit pie."

Mellie raised her eyebrows and peered at Ruby. "That's an extensive list you have there. Ruby knows how to prepare all these dishes?"

Ruby's shoulders straightened, and a look of indignation crossed her face. "I certainly do, ma'am. 'Tis a sad day when I can't cook anything one asks for. When I need something, I tell Mrs. Anderson, and she orders it for me."

"I'm sorry, Ruby. I know what a wonderful cook you are from events in the past. My food at the ranch is plain and simple, so I'm not familiar with some of these foods."

Charlotte frowned and tapped her lips with her pen. "Do you think these are too much for the ladies?" She wanted good food, but not the kind that would make her guests feel like she was putting on a show for them. "What do you suggest from the list, Mellie?"

"Let me see." She peered at the items listed and studied them before she answered. "I think roasted chicken would be fine along with the tomato soup, Waldorf salad, popovers, asparagus, and the pickles." Mellie raised her eyebrows and smiled at Ruby. "We must have some of your homemade pickles. They're too good to pass up." She returned to the list. "And to top it off, how about your butter pound cake, Ruby? That's a wonderful cake."

"And I can have a berry sauce to top it."

Charlotte sat back and grinned. "Now that sounds like a

menu anyone would like. Are you sure Mrs. Anderson can supply you with everything you need?"

"Yes, ma'am."

"That's it then. Thank you, Ruby." Now it was time to present the rest of her idea to Mellie. As soon as the kitchen door closed behind her cook, Charlotte poured a cup of tea, pleased to see steam still rising from the amber liquid. She handed a cup and saucer to Mellie then poured one for herself.

"Now that the menu is taken care of, I have a few more ideas to present for your opinion. I love Christmas, and with the house decorated, it gives a really festive mood to everything." She leaned forward with her hands clasped on the table. "What do you think of the idea of making this luncheon an annual affair and call it the Mayor's Wife Christmas Luncheon? It could be a buffet, and all the ladies of the town would be invited. If my house isn't large enough, we could have it in the town hall."

"That's a wonderful idea, but that's a lot of food now that we're growing so fast."

Charlotte had considered that fact, which was the reason for the town hall suggestion, but she also realized that many of the original families might not be as excited about such an event.

"I plan to hire someone to help Ruby with the food, especially if we hold it in the town hall, but here's the best part: I know a lot of our families in the outlying areas don't have much to spend, and some are barely getting by. There's a new orphanage in Guthrie, and they need help. So I'm going to ask those who can to bring a new toy to the luncheon, and then we'll have a committee to wrap them and take them out to those families and to the orphanage."

A grin spread across Mellie's face, and her face beamed. "That's a wonderful idea. Reminds me of when we had that ice cream social to help raise money for the farmers. We can combine it with our two churches and their Christmas baskets of food for the needy. Let's don't wait. Let's see if we can implement something like that this year."

Charlotte's heart filled with gratitude for her friend. When the idea had first occurred, this year was her first inclination, but she had been worried about the time they needed to implement the idea. Now that Mellie suggested it, the project became more doable.

"We'll need to get right on it and talk with Pastor Weaver. We can also tell the women at the luncheon about the idea and maybe organize a committee. Will you head up such a group, Mellie?"

"I'd be honored, and I'm sure the others will be too. I'm reminded of something else the women want to do because now it will mean more to you. Dove, Lucy, and Alice plan to have a party for Becky and the new baby after it arrives. It will be sometime in January since the baby is due so close to Christmas."

Charlotte's mouth dropped open and quickly closed again. Becky was liked by everyone in town, and this gesture on her behalf proved it. As one of the baby's grandmothers, she would have been included, but now the event became one to anticipate rather than to dread as she would have done in the past.

"That's wonderful of them, but then I know how special Becky is to Lucy. I'll have to let them know how much I appreciate it, as I'm sure Becky will do."

As they talked for another hour, Charlotte regretted even more all the years she'd wasted without Mellie's friendship. No more of that. From now on she planned to make as many friends as would be willing to forgive her and accept her into their circle.

That evening Matt sat with Susannah, Hank, and Amy at the theater. The play, although quite good, didn't capture his interest. Instead, his mother's words from last Sunday kept running through his mind. He didn't want to stand in the way of Hawk finding happiness, and if Hawk cared for Susannah, then Matt had to do something about it, especially since he hadn't been able to see Susannah as any more than a good friend and nice companion.

When he escorted her to the boarding house afterward, he mentally rehearsed how he could explain his decision to Susannah.

"You've been very quiet this evening, Matt. Is something wrong?" She stared up at him with the smile that had captivated him at the dance, but it didn't have the same effect tonight.

This was going to be harder than he thought, and his tongue glued to the top of his mouth. He needed a drink of water. Finally he cleared his throat. "Susannah, I've enjoyed the past few times we've been together, but I believe I've misled you, and it's better if we don't see each other anymore except as friends."

Her mouth dropped open, and her eyes opened wide for a moment before she snapped her mouth shut. The smile had disappeared and been replaced with pure anger. For a moment she glared at him before saying, "It's probably a good thing. I wouldn't want to be strung along for several years like Caroline Frankston." She spun on her heel to head inside.

Guilt swept over Matt. He hadn't meant to hurt her, and maybe this hadn't been such a good time to tell her, but he didn't want to make another trip into town just for that. He'd never been able to understand women and what went on in their minds. Maybe that was the reason Caroline had rejected him.

Susannah's parting words replayed in his head. She didn't want to be strung along for years like Caroline. Is that what he'd done? No wonder Mrs. Frankston disliked him, and now it was too late to do anything about it.

Nestled in his new car, Caroline snuggled under the blanket Stuart had provided to ward off the chill of the night air. Dinner that evening had been a delightful affair, and she'd truly enjoyed her time with Stuart as he regaled her with tales from college days. He hadn't been the least surprised by Steve and Madeline's plans to marry. He had laughed and said that it was about time.

Now he pulled the motorcar into an empty parking space at the park and stopped. It was too cold to get out, and Caroline's curiosity grew as to why they stopped.

His hands left the steering wheel and reached for her to pull her close. She had no time to resist as his arms wrapped around her. "Caroline, I know we haven't been seeing each other very long, but Steve's asking Madeline to marry him has made me think about us and where we're headed."

A lump rose in her throat. She'd expected him to say something along these lines, but now that he had, she didn't want to hear them. She tried to pull back, but he only held her closer.

"You're a beautiful woman, and people like you. You're just the kind of woman I need beside me as I enter the world of politics. You don't need to give me an answer yet, but I do want you to consider being by my side in the years ahead."

Not a word about love. He wanted someone to look good on his arm at those political affairs. Now was the time to let him know what she wanted to do with her life. After her talk with Jo, she had turned to God and sought guidance about where her future lay. Her dream of helping others grew the more she prayed, but she didn't know how Stuart would feel about her plans.

Gently she pushed away from him. "Before I consider anything, I think you should be aware of some things in my own life."

He nodded and lifted his eyebrows. "OK, I'm listening."

"First, I want to work toward helping others. I love my job here at the library and don't want to quit it, but I would like to find ways to help those who are disadvantaged, perhaps by teaching them to read."

"But you won't have time for that if you're on the campaign trail with me, and when I'm elected, you'll be busy with responsibilities in Washington."

Caroline cringed at the words. Still nothing about his love for her. "Is that why you want to marry me? So you'll have a dutiful wife at your side?"

"Well, partly. I've seen you with the children at the library, so I know you'll be a good mother even with a nanny taking care of the children. You come from a background that gives you talent for planning social events and being the proper hostess." He stopped and peered at her. "You haven't told me the rest of your plan."

If he didn't agree with her next idea, he could have no place in her future. "I've neglected my faith and going to church since I've been here, but that's going to change. I plan to attend church every Sunday and eventually hope to be able to lead a class of young ladies in Bible study."

"Attend church? That should not be a problem. The church is a good place for a politician to be seen and to make connections with influential people. There will probably be times when we can't attend because of travel and appearances, and I can't see your having time to teach a Bible class, though."

Those words became nails pounding into her heart. How could she ever plan a future with someone who didn't attend church for the same reasons she did? "God is very important in my life, and I attend because I want to, not to be seen." She grasped his hands in hers. "Besides, you haven't said one word about loving me for who I am. All you've said is how I can be an asset for your career."

Stuart protested. "But I care a great deal for you! Haven't I shown you that?"

"Perhaps," she said reluctantly. Apparently she saw him more clearly than he saw himself. He thought himself in love with her simply because she fit his image of a politician's wife.

Then she realized she'd been doing the same thing, thinking she should love Stuart simply because he fit her mother's conception of whom she should marry. But she'd never be able to marry someone she didn't love with all her heart and soul, nor could she marry someone who didn't love God as much as she did. Those two things were conditions she could not compromise and expect happiness the rest of her life.

"I think it's time for you to take me home. I see no need to continue this conversation."

"But I thought we had a good relationship and that you'd enjoy being the wife of a representative of the United States government. And I don't understand your sudden interest in religion. You've never mentioned it in all the time we've been seeing each other." The indignation in his voice startled her. He sounded like a spoiled child crying over a toy he'd been denied.

When she didn't answer him right away, he grabbed her shoulders and pulled her to him and kissed her. She jerked her head away and pulled back. Her teeth clenched as she spoke. "Take me home this minute."

He released her so abruptly that she fell back against the car door. His eyes flashed with anger, and his words contained pure venom. "I'll take you home, Miss Goody Two-Shoes. Looks like you've made your choice, and it isn't me."

The motorcar roared to life, and Stuart swung around to head back to her place. How could she have been so wrong about someone? He had completely fooled her as to his character. At least she had found out now, and not after she had committed to him.

When they arrived home, Stuart stopped the car but did not get out to open her door. After a few moments, she shoved it open and climbed down to the sidewalk. He never turned his head or said a word, but as soon as she closed the door, he drove off. She stood outside her house with her hands on her hips. Never had a man shown such rudeness toward her.

Caroline unlocked the door and hurried upstairs to her room, where she fell onto the bed. Sobs rocked her body, and she let the tears flow freely. What a mess her life had become. She rolled over onto her back and whispered, "Lord, I don't know what You're trying to teach me, but whatever it is, I don't like it."

With great effort she changed into her nightclothes and crawled under the covers. Matt's face swam before her eyes. Why couldn't he be the one who wanted to marry her?

Chapter 22

*A*fter church on Sunday, Geoff Kensington approached Matt. "I need to have a meeting with your family and the Morrises. I have some good news for all of you, and I've already told your pa and Sam to meet me in my office in fifteen minutes."

"OK. I'll see you there." He pushed his hat back and scratched his head as Geoff strode off down the street. He had said good news, so the well couldn't have run dry. Whatever it was, the man was in a hurry.

Matt mounted his horse and urged Thunderbolt to a fast trot. Ahead he spotted Hawk and Eli.

Geoff stood as the men entered his office. "Sit down, because the news I have is going to knock you off your feet."

A grin spread across his face as he handed papers to Ben and Sam. "A new well came in this past week, and it's even bigger and more productive than what we already have. The money from it will set you up for life. You never have to worry about money again."

Matt gasped, as did the others. Pa and Sam read through the documents and shook their heads. Pa laid his back on the desk. "There's always worry where money's concerned. Having lots of it means a different kind of worry. Are you sure about these figures?"

"Yes, and I've already contacted Mr. Barstow. I should be getting a wire back from him soon." His gaze moved from Pa to Sam and back to Pa. "Do you still plan to send half to the Dawson family?"

Pa stared at Sam a moment before he nodded. "Yes, send it to that bank there in Lawrence just like before. He and his brother are starting up a farm equipment business, and this will go a long way to help them get it established."

Hawk and Eli grabbed for their father's copy of the papers, and Pa handed his to Matt. The more he read, the wider his eyes opened. He'd never seen this much money before in his life. He immediately thought of all that could be done around the ranch with that kind of money. Of course there was enough to do some of that anyway, but more money never hurt.

Pa sat back in his chair and rolled the brim of his hat with his hands. "Sam and I have been talking about what we'd do with some of the money we already have, and with this coming in, we can do more than we talked about."

"And what kinds of things might those be, Ben?" Geoff leaned forward on his desk with his hands clasped.

Sam spoke up first. "For one thing, we need to improve the school. We need more classrooms and more teachers, as well as more books. They don't even have a library there, and they need one."

"That's right, and the town hall could use some remodeling. Lots of people in Barton Creek would benefit from those kinds of improvements." Pa emphasized his words by tapping his finger on Geoff's desk.

Hawk and Eli said nothing, and by the looks on their faces, they were just as surprised as Matt. He'd known these two men were generous, but to take on projects like the school and the town hall would cost a fortune.

Geoff placed the documents back into a folder and closed it. "I suggest we have a meeting with Mayor Frankston as soon as we can set it up and discuss the ideas with him. I'm sure he'd appreciate your willingness to donate funds." He stood and stretched out his hand toward Pa and Sam. "Thank you for coming by. I'll get these signed papers to Mr. Barstow in tomorrow's mail. Meanwhile, I'm anxious to get home and have some of that pot roast I smelled cooking before church this morning."

Pa and Sam shook hands with Geoff. He was right about one thing. Food, any food, sounded good to Matt as his stomach growled with hunger.

Matt followed Hawk and Eli outside. "What do you think of what our pas did in there?"

Eli shoved his hat onto his head and shrugged. "It's their money, so I guess they can do what they want with it. Our percent is not enough to worry about, but I can sure use it to enlarge our stables."

Matt hadn't considered what he might do with his portion, but it'd probably go into savings like the rest had. Eli swung up onto his horse and trotted away, but Hawk remained on the boardwalk beside Matt.

Hawk tapped the boards beneath his feet with the heel of his boot. "One thing I'd like to see done is sidewalks like they have in the city. These wooden things rot and get dangerous."

Matt didn't care about the sidewalks. He had more important matters to discuss with Hawk. His stomach would have to wait a little longer to be satisfied. "I spoke with Susannah last night. We're not going to be seeing each other any longer. None of my business, but I'm sure she could use a sympathetic shoulder." He cut his gaze to catch Hawk's reaction.

The man's expression didn't change. He stared at Matt with black eyes that pierced straight to a man's soul. A moment later he strode away from Matt and mounted his horse. With one last glare at Matt, Hawk turned and headed up Main Street toward the church.

Matt had seen that look on Hawk's face in the past and was glad he was a friend and not an enemy. Others who had crossed the part-Cherokee cowboy hadn't fared so well. Not that Hawk looked for a fight, but most men in town knew better than to be on his bad side.

When the black horse turned the corner, Matt let out his breath. It was up to Hawk now as to what happened with Susannah. Matt had done his part, and now his hunger pains reminded him that dinner waited down at Becky's.

When he arrived, he spotted the Frankston motorcar parked in front. What was Becky thinking to have Rob's parents for dinner at the same time as her own family? He almost turned away to go home, but stopped. The memory of the ham Ma had prepared gave him second thoughts. That and a piece of that chocolate cake from Lucy helped him decide he could stand being around Mrs. Frankston for as long as dinner took, but after that he planned to head back to the ranch.

Both guilt and remorse filled Charlotte at the look on Matt's face when he saw her in Becky's living room. He was a fine young man, and she'd been too blinded by her snobbery to see it. Caroline would have been perfectly happy with him out on the ranch even though she didn't know a thing about being the wife of a rancher.

Mellie rose to greet her son. "We've been waiting for you. Your pa said you'd be along behind him, and he knew you were hungry from the way your stomach rumbled."

Matt's cheeks turned red, and he mumbled something Charlotte couldn't hear. Becky then hugged him, and he followed her into the dining room. Maxwell offered his arm and escorted her to the table.

Ben asked Maxwell to do the honor of asking a blessing for the meal. Her heart swelled with pride as her husband's rich, bass voice filled the air. At the amen, Jake began asking questions about the meeting with Geoff.

The fact that the Hayneses and the Morrises were now the wealthiest families in Barton Creek overwhelmed her. Those ideas developed about ranchers and cowboys so many years ago certainly sounded inane now. How ignorant she had been in those days, and her stubborn pride had refused the truth for all these years.

All through the meal Matt's eyes held only hostility whenever he happened to catch her gazing at him. She deserved it, for she had done nothing but make life miserable for him and just about everyone else in Barton Creek. Although the women had come around and were friendlier now that she had asked forgiveness, convincing this young man of her sincerity would take a lot more time and effort.

After dinner she grasped his arm before he could follow the men into Rob's study. "Please, Matt, may I have a word with you?"

He narrowed his eyes and glanced down at her hand. "I have nothing to say to you."

She didn't remove her hand in hopes of convincing him to listen. Even when he tried to jerk away, she held tighter. "Please listen to what I have to say, then."

He paused long enough to give Charlotte her opening. "First, I again want to apologize to you for the way I've treated you in the past. It was very rude of me, and I had no business doing it. The second thing is that I'm so sorry for ruining your relationship with Caroline. You two would be perfect together. I saw it even back when you were children."

Matt's expression remained unreadable. He didn't plan to make this easy for her.

"I know Caroline cared a great deal for you, but I'm afraid I kept you two apart. I...I was angry with you for not declaring yourself."

His mouth worked as though he were searching for words. Then he frowned. "If Caroline still cares for me, she certainly has a strange way of showing it. I suppose that now my family is very wealthy, I'm suddenly good enough for Caroline." He removed her hand from his arm. "Please excuse me. I have to join my father and whatever they're talking about for improvements in Barton Creek." Before she could protest, he stepped through the door to the study and closed it behind him. That hadn't gone well at all, but what else could she expect after so many years of criticism? Even worse, his words held more truth than she wanted to admit.

"My son can be a very stubborn man at times." Mellie approached and put her arm around Charlotte's shoulders.

Charlotte shook her head. "I hurt him more than I ever could have realized. The more I see of him, the more I know he and Caroline should be together. With her in Oklahoma City and almost engaged to Stuart Whittington, I don't know what to do about it."

"We don't need to do anything. If it's God's plan for them to be with each other, He'll make it happen. All we can do is pray for the right decisions to be made."

Mellie was right, of course, and Charlotte had to accept it. But every mother wants her children to be happy, and all she had done was to make life miserable for both Caroline and Matt.

After the church service Caroline walked out into the bright afternoon sunshine. How ironic that a church had been only a few blocks away all those mornings she thought she didn't have time or didn't feel like attending church. Caroline spread her arms wide and lifted her face to the sun. What a glorious day to be in God's house.

Such peace filled her soul today. After a night of prayer and restless sleep, she had awakened determined to attend church. The message this morning had been as though God had it prepared especially for her. One verse of the morning's passage from Proverbs 16 ran over and over in her mind, especially verse 9. *A man's heart deviseth his way: but the* LORD *directeth his steps.* Now she walked toward home with the brisk wind giving her new energy. For the past two months and more she'd been planning her own life and determining the way to go. Now it was time to let the Lord direct her steps, and He'd take her on the right path.

When she entered the house, all was quiet. Upstairs, the doors to the other bedrooms remained closed, which meant Julia still slept, and Madeline was having Sunday dinner with her parents. She entered her own room and closed the door to keep from disturbing Julia.

Madeline and Julia had both reacted with shock and dismay when she had announced she was no longer going to be seeing Stuart. Julia thought Caroline had lost her mind, and Madeline had voiced anger over hurting Steve's friend, but she had apologized. Madeline wanted everyone to be in love like she was.

After changing into a more comfortable skirt and blouse, Caroline made her way back downstairs to the kitchen. She remembered leftover chicken and rice from lunch yesterday. If she warmed it up, it would make a good meal.

Julia wandered in, her robe hanging and her hair falling

around her shoulders. Not like Miss Fashion Conscious Julia at all. She reached up and tied her robe around her waist. "What's that wonderful aroma coming from the oven?"

"It's the chicken and rice from yesterday and some of the left-over rolls." Caroline placed a plate and silverware on the table. "Do you want some?"

Her roommate yawned and stretched. "If there's enough." She plopped down in a chair.

Caroline filled two plates and set them on the table. After she sat down, she bowed her head for a quick prayer. When she raised her eyes, Julia sat staring at her with a frown.

"You've never done that before."

"And I've missed it. I went to church today and realized how far away from God I had drifted since I came here. I've made some bad decisions while here and chose to do things I don't ordinarily do, so I've decided to change my ways." She paused a moment. "I must tell you about another decision I've made."

Julia stared with her head tilted to one side. Caroline breathed deeply for courage. "I decided not to come back after Christmas. I miss my family and my hometown church, and I have ideas of things I'd like to do to help out in my community. But mostly I plan to confront Matt, tell him how I feel, and then face the consequences. If he has any feelings for me at all, I will stay there and work on developing a relationship."

"This is the cowboy you've talked about before?"

"Yes, and I've never stopped thinking about him. Until I know how he really feels, I will have no peace."

Julia took her hands and squeezed. "I understand, and I think you're doing the right thing."

Tears filled Caroline's eyes. It was all in God's hands now, and whatever He had planned for her, she'd accept as His will for her life.

Chapter 23

*C*harlotte finished dressing for the town council meeting. Maxwell had hinted at a special announcement he planned to make Tuesday morning and wanted her to be present. Since so many of the townspeople would be in attendance, she had been careful in selecting her attire. Gone was the desire to let others know how much better her circumstances were than most of theirs.

Her deep maroon skirt and jacket were of the latest style, but they were simple in cut and adornment. The gored skirt swept about her ankles, and the waistband accented her slender waist. Even her hat was one of her less elaborate ones, with only a few feathers tucked into the side and a bit of veiling around the crown.

Curiosity filled her once again. No matter how hard she had tried at breakfast, Maxwell would give her no hint of today's announcement. It had to be for the good of the town, or he would not propose it. Perhaps electricity would be here before next summer as planned, or maybe the telephone service would be expanded to include long distance for their town. That would be a welcome addition, since she could then talk to Caroline rather than writing her or waiting for a visit.

She shrugged her arms into her coat and pulled on gloves to ward off the chill as she walked into town. The temptation to stop in and see Becky grew when the newspaper office loomed ahead. No time for that now, or she'd be late for the meeting.

The council members were already inside at their places, and citizens of Barton Creek streamed into the building. There would probably be standing room only inside. She spotted Mellie, Emily, and Bea down toward the front when she entered the room. Bea waved and indicated they had saved her a place. She hurried toward it, now seeing that her prediction was true as people began to line the walls to attend this public meeting.

Charlotte took her seat only minutes before the mayor called the meeting to order. Ben Haynes, Marvin Fleming, and Sam Morris were among those flanking either side of her husband.

He stood now before a large group of fellow citizens and smiled as one who had a great secret he couldn't wait to share. "As you know, the *Chronicle* announced we were to have a special meeting today to unveil an important event for our town, and I'm sure that's why we have such a large turnout." He paused to let murmurs and whispers die down.

"We've been a town for some sixteen years, and there's one tradition we haven't taken on. It's one I remember from my youth, and I hope it will bring the same good feelings it once did for me. Last night, the men of our council met and approved the plan we are about to announce."

He paused again, but this time for effect as every citizen sat in anticipation of his words. Charlotte's heart thumped in her chest. From his words and the timing, what he wanted to do dawned on her, and joy filled her heart. He glanced at her now, and when she smiled broadly, he nodded slightly to indicate they were thinking along the same lines.

"What I propose is somewhat late this year, but we can still pull it off. We have voted to have an annual Christmas tree lighting with a concert of hymns and carols, a Nativity scene, and a Santa Claus on the Friday after Thanksgiving. The streets will be decorated for Christmas, and we're hoping merchants along Main Street will join us with special holiday decorations. This year the lighting will be later but will still be just as beautiful. It will be held next week Wednesday, December 18, at seven p.m."

The crowd sat in silence for a moment before someone began clapping. Soon the hall filled with the cheers and claps of the people assembled there. Charlotte gazed across the crowd at the faces of those who made up the town of Barton Creek. Some had been here since the great land rush in '89, and others had come only recently, but this was their town, and they would pitch in with time and effort to make the holiday celebration the best in Oklahoma.

Maxwell held up his hands again for attention. "Now comes the best part. The money to initiate this project has been donated by the Haynes and Morris families. After this year, we will set aside an amount in our budget to help with expenses." Cheers and handclaps again interrupted him, but he smiled and continued. "I've already ordered a tree from Colorado, and it should be here in plenty of time."

He picked up a folder and opened it. "Now to make sure this event happens in a timely fashion this year, we have appointed committees to take care of the different aspects. These people have been contacted and have agreed to take on the responsibility. And I must say, they were sworn to secrecy about the subject matter of this meeting, and from the look and sound of things, they did a good job of keeping quiet."

Chuckles spread around the room as men and women looked at each other to see if one or the other had been in on it. No one had contacted Charlotte, and even Maxwell had refused to share what was going on. At first anger bit at her with vicious nips, but she breathed deeply and remembered her new attitude. This town had plenty of women who could do just as good a job as she could do any day. It was time to let them have their turn in the limelight.

Maxwell perused his list then began naming the committees. Mellie Haynes and Emily Morris were named as co-chairmen of the project and would be responsible for disbursement of funds. The choir directors of both churches were assigned to the music committee, along with a few choir members from each congregation. The decorations committee came next, and Bea and Carl Anderson were named to that post with a committee that included Dove and Luke Anderson, Ruth Kensington, and Lucy Haynes. Charlotte applauded the selection. That group would do wonderful work.

He continued naming groups for food, setting up the Nativity scene, procuring a Santa, and providing concessions. Each time Charlotte marveled that the group of men on the council had come up with exactly the right people for each committee. She hadn't been named to any of them, but she'd be busy at Maxwell's side helping him do his part in overseeing the entire project, and that's exactly where she wanted to be.

After the meeting concluded, Mellie detained Charlotte for a moment. "It's almost noon. How about dropping by the *Chronicle* and seeing if Becky will have lunch with us? Ben won't be ready to leave anytime soon as he and the other men discuss the project further."

"That sounds delightful, and we can go to my house, as Ruby has lunch already prepared. I'm sure she'll have plenty."

"Then we can have a really nice visit with our soon-to-be mother." This would be the perfect time to talk about the baby shower in January and get Becky's thoughts and ideas. She and

Rob already had a well-stocked nursery in their home, but gifts from friends would always be appreciated.

The wind had picked up, causing both Mellie and Charlotte to pull their coats tighter about their bodies. Maybe walking to the Frankston's house wouldn't be such a good idea for her daughter, but Mellie did want to visit with her. Only a few weeks away from the baby's arrival, and Becky still held on to her position at the newspaper. If she didn't quit soon, she just might have that baby in the office. That scene brought a shudder from Mellie.

Charlotte poised her hand over the door handle at the *Chronicle* office. "What's wrong? Are you too cold?"

"No, no, I'm fine. It was just a thought I had. Let's go on in."

Becky stood to one side with Amy in deep discussion, with Becky doing the talking and Amy the listening. When the door clanged shut behind them and the overhead bell jangled, Becky turned around. She hurried over to where they stood at the railing. "Ma, Mrs. Frankston, what are you two doing here?"

"We came to see if you'd like to have lunch with us. Charlotte has graciously invited us to her house." Despite the cold outside, the offices remained warm and cozy. Becky's face glowed, and her swollen belly announced to one and all that a baby was due soon. Her daughter had none of the usual clumsiness of late pregnancy, and she had not complained of backaches, swollen ankles and feet, or sleepless nights. Apparently impending motherhood agreed with her.

"I'll get my coat. One of Ruby's meals is too good to pass up."

Charlotte helped with the coat and knit her brows. "Are you sure you should be walking in this cold wind?"

"Oh, yes. Dr. White said I'm healthy as a horse, and good exercise will never hurt me if I'm careful and don't get in a hurry." She opened the door then turned back to the room.

"Amy, I'll be back in an hour or so. Be sure to let Mr. Lansdowne know where I am in case he needs me. The number is right there on my desk."

Becky hooked her hands onto the arms of Mellie and Charlotte and walked between them down Main Street.

"I'm so excited about the plans for Christmas. When Dad Frankston gave me the news for the paper, I almost burst with the news, but I promised to keep silent and just write my article. I did, and it's ready for the morning edition."

Mellie said nothing and listened to her daughter babble on about how much the town had grown, how many people lived here now, and how many improvements were being made. Becky was perfect for the newspaper business. Her interest in anything and everything going on in the country, the state, and her town gave her stories a flair. Nothing seemed to dampen her enthusiasm for life. Matt was her quiet one. The siblings were both stubborn, but Becky could listen to reason. Once her son made up his mind about something, not much, if anything, could change it.

This whole business with Caroline stemmed from his dislike for Charlotte. Becky stood up to her and went her own way, but Matt kept his feelings inside and chose to let things be. If he could only see that Charlotte had changed, then perhaps he'd change his own attitude and decide to let Caroline know his true feelings for her. Still, Mellie had turned it all over to God, and He was in control of whatever happened now.

When they were seated at the lunch table with steaming bowls of vegetable soup and a salad, Becky finally stopped talking long enough for the blessing and to eat.

Mellie tasted the soup and found it to be delicious with a bit of flavor she couldn't quite identify. She'd have to ask Ruby about it later. But other things filled her mind at the moment. "Becky, how long is Mr. Lansdowne going to let you keep working at the paper? It seems you'd want to stop and get everything ready for the baby."

"I plan to stop soon as I write the story about the Christmas tree. Molly will be here next week, and I'll go through all the procedures with her. Then I'll have at least a week before Christmas to finish up my gifts and then another few days before this little one is due to enter this world."

Charlotte shook her head and buttered a roll. "Don't you think that's cutting things a little close?"

"Not really. Dr. White said first babies are usually late, so I figure I'll have at least two weeks and may even have a New Year's baby."

Mellie remembered her own experience with having babies and prayed Becky would have an easier time of it. Of course she would be in the hospital and not at home, so that should make it a better labor. She had voiced her concerns to Dr. White and told him about her own problems with giving birth, but he had assured her Becky was in excellent health and should have no problems.

Then she remembered Lucy's request for Becky. "Dove, Alice, and Lucy want to give a shower for the new baby in January. Isn't that nice?"

"Yes, but it really isn't necessary. Rob and I have everything we need. We ordered whatever the mercantile didn't have in stock from the Sears Roebuck and Montgomery Ward catalogs, and you and Mother Frankston have supplied the rest."

Charlotte leaned over and rested her hand on Becky's arm. "Now, dear, this is something they want to do for you. They're your friends, and this is the way they can show you how much they care."

Mellie agreed. "Yes, you must let them express their love with this gesture. I'm sure there will always be some item you didn't think of or something new will appear in a catalog that you can't live without. Besides, by then you will know if the baby is a girl or a boy, so the appropriate clothing would be in order." Young couples today needed or thought they needed so much more than she and Ben had when Matt was born. A cradle and baby clothes were all they needed until the infant grew older. Now it was baby cribs, prams, special chairs for the table, and who knew what else.

Becky sat back and patted her stomach. "Well, it would be a nice way to let everyone see our baby at one time, and there will be good food as well, so I suppose it will be OK. But we have to have it here in town."

"Of course. Dove is planning for it to be at her house. That way if the weather is bad, you won't have far to go with the baby. I believe she and Lucy are already working out details."

"Thank you, Ma. I do appreciate their thoughtfulness." Her face brightened with enthusiasm and her eyes sparkled. "Now, tell me what happened at the meeting. Who's going to be in charge of the committees? What activities are planned? I have to write a story about it and couldn't even get inside the building. That's one reason I was so glad to see you two because I knew you were there and I could get all I need from you."

Mellie had to laugh at how quickly her daughter changed from discussing a baby party to her work as a reporter. "Don't worry, we'll tell you everything you need to know." Seeing her daughter so happy and excited about both her baby and her work filled Mellie with love and pride, but her heart ached for her son. If there were some way she could take away the sadness lurking in the eyes of her son, she'd be much happier about the coming holidays.

Chapter 24

Charlotte's nerves bunched up in knots, and her mind worked overtime to make sure all was ready for her luncheon today. With the tree lighting a week from today and Christmas the next week, she and Ruby had adorned the house with fresh greenery, red ribbons and bows, and ornaments. A large tree stood decorated in the living room, and her wreath hung on the door to welcome her guests. She rearranged a piece of greenery and reset a candle on the mantel. Everything had to be perfect.

Ruby had done an outstanding job with the decorations for the tables. The new florist in town had ordered flowers from out of state, and Ruby had arranged the red poinsettias in baskets with additional greenery to set as the centerpiece for the dining table. Red glass balls and white candles completed the decorations.

The table, set for twelve, glistened and sparkled in the sunlight pouring through the windows. God had blessed her with a beautiful day to entertain. She had prayed all week that the women of Barton Creek would be receptive to her apologies and gestures of friendship. So far none of them had rejected her statements of remorse. The big test would come when she spoke at the Women's Guild at church.

Satisfied that all was ready, Charlotte read over her guest list once more. In only a few minutes they would enter her home and listen to her words of apology. Afterward they would partake of the meal Ruby had prepared.

The doorbell rang, announcing her first arrivals. Charlotte opened the door to greet Mellie, Lucy, and Bea on the porch. Emily, Dove, Marie Fleming, and Sarah Perkins were right behind them. In a few minutes, all eleven women were seated in the living room. After a few pleasantries and admiration for the decorations, Charlotte raised her hand.

"Ladies, if I may have your attention, I want to explain the purpose of this luncheon."

All except Mellie leaned forward slightly with curiosity written on their faces. Even the ones to whom she had already apologized appeared anxious to hear her words.

"I've told a number of you how sorry I am for my behavior for so many years. I've missed out on the opportunity to get to know you and have you as friends, but I hope to rectify that in the days ahead. I have not behaved as a Christian should, and that is my deepest regret. I pray you will forgive me."

She paused to let her words take effect on the others. Mellie sat across from Charlotte and smiled broadly. She nodded to let Charlotte know that the brief speech had gone well.

Marie Fleming was the first woman to respond. "Charlotte, I've known you since the early days of our town, and you said then that you weren't happy to be here. You still wanted to be in St. Louis, your home. I've seen you ignore people and hurt feelings, but underneath I sensed it was your own unhappiness that caused your behavior."

Charlotte blinked back tears as the truth in Marie's words sank in and lodged in her soul. If others saw this in her, then maybe they would forgive her.

Bea Anderson clasped her hands in her lap, and Charlotte noted tears staining the woman's cheeks. "Charlotte, at one time I sided with you in passing judgment on others, but after Catherine came here and I learned to forgive, I could no longer support you. I've been praying for you for ten years now, and today is an answer to those prayers."

Emily and Dove both came to her side, and Emily hugged her. "Charlotte, I'm so proud of you for having the courage to admit your mistakes. This is an important day for our town."

Dove grasped Charlotte's hand and gently squeezed it. "I'm sure I speak for all the ladies present when I say I forgive you and look forward to the years ahead of us."

The others all spoke at once, echoing Dove's words. Charlotte swallowed the lump in her throat and silently thanked the Lord for the love of these women. After a moment she cleared her throat and called again for their attention.

"I have two more things I'd like to say before we go in and enjoy Ruby's delicious meal. You are aware of Mayor Frankston's plans for a tree-lighting ceremony and program, and I want to say now how proud I am of the committees he selected to put it all together." She smiled at Emily and Mellie. "And we can't thank you two women enough for the generous gift your husbands have given us to pay for it. You will be wonderful for the committee, and if there is anything I can do to help with decorations or the program, please let me know."

The ladies all nodded and murmured their agreement. Mellie spoke up, "We'll be looking to you for suggestions and ideas, I'm sure, but you said there were two things. What is the other one?"

The encouragement in Mellie's voice and eyes filled Charlotte with hope that the others would be as receptive to the idea as Mellie had been earlier. Charlotte cleared her throat then plunged ahead with her idea. "I plan to make this luncheon at Christmastime an annual affair, but next year and beyond, it will include all the ladies who can come. We'll have it at the town hall and plan it in connection with our Christmas tree lighting celebration. There will be no cost, but the price of admission is one nonperishable food item and one new toy. Those items will be collected then distributed to families who may not be able to have their own Christmas."

Once again murmurs of approval and interest filled the room. Lucy said, "I think it's a wonderful idea, but how will we know which families may need help? We don't want to embarrass them by asking."

"I've already spoken to the pastors of our two churches, and they both have agreed to supply us with names of families we can help. It will be done much the same as we did years ago with the farmers' benefit. The baskets or boxes will be left on the porches or by the door of each family in secret so they can't refuse the gift."

Lucy nodded her head. "Now that sounds like a plan, and every one of us must do all we can to insure the success of such a venture."

Nods and words of approval and acceptance filled the room as well as Charlotte's heart. She should have known these ladies would be more than willing to participate in such an endeavor.

Ruby appeared at the door, and Charlotte inclined her head in acknowledgment. "And now, ladies, I believe Ruby is ready for us in the dining room." She stood and swept her hand toward the other room. "If you'll join me, we will partake of God's bounty for this day."

As the ladies took their places, Charlotte blinked back tears of appreciation and love for these women who were leaders in the community. Because of their future participation, Barton Creek would become an even better place to live.

Matt joined Eli and Alice as they moved a group of horses back to the Hayneses' ranch. Pa had instructed him to pick out six of the ones brought back from Wyoming and buy them from Eli. "I think these are some of the finest horses we've seen for a while."

Alice rode beside her husband and said, "Yes, they are. What does your father plan to do with them?"

"We have a few that need to be put to pasture. Daisy is too old for much of anything now except riding around short distances. Even then she seems to tire quickly. The two that have been our team horses need to be replaced, as well as a few others."

"I bet Becky is sad to see Daisy get so old. She loved that horse when we were growing up. She was a little younger than I am, but I could never outride her. Your sister is quite the horsewoman."

Only in the past five years had Alice become the horse-woman she was now, but she had always enjoyed being around the animals. She'd made a fine partner for Eli with his horse ranch. "And I remember Becky beating me a few times. She'd race back to the barn telling Ma and everyone who'd listen how she'd outrun her brother."

Eli rode up ahead to head off a mare easing out of the herd. Alice moved closer to Matt. "I remember so many good times you, Caroline, Eli, and I had when we were younger. I always believed you and she would marry. Please don't think me nosy, but what happened?"

Matt twisted his mouth. He didn't want to be rude, but neither did he want to answer her question. "Why would you ask me that?"

"Because I care about you both, and I know how much she loved you and still loves you."

The same thing he'd heard from Becky and Ma, and even Mrs. Frankston, but the answer was still the same. She had a funny way of showing it. "Then why did she run off to school? And then to Oklahoma City?"

Alice stared at him until he turned away. "*You* don't even know the reason," he accused her. "I've been rejected twice, and that's enough. The thought of having Mrs. Frankston for a mother-in-law didn't help any." He hadn't meant to tell her that much. It had just slipped out.

She reached out and grabbed his horse's bridle to stop him. "You listen to me, Matt Haynes, and you listen good. Caroline went off to college because her parents insisted. They convinced her it was in her best interest."

He tried to speak. "But Mrs. Frankston just wanted her away—"

"No, don't say anything until I've finished. Of course Mrs. Frankston probably did want to get her away from you, but that's beside the point. Caroline loves you, and when you kept stalling and then quit paying attention to her, she decided to take her chances in Oklahoma City."

"And she found someone else there."

"Matt Haynes, you're the most stubborn man I know. Mrs. Frankston is in town now telling Ma, Dove, Mrs. Morris, and a bunch of other women that she's sorry for the way she's treated everyone these past years."

That's what Ma had said this morning, but he still had difficulty believing a person could change her ways like that so quickly. "And why aren't you there?"

"Because I've never had a real problem with her. I didn't care what she thought about me or my marriage to Eli. I don't let women like her dictate how I will live my life. And you shouldn't either."

He couldn't be as forgiving as Alice and his ma. Too much had happened, and he'd seen too many people hurt. Besides, what he'd said about Caroline finding someone else had happened, and he didn't have a chance with her now.

"Matt, I wish I could shake some sense into you. You're a grown man, but you're acting like a child who didn't get what he wanted for Christmas. You love Caroline, she loves you, so do something about it."

"I told you she's found somebody else." He was ready to end this conversation and tried to pull away, but Alice held firmly to the bridle. If he yanked any harder he might hurt his horse, and that wouldn't do. He glared at Alice in hopes she let go, but she didn't.

"Last time I talked with her there were no wedding plans in the future, and until that happens, she's still available. As for her mother, you'd better be thinking about forgiveness yourself. Look at what my mother did ten years ago. What happened to her in that Indian massacre was horrible, but when she was finally able to forgive what happened in her past, she reaped rewards far greater than she could imagine. She wouldn't have Dove and Eli in the family, and she wouldn't have those two grandsons either."

His mind understood her words and what he needed to do, but his pride wouldn't cooperate. Alice let go of the bridle and called to Eli. "Let's go home. Matt needs some time alone. He's got a lot of thinking to do."

Eli returned and reined in his horse. "I saw you two talking, and from the look on your face, I decided to stay out of it. I know when you're angry."

"I was telling him he had to forgive Mrs. Frankston like your family forgave Ma and that he needed to let Caroline know how he feels about her."

Eli rubbed his chin then tipped his hat at his wife. "You listen to this little gal. She knows as much about people as she does horses. Whatever she told you, consider it."

Matt stared after the couple as they rode back to their home. He turned to gaze at the land around him. A blue sky with scattered white clouds, cold air, the sun's warm rays, wide, open spaces dotted with cattle, mountains off in the distance, and a group of horses to take home all spoke of God's creation and power in the world about him.

He lifted his face to the sun and let the heat wash over him. God was still in heaven, and He was still in control of the universe, but He had given man free choice to be obedient or to go his own way. Right now, with that free choice, Matt controlled his own destiny.

Forgiveness. He had to choose to forgive Caroline's mother, and unless he did, he'd be setting himself up against God Himself. God forgave Jake for shooting a man, He helped Mrs. Anderson forgive her past, He forgave Geoff for his trickery in trying to buy the land that now produced the oil he sought, and He forgave all who had come to Him seeking mercy.

Matt squeezed his eyes shut. "Lord, help me forgive. Give me the strength I need to forgive Mrs. Frankston and to find Caroline and tell her how I feel."

Peace filled him as he headed the horses into the corral at the ranch. Why had he waited so long to do what he had learned as a child? Once again man's stubborn pride had cost more than he wanted to admit.

When he locked the gate, he sat still in his saddle for a moment. God had opened Matt's heart to the mercy and grace that only He could give a sinner. Now it was time for him to show that same mercy and grace to others.

Matt swung off his horse and led him into the stables. In less than two weeks Caroline would be home. But that time loomed ahead and seemed more like months than days.

Chapter 25

Charlotte opened the front door and stepped out onto the porch. The day of the Christmas tree lighting ceremony had dawned with only a slight chill in the air—perfect weather for all the activities of today. If she leaned far enough from the railing at the end, she could see the decorations on Main Street.

She rubbed her arms to ward off the cold creeping in and hurried back into the house and to the dining room. Maxwell had finished his breakfast and now read the morning paper.

"It's a glorious day," she greeted him. "The tree is beautiful already with all its decorations, but it's going to be spectacular tonight when you flip the switch and light it."

"I'm going to test that generator again to make sure it will work tonight." He shook the paper to straighten the pages. "Becky wrote a very nice article about all that went on yesterday with the decorating."

Ruby entered with a tray, ready to remove the breakfast dishes. "I'm sorry. I'll come back when you leave. I didn't realize you were still here."

Maxwell waved his hand in the air. "No, that's fine. We're done." He pushed back from the table. "I have to get to the office anyway." He kissed Charlotte's cheek. "I'll see you later this morning."

After he left, Charlotte headed upstairs for her morning Bible reading. Today's passage began with Psalm 139. As she read the familiar words, tears misted her eyes. God knew her and had planned her life from the very beginning. Before she had even been born, He had known the number of her days. There was nowhere on Earth she could go to get away from His presence, and that gave her comfort she had lacked for many years.

When she reached the last two verses, her tears became weeping. The last sixteen years had been spent in disobedience to the teachings she had grown up observing. God had searched her heart and purged it of its wicked ways. Now she could meet the townspeople with a clear conscience and a loving spirit.

To be sure, the road to her recovery had not been without its bumps. The memory of her meeting with the Altar Guild at church caused a shudder to course through her body. The looks of distrust and skepticism on their faces almost made her turn around and leave without apologizing, but Mellie had stood by her, as had Emily and Bea. Admitting her mistakes and telling the others how much she regretted her actions in the past had been one of the most difficult things she'd ever done, but the results had been worth the effort.

If it hadn't been for Mellie's assurance that Charlotte did mean what she said, it might have turned out differently, but with Emily and Mellie beside her, Charlotte had finally convinced the women to accept her words of remorse.

After her prayer time, she cleansed her face and refreshed her hair before going down to get her coat. The Whites had moved into their new home, and Charlotte arranged for several women from the church to deliver food for them today and tomorrow so Anna could unpack and get everything settled and take care of her baby.

Thinking of Anna White's baby reminded her of Becky. At least today would be her last day at the newspaper. How the girl could wait until so close for the time for the baby's birth mystified Charlotte. Even worse was the fact that Mr. Lansdowne allowed her to continue to work. When Becky changed his mind about women's rights and suffrage, she'd changed it all the way. For her part, Charlotte would never understand why women would want to vote or do the jobs men usually did.

After picking up a dish of baked chicken and vegetables from Ruby, Charlotte walked to the livery to get the carriage Maxwell arranged for her.

Jonah helped her up into the rig. "When you gonna start learning to drive that there motorcar the mayor done bought?"

"I'm not planning to drive it at all." Actually, the monster frightened her more than her first encounter with horses. She planned to keep her distance except when riding in it...with Maxwell driving. She flicked the reins and drove away.

At the Whites' new home, she wrapped the reins around a fence post and met up with Marie Fleming. Grace Weaver, the pastor's wife, waited for them at the steps to the porch.

Anna White opened the new leaded glass front door. "Good morning, ladies. I was just putting baby Glory down for her morning nap when I heard voices." She stepped back and welcomed them to her home. "Pardon the boxes and things. We still haven't unpacked everything."

Charlotte handed over the dish she carried. "And that's why we've come to bring you food for today and tomorrow. We know that moving into a new house this close to Christmas can be a real burden, so we wanted to lighten the load."

"Oh, my, that is so generous of you, and I'm sure Roy will be most appreciative to have a real meal and not another fried egg sandwich."

After the dishes were deposited in the kitchen, she led them into the parlor. Grace headed for the door. "You must have a million things to do, and I need to get back to the church to make sure we have everything we need for tonight's concert.

The choir robes were just washed, and I need to hang them up to get out the wrinkles."

Charlotte joined Grace at the door, and Marie hugged Anna. "If you need me to help unpack, I'll be glad to stay."

"No, that won't be necessary. I'm not sure exactly where I want everything just yet." As they were leaving, Anna stopped them on the porch. "By the way, I forgot to tell you. We had a letter from Doc and Clara. They plan to be back in time for Christmas. In fact, I believe Clara wants to be here in time for the birth of Becky's baby. Won't it be wonderful to have them back after a year of being gone?"

Grace and Marie agreed, but Charlotte's heart went cold. The Carters were returning to Barton Creek. After all that had happened before the couple left to visit family back East, Clara Haynes Carter was one woman she most dreaded seeing again. The outspoken Clara had said her piece about Charlotte's behavior more than once, especially where Becky and Matt were concerned.

Everyone in town may call her Aunt Clara, but she was the blood aunt of Ben Haynes and great-aunt to his children. Charlotte had been the recipient of Clara's scolding on a number of occasions, but she deserved an apology as much as any one of the other ladies.

Charlotte said her good-byes and climbed back into her buggy. Just when things were beginning to come together in a wonderful way, God had put another obstacle in her path. She sighed and accepted the fact that God wanted her to be completely His, and until she sought forgiveness from Clara, there would be no peace. How she wished Caroline were with her now instead of in Oklahoma City.

Matt prepared to go into town with his parents for the tree ceremony. Ma and Pa had been excited all day about the event, and some of it had rubbed off on Matt. He finished saddling his horse and led him outside. Pa had hitched a team to the buggy and waited for Ma.

When Ma emerged from the house, she wore her Sunday best. Her brimmed hat sported a large flower, a few feathers, and some kind of sheer material around it. This occasion must be really important for her to wear that hat on a weekday. She waved at him and climbed up into the buggy seat with Pa's assistance.

All the way into town, his mind filled with images of Caroline. Of course she couldn't come home in the middle of the week, but it would have been nice to have her here. What he planned to say to her when she did come home would be either the beginning of a new relationship or the ending of it altogether. Just as well she wasn't coming since he hadn't yet worked out exactly what he wanted to say.

If she decided to stay in Barton Creek, he wanted her to be happy, and he had the means now to give her anything she wanted. A new house would be the first thing on the list. She always had loved helping people, and she said she loved her job at the library. Those were two things he needed to think about for the future.

A chuckle began deep inside then turned into full-blown laughter. Here he sat on his horse planning their life together when he didn't even know if they had one. If she'd already agreed to marry Stuart, he wouldn't stand in her way. If that made her happy, then he would have to accept it.

He laughed again at the thought of what Aunt Clara would

say about his predicament. She'd fussed at him too many times to count because he wasn't paying enough attention to Caroline. She didn't like Charlotte Frankston either, but she tolerated the woman after Becky married Rob. That's what he should have done. Their former pastor, Reverend Larson, had once said that God's foresight and workings are seen only in hindsight by man. Now his own hindsight told him he could have tolerated Mrs. Frankston for Caroline's love.

They neared the town, and the glow in the sky meant that every store, shop, and building on Main Street had kept their lights on for the event. Pa had told him about a new generator that produced electricity the mayor had ordered to be used tonight. When he'd been in the mercantile last Saturday, Luke had shown him the dozens of light strings that would be put on the tree.

Pa and Sam Morris had spared no expense for the celebration, and excitement filled the air as people milled around waiting for the festivities to begin. Matt swung down from his horse and waved at his parents, who headed down to the livery to leave their buggy.

He spotted Becky talking to several people with a tablet and pencil in hand. He shook his head at the sight of her going from one person to the next. He caught up to her and grabbed her arm. "I can't believe you're still working. Where's Rob?"

"He's with his father over by the tree. And this is my last assignment. I had to write about tonight. Tomorrow I stay home and wait for this baby to finally decide to be born." She patted her swollen stomach. "I hope it's after Christmas."

She held up her tablet. "Now tell me, Mr. Matt Haynes, what are your thoughts concerning this occasion and the fact that it will become an annual affair?"

Matt grinned and shook his head. OK, he'd humor his little

sister. "I think it's quite an auspicious occasion and one of which Barton Creek can be extremely proud. Mayor Frankston and the committees have done an outstanding job of organizing the town on such short notice. And we mustn't forget the generosity of Ben Haynes and Sam Morris. Their philanthropy is to be applauded."

Becky's mouth dropped open. "Matthew Benjamin Haynes, where did you learn to speak like that? Do you even know the meaning of some of those words you used?"

He loved the surprise on her face and reached over to tweak her ear like he had done when they were children. "Of course I do. I didn't sleep through school, you know, and I have read a lot."

She jerked her head away and frowned. "Quit that. You know I hate it."

"And you still react just like you did when you were little. Nice to know that some things never change."

This time she punched him in the arm. "You may be my big brother, but I can still outride you any day."

The picture of her galloping on a horse right now brought laughter that made him clutch his side. "I don't think so. At least not for a while, and probably never."

"Humph, we'll see about that." She turned away. "I see Ma and Pa, and I want to get their statements too."

Matt grabbed her arm. "Wait just a minute. I need to tell you something, but you have to promise not to say anything to anyone else about it."

"Uh-oh, now you do have my attention." A smile curved her mouth and brought a sparkle to her eyes. "Is this about Caroline?"

"Yes, but I don't want anyone else to know in case things don't work out. You promise?"

She crossed her heart with her right hand then held it in the air. "I promise. Now tell me before I split open with wanting to know."

"I've decided to ask Caroline if she'd consider moving back to Barton Creek and marrying me." There, he'd said it, and now he'd have to follow through no matter what.

Becky reached out and hugged him around the waist. "Oh, I just knew you'd come to your senses. She loves you, and she'd go anywhere you asked her to go."

"I'm praying that's true, but I need your help. I want her to have something for staying here. She loves her work in the library, and she's always doing things for others, so think of something that she can do here that will give her the same satisfaction."

"Being married to you would be enough, but you know, a library here in town would be a good thing to have. I'll see what else I can come up with."

"Thanks, I figured you'd have some good ideas." He glanced around and noticed most of the crowd now gathered where the fifteen-foot-tall tree stood waiting to be lighted. Rob hurried up to them and grabbed Becky's arm.

"Come on, honey. Father is about ready to flip the switch to light the tree."

She went with Rob but turned her head and mouthed the words, "Good luck."

He spotted Susannah with Hawk. Ever since he'd told Susannah he wouldn't be seeing her again, he'd worried about how she'd been feeling. She'd been so angry when she'd turned on her heels and run away. Now it appeared that Hawk had taken Matt's place with the schoolmarm, and that was how it should be. They both looked happy, and that was good.

All conversation ceased as Mayor Frankston counted down

from five to one. On one he bent over and turned on the generator. The electric lights Mr. Anderson ordered from the Eveready Company came to life with little white lights covering the tree and lighting up the park with their twinkle and glow.

The crowd cheered and clapped. The committee had outdone itself with the decorating and had produced something the town could enjoy for the Christmas season. But best of all, just a few more days and Caroline would be home.

Chapter 26

*C*aroline waited until after lunch to seek out Mrs. Caskey and speak with her about leaving the library to return home. The time had come, but Caroline still hesitated. Everyone at the library had been so kind to her and helped her learn the system quickly. Her love of books had definitely been an asset as a library aide. She'd miss the work and the people she had met, but she'd made a choice and had to follow through.

Her thoughts turned to Jo. The confidence the young woman had in herself now had been more than worth the time and effort Caroline had given her, and the clothes only made it better. She mentally checked off things in her closets at home. So many of them had not been worn in a while since Mother kept ordering new ones. One of the projects she hoped to discuss with Mrs. Weaver at the church concerned a way to get clothing to families who were in need.

If she became Matt's wife, her clothing would need to be much more practical, and she would certainly have less need for many of her garments. She did hope to be able to go into town several times a week to help at the church and possibly have a class teaching social graces and proper etiquette to young girls and perhaps even boys. Even if she didn't marry Matt, she would still implement the project. Father would be happy to give financial backing to such an undertaking. After it was established, donations would take care of the rest.

She shook off the daydreams and picked up a book that

needed to be reshelved. The library had been quiet all week since the college had dismissed for the holidays. Classes wouldn't start up again until mid-January, so Mrs. Caskey would have plenty of time to find a replacement.

When she spotted Mrs. Caskey headed into her office, Caroline followed. She knocked on the door frame to the office. The head librarian glanced up. "Ah, Miss Frankston, what may I do for you?"

Caroline walked to the desk and eased into a chair facing Mrs. Caskey. "As you know, I'm leaving on the Sunday evening train to go home for the holidays."

Mrs. Caskey peered over the rims of her glasses then reached up and removed them. "I think I hear a 'but' coming in there somewhere."

"Yes, that's what I need to tell you. I will not be returning to the library to work after Christmas." Caroline held her breath and waited for a response. She should have given a longer notice, but she had wavered all week about her decision. Last night she finally accepted that going home was the only way to know in which direction her future may lie.

Mrs. Caskey's eyes lighted up, and a huge smile filled her face. "So, Mr. Whittington has proposed. I knew I would lose you to him sooner or later, and I'm quite happy for you. He's a young man on his way up in this world."

Caroline bit her lip and hesitated to dispel Mrs. Caskey's assumptions, but it had to be done. "No, I mean, yes, he did propose marriage, but I declined. I decided his was not the kind of life I wanted. Our religious beliefs are not the same at all, and his expectations of a wife are not what I want to do with my life."

Mrs. Caskey studied her a few minutes then leaned forward. "I didn't think I saw the sparkle of love in your eyes for that young man, as handsome as he is. I'm sorry to lose you, because you've been wonderful helping the students with their research, and I've seen how Josephine has blossomed under your tutelage. You have a gift of service and helping others, and I hate to see it go to waste."

"Oh, it won't, I assure you. I have a number of things I'd like to do back in Barton Creek that will help young women like Jo."

Caroline spent the next ten minutes explaining some of her hopes and ideas in helping others with their lives and doing it through the church. The more she talked, the more things she thought of that she could do.

Mrs. Caskey laughed when Caroline finished her spiel. "I can see the excitement in your face. I wish you the very best in your endeavors. Tell me, does your town have a library?"

The question stopped Caroline for a moment. A library in Barton Creek hadn't entered her mind. "Why no, we don't, and we need one." But the task of establishing a library was beyond her comprehension at the moment.

Mrs. Caskey stood and came around her desk. "Well, if you ever decide to build one or find a place for one, give me a call or come back for a visit. I'd be glad to help you any way I can."

"Thank you, Mrs. Caskey. I'm sorry to spring this on you on such short notice, but I didn't really make up my mind for sure until last night."

The librarian waved her hand. "Pooh, don't worry about that. With the students gone and it being the holidays, I'll have plenty of help and time to find someone to replace you. You go on home and have a wonderful Christmas with your family."

A few minutes later Caroline met Jo in the employees' room. She'd already told her about the plans for Barton Creek, and Jo had been very excited about them.

"I can't believe you won't be coming back. I'm really going to miss you."

"And I'll miss our little meetings, but you'll have to come visit me in Barton Creek. It's a small town, but you'd love it."

"I'm sure I would. I'm going to have dinner with Jimmy's parents this week. I think he's getting more serious about our relationship."

"Oh, that's wonderful. How nice it would be to marry and be able to stay here in the city. I'll be praying for you."

When Jo's eyebrows raised, Caroline said, "Yes, I've realized how far away I was getting from God and went back to church."

Jo hugged her. "That's the best Christmas present ever."

Caroline returned the hug then noticed the time. "Oh, dear, if I don't hurry, I'll miss my trolley." She hugged Jo one more time before gathering all her belongings and heading home.

On the steps outside, she paused for one last look at the building she'd come to love. Rather elaborate for some tastes, the high arched columns at the entrance gave an air of elegance that Charlotte deemed to be very distinguished and stately. She turned and ran down the street to the trolley stop. No time to think about what was behind her now; she had her whole future ahead, a future she prayed would include Matt Haynes.

Mellie rode in the carriage beside Ben reading Aunt Clara's last letter one more time. She and Doc would be arriving on the train from St. Louis today. The letter had only arrived yesterday, so she'd had no time to prepare Clara and Doc's house for them. Of course, Anna White had left it in excellent condition, but Mellie still wanted to air it out after being vacant and closed up for several days.

She had boxed up a number of Christmas decorations to

decorate a tree Ben had cut for her to put in Clara's living room as a welcome home surprise. Ten years ago Aunt Clara arrived in Barton Creek right after New Year's Day. What a shock that had been. Her letters had been delayed for some reason, and no one expected the feisty little woman to arrive on the doorstep. Her stay in Barton Creek had been memorable to say the least. After people grew accustomed to her outspoken ways, they came to recognize the wisdom she imparted, and they all loved her.

The best thing happened when Aunt Clara, a spinster, married widower Doc Carter. They were perfect for each other and were as much in love as any younger couple Mellie had known. When he retired and turned his practice over to Roy White, he and Clara had traveled back to their homes in Pennsylvania and Massachusetts. Now they were returning to spend their remaining years in Barton Creek, and Mellie looked forward to many happy days with them.

When they arrived at the house, Ben left her there while he attended to business in town. One good thing about having experienced and trustworthy cowhands at the ranch was being able to leave them in charge and come into town for business or visits. Matt and Hank knew what to do, and Monk could tell them anything they didn't. That old man would probably die on his horse out looking after cattle.

Catherine Claymore hailed Mellie from down the street and hurried to meet her. "I came to help you. Clara and I became good friends and neighbors, and I'm so glad they're coming home."

"I can use the help. Come on in." Mellie unlocked the door, and Catherine followed her inside. "The first thing is to open the windows. Only a few days closed up and it smells musty."

Even with the outside temperature in the mild range, cold

permeated the house. She and Catherine went about airing out the place and found a few logs for the fireplace. After she started the fire and the logs were sending out their warmth, she checked on the supplies in the kitchen. Bea Anderson had brought in groceries yesterday so the pantry wouldn't be completely empty, and the icebox held a fresh block of ice for keeping the milk and butter cool.

After removing the sheets and coverings from the furniture, Catherine dusted her hands together then removed her apron. "Looks like it's all ready for them."

"One last thing to do." Mellie opened the back door and grabbed the tree Ben had left there for her. "We have a tree to decorate."

"What a wonderful idea! I love decorating trees. The sheriff found a really big one for me to use at the boarding house, and we all decorated it."

Catherine ran the only boarding house in town and served some of the best home-cooked meals one could find. She and the sheriff had married about the same time as Doc and Clara, and the two women had become fast friends.

Mellie opened the box of ornaments and tinsel she had brought, and for the next half hour they decorated the tree. As they worked, Mellie observed Catherine and marveled at the miracle that had brought her to town and the wonderful reunions that took place. Looking at her now, it was hard to believe she'd spent so many years as a captive in an Indian village. Bea, her sister, had thought her to be dead after being carried off by an Indian brave. The memory of the reunion between Catherine and Bea ten years ago still brought tears to Mellie's eyes, and then to discover that Catherine and Emily Morris, a Cherokee, had been on the same reservation only added to the joy of the reunion.

God worked in mysterious and wondrous ways to bring about His plans, and Catherine's arrival at the precise time she did made a tremendous difference in so many lives. Mellie reached over and hugged Catherine.

Catherine laughed and hugged Mellie in return. "Now what was that for?"

"Oh, I was just thinking about when you came to Barton Creek. If you hadn't come, Dove and Luke wouldn't be married, Emily would still be an outcast, Alice and Eli wouldn't be married, and Bea Anderson would be a bitter old woman. What a difference you made in so many lives."

"It was all God's timing, because I had been searching for Bea for so many years. God knew just when she would need me and led me to her."

Truer words couldn't be spoken. Now if that same timing could happen with Matt and Caroline, Mellie's happiness would be complete.

"Oh, dear, look at the time. I'm supposed to meet Ben at the station, and I hear the train whistle now. We better get ourselves down to the depot." She stowed away the box then locked up the house.

She and Catherine walked as fast as their health and age allowed and arrived just as the passengers stepped off the train. Mellie reached Ben's side at the same moment Clara preceded Doc down the train steps. Mellie stretched out her arms, and Clara reached for her niece. "Oh, I'm so glad you're home. We've missed you so much."

Clara laughed and stepped back to grasp Doc's arm. "It's good to be home. We had a wonderful trip, but now we're ready to settle down and enjoy life in Barton Creek."

Ben and Doc shook hands, and Catherine hugged Clara. The two older women laughed and talked while Mellie looked on with tears in her eyes. She'd missed the feisty Clara more than she had admitted to herself all year.

Ben helped Doc with the luggage while Mellie walked with Clara to the buggy. Catherine hugged Clara again. "I have some errands to run at the mercantile and bakery, but I'll be over later today to have a real visit."

She made her way across the street, and Mellie climbed up to sit beside Clara. "So much has happened in the past year, and you're just in time for Becky and Rob's baby. It's due any day now."

"Has my great-niece quit that newspaper job to stay home?"

"Yes and no. She's at home for now but plans to go back later in January."

"And just who is going to be taking care of that baby? She can't take the child to work with her every day."

"Lucy's aunt Hilda is coming into town to stay with Becky and Rob and be nanny. Mr. Lansdowne told Becky she could go home anytime during the day to feed the baby." That had been so unlike the man who had hired Becky that Mellie ended up asking him herself if he meant it. He told Mellie that Becky was the best reporter and editor he'd ever had, and he didn't want to lose her.

"Well, I hope she'll let me help take care of the baby too. After all, they'll only be a few doors down the street from us."

"I'm sure she will." And if Becky didn't, Aunt Clara would find a way to do it anyway. Now Mellie was anxious to see her aunt's reaction to her news about Charlotte Frankston. "We've had some real excitement around here the past few weeks."

"Is that so? Hmm, has Matt proposed to Caroline yet?"

"No. She moved to Oklahoma City and is working at the library there. But the news concerns Charlotte." Mellie paused for effect.

"And what has that woman done now? Hasn't she hurt or snubbed just about everybody in town already?"

"That's the good news. Charlotte has apologized both personally and publicly to all the ladies of Barton Creek, and especially Emily and Dove."

Aunt Clara sat back with the satisfaction of a cat lapping cream. "So she finally acknowledged the corn. It's about time. Probably took her days to get all that apologizing done."

Mellie stifled a laugh at the use of the old-fashioned term. She hadn't heard anyone say that about corn since her early days in Kansas. Trust Clara to come up with something like that. "Not quite. She took care of it with a luncheon for some of us, and then she met with the ladies at the church and made amends there."

"Humph, then what's wrong with Matt? That's the last obstacle in his way of proposing to Caroline."

"There's more to it than that. Caroline is seeing a young man in Oklahoma City. We met him at the inaugural ball last month. She'll be home for Christmas, and it wouldn't surprise me any to find out she plans to marry Stuart Whittington."

"Then somebody needs to talk some sense into those two young people. Matt's been in love with Caroline ever since I came to Barton Creek. It's time for him to stand up for what he wants and go after it."

"I believe Matt will do what is right, and if they are supposed to be together, it will all work out." She believed that with all her heart, but it would take both of them waking up to the fact that they loved each other at the same time. For that she would pray in earnest for the next few days until the two saw each other at Christmas.

Chapter 27

*C*aroline dashed home from church in the rain, her shoes splashing water on the sidewalk. The rain had begun yesterday evening and had not let up. Even with her umbrella, rain pelted her coat. What a day to be traveling. Her train departed in just a few hours, and if the rain didn't let up, she'd have to leave some of her luggage here and come back for it after Christmas.

When she reached home, both her roommates still slept. A few weeks ago and she would have been with them, but now she didn't want to miss another Sunday in the Lord's house.

Her bags stood by her door, packed and ready to go. She contemplated them now, trying to decide which ones to take and which ones to leave. All of them would have been no problem without the stormy weather, but now they would be too much to handle. The larger case should be plenty for a few days. Besides, she did have clothes at home she could wear. Her personal items such as the lamp, pictures, and other pieces of décor brought from home could wait until she and her father returned for them after Christmas.

With that decision made, she lugged the bag downstairs to the front door. As much as she would miss her new friends and this house, moving back to her old room and beginning new ventures in Barton Creek excited her more. She had written to Father some of her ideas, but she had not as yet heard back from him. That wasn't so bad since it would be better to discuss them face-to-face anyway, but she had wanted to let him know so he would have time to think about her proposals.

Arrangements for a cab to take her to the station had already been made. She had time for a quick lunch before it was due to arrive. She found some leftover ham in the icebox and prepared a sandwich. With an apple and glass of milk, she could make the trip with no hunger. Then when she got to Barton Creek, Ruby's good food would be waiting for her.

The doorbell rang, and Caroline spotted the cab out front. At that moment Madeline and Julia raced down the stairs, their robes and hair flying behind. Madeline reached her first and wrapped her in a hug.

"You can't leave without our saying good-bye first. I can't believe you're actually planning to move back to Barton Creek. We're going to miss you so much."

Julia echoed her roommate's words and hugged Caroline too. As a teacher, Julia would be in Tulsa for the holidays and would not be there when Caroline returned for her other belongings. "I guess I won't see you until the wedding in February. That's a long time."

"Not so terribly, and we'll see each other when we're fitted for our dresses and for the parties before the wedding."

Madeline wrapped her robe tighter around her body. "I see the cabbie waiting, so we'd better let you go. I'll see you when you come back with your father next week, and we can talk more about the plans for the wedding."

Caroline hugged each of them again then opened the door to the cabbie. Both friends disappeared toward the kitchen. The cabbie picked up the bag and hurried out to his vehicle. She followed, carrying her umbrella overhead. The driver helped her up into her seat then climbed up into his. She shivered and attempted to dry her hands and face with a handkerchief. That poor cabbie must be miserable sitting in the rain and guiding the horse through the water-filled streets.

When he helped her down at the station and set her bag on the walk, she handed him several coins for the fare plus an extra bit for his time and effort in the horrible weather.

Once inside, Caroline hurried to the area where her train would begin taking on passengers shortly. All around her people milled about, and she could hear snippets of conversation about the storms in the area. At least she'd be on the train and out of the elements. A conductor announced the boarding of her train, and she moved out to the platform. Because of the holiday, extra cars had been added to the train coming from Texas that would carry its passengers to Guthrie, Barton Creek, and then on into Kansas and Missouri.

With ticket in hand, she made sure her suitcase was loaded onto the baggage car before she stepped up to board her car with the smaller one in hand. The bench seats were filled with passengers, but she spotted one back near the rear exit and headed for it.

An elderly couple sat across the aisle, and she greeted them before settling herself. A few minutes later, a woman stopped in the aisle. "Is this seat taken? I hope not. I'd much rather be seated beside a woman I don't know rather than a strange man."

Caroline smiled and scooted to the window. "No, I'm alone, and you're welcome to the seat."

The woman nodded and planted herself beside Caroline. "Are you going all the way to Missouri? If you are, we'll make the long trip together."

"No, I'm getting off in Barton Creek. That's where I live." Caroline perused the woman seated next to her, and from the sour expression on the woman's face, relief filled Caroline's soul that she'd be getting off early. Still, she could be courteous toward the woman, and perhaps she would become friend-lier. "My name is Caroline Frankston, and I'm going home for Christmas."

The woman frowned a moment and didn't reply. With no change in expression, she finally said, "I'm Miss Prudence Merriweather. I'm going back to Missouri to see my family."

The emphasis on the "miss" didn't escape Caroline's atten-tion. *Lord, please don't let me be a spinster like that.* "My mother is originally from St. Louis. She and my father married there then moved to the Oklahoma Territory in the land run. My mother's family's name is Sinclair. Perhaps you've heard of them." If Caroline guessed right, Miss Merriweather would be about the same age as Mother and her sisters.

Miss Merriweather's eyes opened wide and she raised her eyebrows. "You mother is a Sinclair? I knew Kathleen and Marian. We weren't friends, but I saw them at parties and other events. So you must be Charlotte's daughter. I heard she'd moved out here with her husband and children."

If this woman knew her aunts, how did she get so far away from Missouri herself? Curiosity filled Caroline, but good manners forbade her from being nosy and seeking information. A while later she realized she needn't have worried. The woman talked nonstop about everything, including herself.

"My parents know your grandparents quite well, but my sister and I didn't socialize with Kathleen and Marian. I came west to be a teacher and have spent my years in Oklahoma City teaching fourth and fifth year students."

She droned on about how children were not taught to behave like they should and how she had to discipline them. Caroline listened until Miss Merriweather finally began to run down.

"So you see, I'm here because I couldn't face being rejected by the one man I loved in St. Louis. I'm only hoping I don't happen to meet him or see him on this trip home. He's married with a family of his own."

How different that story from Caroline's own. She was going home hoping to see Matt, not avoid him. Everything about her future hinged on his acceptance or rejection of her after she revealed her love for him. She turned her face toward the window where the rain pounded against the glass. The skies were darker now than they had been before, and the wind blew the rain in every direction.

Caroline bit her lip and prayed that the storm would let up, but when they reached Guthrie, it rained even more. Passengers disembarked and huddled under the overhead protection and greeted the people who had come to meet them.

A few others boarded, and when the conductor came through for their tickets, he announced that there would be a delay in getting to the next stop as the storm would slow them down. That meant at least an hour if not more before they'd reach their destination.

The elderly woman across from them leaned forward. "Would you two ladies like to have some cookies? I made them myself."

Miss Merriweather reached for the basket, took two for herself, then handed them to Caroline. She picked out two then handed the basket back across the aisle. "Thank you. This will be a nice snack." Hunger pains rumbled in Caroline's stomach to remind her of her meager lunch. Perhaps the woman would offer more later. She settled back against the seat and closed her eyes. If she feigned sleep, perhaps Miss Merriweather wouldn't be so prone to talk.

After church Matt rode through the rain to follow his parents to Aunt Clara's house for dinner. Ma had said she had to be at church whether it was raining or hailing or both. Matt snickered. The real reason was she couldn't stand to be away from Becky for very long. The doctor said the baby could come at any time, and Ma wanted to be right there when it did.

The rain didn't bother him. He'd been through storms worse than this out on the range with the cattle, making sure the lightning and thunder didn't spook them. With raindrops dripping off his hat brim, he peered ahead to Clara's house. His aunt had left the church a little early so she could be home to take care of dinner for the family. She didn't want any strain on Becky at the moment.

A train whistle sounded in the distance as he tied up his horse under a tree by Aunt Clara's house. That would be the one from Denver headed for Tulsa and then up through Missouri into Illinois. Caroline was due to arrive in several hours from Oklahoma City. His breath caught in his throat and his heart pounded. If she rejected him this time, he was through with women for good. He would never leave himself open to that kind of hurt again.

Head bent, he ran to the house, dodging raindrops.

The rain continued through dinner, and Matt began to worry. "With the weather like this, the train will probably be delayed from Guthrie."

Pa glanced at his watch. "It's not due for over an hour. It should let up by then."

Ma pushed through the door from the kitchen with Aunt Clara on her heels. "This dessert should take your mind off your troubles for a while." She set the huge chocolate cake in the center of the table. Aunt Clara added plates and forks beside it.

Chocolate cake usually did take his mind off anything bothering him, but not today. He pushed his plate back and stood.

"I'm going out to check the sky. Seems it's getting darker."

He strode outside to the porch. The storm still hadn't let up, and the sky did appear darker than when he'd last looked. A greenish tinge to the atmosphere and the hail that now began to fall warned that a bad storm could be headed this way. It may not be the season for tornadoes, but he didn't want to take any chances.

He hurried back inside. "The skies are dark as evening, and hail's started. I think we need to get down into the cellar."

Becky moaned from the sofa. "Do I have to move? I don't think I can get up."

Rob placed his arm under her shoulders. "Yes, you have to. Come on, we'll help you." He glanced up at Matt with a plea for assistance in his eyes.

Matt stepped to the other side of his sister and helped Rob lift her from the sofa. Together they managed to get her to the cellar steps with Aunt Clara giving instructions all the way. "Be careful. Don't drop her. Watch out for the table there."

Pa and Jake waited at the bottom to help Becky down the last few steps. They settled her on a bench in the cellar, and Doc lit all the lanterns. At least they did have Doc with them if anything happened.

They all sat huddled below the kitchen and listened to the storm. Matt picked up Micah, and Charley clung to Jake. The eyes of the two boys opened wide with fear, but little Amanda slept peacefully in Lucy's lap. Out of nowhere came the image of Jesus in the boat in a storm. He slept while the others worried. Peace stilled Matt's anxiety. They would be safe because the Lord was in the room with them.

After ten minutes, Matt had not heard the roar that accompanied a tornado. He'd never forget the sound after the one that had destroyed their home years ago. Hank, Monk, and the boys would take care of the ranch and the livestock if the storm had headed that way. Matt stood and stretched. "I'm going to take a peek and see what's going on. Sounds like the winds are quieter now."

Pa rose from his seat. "I'll go with you."

When Matt opened the door to the kitchen, he saw light. Rain still fell, but the sky had brightened and the house was intact. From downstairs a groan floated upward. That sounded like Becky. He leaped two steps at a time back to the bottom.

Rob sat next to Becky holding her hand, and Doc stood nearby with his watch. He glanced up at Matt. "I think labor is setting in. She says she's been having contractions for the past half hour but didn't want to say anything with the storm."

Just like Becky to have her baby in the middle of the worst rain they'd seen in months if not years. Lucy and Jake ushered their children up to the living room, and Ma knelt beside Becky with Rob.

Aunt Clara stood with her hands on her hips. "Time to get organized here. This baby will take awhile since it's her first. Matt, go upstairs and call Dr. White. Tell him we're bringing Becky to the infirmary. Then call the Frankston home and tell Charlotte to meet us there because she's about to become a grandmother."

That he could do. He didn't intend to stay in the cellar and watch his sister in pain. When she screwed up her face and moaned, it sent shivers all through him. He bounded up the stairs to the hall where the telephone hung on the wall.

After he made the calls, he sank onto the sofa. Doc and Rob carried Becky up the stairs, and Jake helped them get her covered to protect her from the rain then out to the wagon to take her to the infirmary. She should have stayed put and let Dr. White come to her. After all, she had Doc and Clara to help her.

They'd delivered hundreds of babies and knew what to do, but then what did he know about birthing babies? Nothing.

Lucy went about to find cookies and milk for the boys. Amanda still slept on the floor on a quilt in the living room. Lucy grinned at Matt and poured two glasses of milk. "I take it that was a little too much for you, huh? She'll be fine. We'll wait and go over to the hospital in a little while. Becky doesn't need anyone but her mother and Rob with her right now." She took care of her children then returned to the sink to finish up the dishes left from dinner.

Matt grabbed several cookies and put them on a plate and filled a glass with milk. Jake came through the back door and shook the rain off his coat. "Just saw Sheriff Claymore, and the storm passed to the south of us. He says he thinks a small tornado touched down, so he's taking a few men out to check on the ranches down that way. Everything in town is fine, and the rain's lettin' up."

This was more than he'd bargained for on a rainy Sunday afternoon, but at least the town was spared. Then he remembered. Caroline! Who was going to meet her train? Mr. and Mrs. Frankston wouldn't want to leave the hospital with Becky in labor. He glanced at Lucy now sitting at the table with her children and reading to them. He couldn't ask her to go, and Jake wouldn't do. Matt shook his head. He'd have to go himself.

He put his glass and plate into the sink. First he'd have to make a stop at the hospital to tell Mr. and Mrs. Frankston he'd meet Caroline unless one of them wanted to. Even so, he'd still be there when that train arrived. He couldn't wait one more day to make things right with the woman he loved.

Chapter 28

Caroline dozed for a few minutes, but the hardness of the bench seat made getting comfortable rather difficult. She glanced out the window only to see more rain pounding against the window and a sky as dark as evening just after the sun sets. She furrowed her brow and leaned against the window, but she could see nothing of the landscape. Such poor visibility was sure to slow the train down even more.

Miss Merriweather's eyes were closed, but Caroline was unable to tell if the woman was sleeping or praying. Caroline leaned forward to find the elderly couple across the aisle with their heads together and their hands clasped. She turned back to the window concerned about what she could and couldn't see. Fear snaked its way through her veins, and her teeth dug into her bottom lip. Things didn't look good out there. She prayed God would keep them safe.

The words had barely left her thoughts when a screeching filled the air and sparks of light flashed by the windows. Caroline clutched the edge of the seat as the train tried to slow down. Beside her Miss Merriweather screamed. The sound pierced the air of the car and caused others to do the same. Fear lodged in Caroline's throat and stifled her own.

In the next few seconds the car began to sway and then fell to its side, still sliding along the ground. Caroline felt herself tumbling and reached out to grab whatever she could to stop the fall. Miss Merriweather grabbed on to Caroline, and together they fell against the edge of the seat and then on top of the older couple.

Glass shattered and shards flew everywhere. One hit Caroline's forehead, and blood spurted out and ran down her face. Pain gripped her body as she rolled over the back of a seat and onto the floor. Her arm twisted under her, and this time the pain caused her to scream out.

Then the train stopped with the car on its side and rain pouring in the broken windows on the up side and people piled against the crushed windows and splintered wood of the down side. Caroline raised a hand to wipe away the blood dripping into her eyes and tried to get her bearings. Legs, arms, and bodies lay in a contorted heap up and down the aisles. Sobs and screams of pain filled the air around her. When she tried to move, Caroline realized her left arm was pinned beneath a broken seat, and she couldn't move it.

Miss Merriweather lay beside her with blood staining her dress and her hair falling loose. Her eyes were closed but her chest moved, so Caroline presumed her to at least be alive. The elderly couple didn't move, and because they were on the side that hit the ground, she feared for their lives. Tears filled her eyes and mixed with the blood to blur her vision. She had no idea how far they were from Guthrie or if they were closer to Barton Creek. Whichever it was, surely somebody would come to their rescue before too long.

Moans and groans now mingled with the sobs, but the screams had diminished. Questions as to how many cars were involved and what had happened filled Caroline. Someone had to come to help or some of these people would die.

A man with a lantern leaned through a window above her. She recognized the conductor and called up to him. "We need help down here."

"Help is on the way. We wired back to Guthrie, and they'll be sending a rescue team out. Can you hang on 'til then?"

"I can, but I'm not sure about the others. I think several are dead and more are injured. I can't move because my arm is pinned under the seat." And as long as she didn't try to move it, the pain was bearable.

"OK, I have to go check the other cars."

"Wait! What happened? Why did we derail?"

"Engineer said he saw a tornado ahead and then trees across the tracks. Before he could stop, we hit the trees and the train derailed. The engineer is badly hurt, but the telegraph still worked, so we were able to get the word back to Guthrie. Gotta go now."

At least the sky had lightened and she could see better around the car. As her eyes beheld the scene of blood and twisted bodies, she wished for darkness.

Miss Merriweather moved beside her then opened her eyes. A grimace crossed her face. "Ow, my legs hurt."

"I'm sorry. It's because I'm lying on top of them and can't move out of the way." Caroline looked down to see if she could ease up enough for the woman to move. From the odd position of the ankle and its angle, Miss Merriweather would not be moving by herself. Still, if Charlotte could ease off that leg, the pain might not be so bad for the older woman. She lifted her weight just a trifle, and pain shot up her arm like lightning.

"It looks like we'll have to stay put until help arrives. Try to relax and not think about the pain." Easy to say, but if their injuries were not treated soon, more damage could be done.

Caroline closed her eyes to pray when she heard a groan nearby. She opened her eyes to see the man of the elderly couple blinking his eyes. Thank the Lord, he was alive, but his wife still did not move. She had been in the aisle seat and now lay sprawled across her husband with her head against the window and bleeding.

The man wrapped his arms around his wife and whispered her name over and over. Caroline's eyes misted over, and tears rolled down her cheeks. To see such love filled her own heart with longing for what she may have let slip through her fingers. If Matt no longer cared for her, then so be it. However, she couldn't go on without telling him of her love. "Thank You, Lord, for sparing my life and giving me the chance to see Matt and my family again."

She didn't realize she'd spoken aloud until she heard someone say "Amen." That's what they needed…prayer. This time she spoke louder so all around could hear. "Dear God, we're in a mess, but You know that, and You're sending help to us. Give us the strength and courage to hold on until that help arrives. Keep our injuries from becoming worse. Help us to think of those we love and seeing them again to help relieve our pain. Lord, touch the serious injuries so that they can be treated and their lives saved. Watch over us until help comes. In Your name we pray, amen."

A few more amens resounded, and sobs mixed in with the groans of pain. Although it seemed like they'd been wrecked for hours, no more than ten or fifteen minutes could have passed since they derailed. No telling how long it would take rescue workers to arrive, but they must all have patience and wait.

Impatience and running ahead of God is what landed her on this train to begin with, but no more. From now on she'd do the following and let God lead her wherever He wanted her to go. The next place she wanted Him to lead was out of this train car and straight back to Barton Creek.

Matt entered the infirmary to find Mr. and Mrs. Frankston seated in the waiting area with Ma, Pa, Rob, and Aunt Clara. "Anything happen yet?"

Ma shook her head and gestured for him to come sit beside her. "It'll be awhile according to Dr. White."

He turned to Mrs. Frankston "Caroline's train is due in less than an hour. I know you don't want to leave Becky, so I'll pick up Caroline and bring her back here."

She reached out and grabbed Matt's hand. "Thank you. We do want to stay here with Becky and Rob."

Pa stood and came toward Matt. "Take our rig down to the station. She'll have luggage and other belongings. That way you won't have to walk and carry it all."

"Thank you. I'll do that." At that moment Becky yelled out something indistinguishable. Rob grimaced and squeezed his hands together. Matt frowned at his brother-in-law. "Shouldn't you be in there with her or something?"

Aunt Clara snorted. "Not on your life. He'd only be in the way. The doctors and Ruth have enough to do without a nervous papa messing things up."

This time Becky yelled, "I don't want to do this. Stop it now!"

Rob turned a green that rivaled the earlier skies. Matt didn't feel so good himself. He had to get out of there. "I'm going to make sure the horses are OK after the storm and that the buggy's not damaged."

He turned on his heel and strode out of the building before anyone could say anything to stop him. Not that they would have been about to anyway. They were all too busy worrying about Becky.

If that was what it was like for a woman to have a baby, how could they keep having them? He'd always wanted children, but after seeing Rob, Matt didn't want to go through anything like that. Of course it might be different if his own wife was the one having a baby, but how could he let her go through such pain? Jake and Lucy had three children, and he loved those children, but he had no idea what Lucy had endured in order for them to be here.

Although soaked, the carriage looked none the worse for the storm, and the inside was fairly dry. With the rain now down to a slight drizzle, Matt led his horse and the buggy team down to the stable. He dismounted and entered the stables that emitted a strong odor of wet hay and horses.

"Hey, Jonah, you here?" Matt peered around and heard Jonah before he appeared.

"I'll be right with you, Matt."

A few seconds later the burly man stepped out from one of the stalls. "Just getting one of my tenants situated. How can I help you?"

"I need these horses fed and warmed. They've been out in the cold since the storm."

"That I can take care of. Got plenty of room now since more people are getting those horseless motor things. Think I'll start me a garage just for them." As he talked, he started to unhitch the team.

Matt stopped him. "Jonah, I'm meeting the train to take Miss Frankston back down to the infirmary, so just keep them hooked up and warm them up a bit."

The old man scratched his chin, his eyebrows hunched together. "Now who's in the infirmary? Someone in the mayor's family sick?"

Matt laughed and clapped Jonah on the shoulder. "Becky's

having her baby, and the whole family's there, so I'm meeting Miss Frankston."

"Becky's havin' a baby, and you're meetin' the train." Jonah's rheumy eyes peered at Matt. "'Bout time you got that Miss Caroline to stay home. She don't need to be off there in that city."

"That's what I'm hoping to do, Jonah, and you could be praying for that to happen."

"Well, ya know I'm not much of a prayin' man, but the Lord does listen when I do, so I'll say a few words for ya."

"Thanks, Jonah. Soon as I hear that train whistle coming, I'll get my rig and be ready for Miss Frankston." That shouldn't be too long. The train from Guthrie was always on time. He headed back out for the street and met Dove and Mrs. Anderson outside.

The rain had stopped, and both ladies were walking in the direction of the hospital. Dove grabbed Matt's arm. "Is it true Becky's having her baby?"

As usual, the news traveled fast around town, especially where the mayor's family was concerned. "Yes, she is. Looks like it'll be an early Christmas present for the family."

"Then we'll go down and check to see if they need anything. Where are Lucy and the children?"

"At Aunt Clara's house."

"Good, then we can go pick up the boys and Amanda then bring them back to play at my house with Danny and Eddie. If you'll excuse us, we'll be on our way."

He stepped back to let them pass. Lucy would probably appreciate the gesture. Just like neighbors and good friends, Dove and Mrs. Anderson wanted to make things easier for everyone during this time. As long as he didn't have to stick around and listen to Becky's screams, he'd be fine. He could find lots of other things to do so he didn't have to be at the infirmary.

He sauntered down to the station. The sun peeked from behind the clouds, causing the rain puddles in the street to sparkle in its rays. At least he wouldn't have to worry about Caroline getting wet now. He strained his ear toward the south, but no train whistle sounded in the distance. The train had probably been delayed by the rain. He decided to sit inside the station and wait for her.

All the words he wanted to say to her today rolled through his mind like tumbleweeds on a windy day. The first thing would be to tell her about Becky and take her to the infirmary to be with her parents. Ten minutes later the train hadn't arrived. When he inquired, the ticket agent said they'd had word from Guthrie that the trains were late leaving and the weather would slow the train by maybe an hour. With the weather like it had been, that sounded logical.

He headed back to the infirmary to check on Becky so he could have the correct information to give Caroline. Maybe the baby had been born by now.

When he entered the waiting room, everyone still sat where they had been before. Mrs. Frankston jumped up. "Where is Caroline? Wasn't she on the train?"

"It hasn't arrived yet. The man at the station said it'd be late because of the weather. I'm going back down there to wait on her. What's happening here?"

Mrs. Frankston shook her head and grasped his arm. "Nothing yet, and it will likely be awhile yet. Dr. White and Doc Carter are both with her, so she's in good hands." She tugged on his arm. "Come over here a minute. I have something to say to you."

He didn't want to hear anything she had to say to him today

or ever. The last thing he wanted today was to hear this woman utter sentimental and insincere platitudes about how he and Caroline would be so good together.

Mrs. Frankston bit her lip and stared up at Matt then turned to Aunt Clara. "I'm so sorry for the way I've treated you and your family. Please, Clara, can you find it in your heart to forgive me?"

Aunt Clara opened her eyes wide and rocked back on her heels, grinning a smile so broad it took up her face. She strode toward Mrs. Frankston. "Now that's what I've been waiting to hear ever since Mellie told me you'd apologized to the ladies in town." She wrapped her arms around Mrs. Frankston. "Of course I forgive you."

Mrs. Frankston returned the hug with a stunned look on her face. Matt pressed his lips together to keep from laughing. Guess she hadn't expected that reaction from Aunt Clara.

When his aunt released Mrs. Frankston, she turned back to face Matt. "I could tell by the look on your face you didn't believe me the other day, but I want you to know right now that I meant every word. I could also see that you still care very much for her, and if you love Caroline, you should do everything in your power to convince her to stay here and marry you. Mr. Frankston and I will do all we can to help you both."

He studied her face a moment, but all he saw was sincerity, and after the scene with Aunt Clara, all his long-held cynicism and skepticism melted away, and compassion for this woman—Caroline's mother—filled his heart instead. "Thank you, Mrs. Frankston. I intend to do just that when she gets here."

Doc Carter stepped through the door from Becky's room. "Well, folks, we have us a bouncing baby boy. Becky's fine, and Rob, you can come in and meet your son."

Everyone cheered and clapped as Rob jumped up and

followed the doctor. Cries now came from the room, but they were from a newborn this time, and to Matt, those lungs sounded mighty healthy.

He turned around to leave with relief flooding his soul. The last barrier to his relationship with Caroline had just been broken down—*and* he was an uncle.

At that moment Mr. Weems, the telegraph operator, burst through the door. "There's been an accident. The train from Oklahoma City derailed between here and Guthrie. Lots of people injured and some killed."

Chapter 29

*S*tunned silence followed Mr. Weems's announcement. Matt absorbed the news, fear running through him faster than a hound after a coon. Caroline was on that train. All his thoughts jumbled together, and for a moment he couldn't think at all.

Mayor Frankston grabbed his wife's hand. "When did this happen, and where is the train now? My daughter is on it."

"Far as I can tell from the message, it's just north of the Cimarron River. The storm felled some trees over the track. Sheriff Claymore is gathering a group to go up and lend a hand with the rescue."

Matt could go with them. He had to find Caroline. He headed out the door then stopped and turned back to Mr. and Mrs. Frankston. She leaned against her husband, sobbing, "My baby, my baby is on that train."

"I'm going to go find her, Mrs. Frankston."

The mayor nodded and patted his wife's back. "Thank you, Matt. Do you want to take the motorcar? It might be faster."

"No, sir. With all the mud from the rain, the roads won't be good, and I might get stuck. My horse can get through it quicker because we won't have to stay with the roads." He jammed his hat on his head. "I'm going to find her no matter what. I'll try to send word soon as I do."

Ma grabbed him in a bear hug. "Oh, Matt, please be careful. No telling what kind of weather you might find."

"I will, Ma. Give Becky and that new little nephew of mine my love."

Then he ran out the door and down to the livery to get Thunderbolt. What an apt name for his horse for this day. He waved at the sheriff. "I'm going with you soon as I get my horse."

Jonah had the black stallion saddled and waiting. "I figured you'd be a-needing him to go with the sheriff's men."

"Thanks, Jonah." Matt swung his leg up and over the saddle then joined the men ready to leave.

Sheriff Claymore said, "We're going to ride hard and fast as the conditions will allow. No telling what we'll find when we get there, but we want to help in any way we can. Most likely they'll be taking the injured back to Guthrie." His gaze panned the group of men and landed on Matt. A slight nod indicated an understanding of Matt's purpose in riding with them. "OK, men, let's go."

Voices sounded through the window, and a lantern appeared. "Can anyone hear me down there? Can anyone answer me?"

Caroline joined her resounding yes with several others around her. "Good, we'll send someone down to check on you."

A few minutes later a man lowered his body through the window. He studied the conditions a moment and turned his head side to side looking for a place to drop. He rested one foot on a seat back then lowered the other to a small space beside Caroline. When both feet were situated, he glanced from passenger to passenger. He then looked straight at Caroline.

"I'm a doctor. I see the gash on your head. Are you injured anywhere else?"

Caroline grimaced and tried again to move her arm. "I think my arm is broken. It's pinned beneath this seat, and my legs are trapped, but they're OK. The woman under me can't move, and I think her ankle is broken."

Another man joined the doctor. He blew out a breath and pushed his hat back on his head. "We have a mess down here. Where do we start?"

The doctor situated his hands on the seat holding Caroline's legs down. "Give me a hand here. If we can get her out, we can have room to reach some of the others."

Prudence Merriweather's eyes fluttered open, and she moaned. "I'm dying; get me out of here. I can't feel my legs."

"Yes, ma'am. We'll get you soon as we can." He grunted and pulled on the seat with the other man lifting the other side.

The weight lifted, giving Caroline blessed relief. The seat pinning her arm moved too, and she was able to free it. She bit back the pain and pulled her legs, and with her injured arm against her body, she rolled to her right side. From there she was able to pull herself up and balance on another bench seat. "My legs are OK. Can you get to her now?" Despite the pain in her own arm, Prudence needed help first.

The doctor yelled up to someone near the window. "Hand me down my bag and something to make a splint." He turned back to Caroline. "I'm going to clean up that gash then give you both something for pain before I splint your arm and her ankle. After that we'll try to get you out."

He crawled past her to the elderly couple. The old man shook his head and caressed his wife's hair. "I'm OK. Just a bunch of bruises, but I couldn't save her. The impact against the window and the ground broke her neck. She's with Jesus now."

Tears streamed down Caroline's cheeks, mingling with the blood there. She had feared the woman hadn't survived, but to hear the truth hurt to the core of her being. Such a short while ago the woman had shared her cookies and looked so happy.

Then she remembered seeing them with their heads bowed together and the man's lips moving. The man and his wife had been prepared, thank God.

One glance around the car and she realized more bodies would be found. Those not seriously injured began helping those who were in the most pain.

The doctor opened his bag and removed what looked like a pair of scissors and pulled something from her head. This time she screamed at the pain.

"I'm sorry, but I had to get that piece of glass from your forehead." He moved his hand to show her the shard just removed. It was covered in blood and was at least an inch wide with a pointed edge. "I'll have the nurse up top clean it out more. Now take this."

Caroline swallowed the pill and let him put a splint on her arm. He then did the same for Prudence's ankle and gave her a pill.

"They're sending someone else to take people out, so I'm going to check on some of the others now. That pill should do its work quickly."

He was right about that. It was certainly stronger than the aspirin Madeline gave her, because its effect was almost immediate. The next thing she knew strong hands reached beneath her arms and pulled her up through the window, now cleared of all broken glass. Two other men carried her to a stretcher on the ground.

There she lay while more of the injured were removed and placed on stretchers. Those who had not made it were placed off to the side and covered as best as possible. Caroline shut her eyes against the scene and breathed a prayer for the families waiting for them to arrive.

Her eyes opened wide. Family? She had to get word to her

family that she was OK, but she wouldn't be home tonight and maybe not even tomorrow. At that moment a woman leaned over her with a damp cloth.

"The doctor wants me to clean up some of the blood on your face and cleanse the wound."

Caroline shivered as the cold cloth dabbed at her forehead. At least she still wore her coat to ward off the December chill.

The woman stopped then wiped across the cut with something that burned. Caroline yelped, and the woman said, "I'm sorry, but I had to clean it out. You have a nasty cut, and I had to use an antiseptic. It's clean now, but you're going to need a few stitches when we get you to the hospital."

From the pain and amount of blood, Caroline had known the cut was bad, but stitches meant it was deep and would leave a scar. She didn't want to think about it now with the pain medication causing her to be sleepy. She peered up at the woman placing a bandage on the wound. "Thank you. It doesn't hurt as much. Are we going back to Guthrie?"

"Yes, and the first vehicles have arrived to transport the injured." She patted Caroline's arm. "You may have a scar, but you'll be fine. Now get some rest. I have to take care of the others."

Caroline closed her eyes again, aware of more movement but too sleepy to reopen her eyes and check what was happening. Her body relaxed as strong hands lifted her and carried her to an ambulance.

Many Barton Creek citizens lined the streets and walks as the men thundered out of town, splashing through mud and water to get on with their mission.

Matt rode with grim determination to find Caroline. An image of her injured and lying in the rain or mud and in need of help or even...no, he wouldn't go there. Caroline had to be alive.

Alice was right. He'd been foolish to let Mrs. Frankston keep him from the girl he loved. Now his heart stood ready and willing to forgive all the past hurts and look to the future. Even what he thought were rejections by Caroline had been no more than her attempt to force him into action, and he'd done just the opposite.

Because of what Alice had told him, he now knew she'd gone off to college to please her parents, not as a rejection of him. But she'd gone to Oklahoma City because he hadn't the gumption to let her know he loved her. What if he was too late and Stuart had already claimed her hand and planned to marry her? That didn't matter at the moment. Caroline had to know the truth. He'd deal with Whittington later.

Evidence of the storm's passage lay all around them in uprooted trees and debris dropped by the storm. Two washtubs lay upside down pushed up against some bushes; other pieces of furniture and equipment littered the ground in spots. When they reached the scene of the accident, the huge tree across the tracks with the engine smashed into it explained how the train crashed and derailed. Men climbed over the cars lying on their sides and pulled victims through the windows.

The sheriff indicated to his men where to tie up the horses and get busy with helping those already there. Matt wrapped Thunderbolt's reins around the remains of another tree and headed over to hunt for Caroline.

A row of bodies lay to the side. Some were covered; others were not. He didn't want to go there.

He climbed up on the overturned car nearest him and helped pull a man through the window. They lowered the unconscious form to two men waiting below. Then he worked steadily for the next hour, moving the dead and injured, and looking and calling for Caroline.

After all the cars were empty, there was still no sign of Caroline. Ambulances, wagons, and carts left with the injured. The dead still lay where they had been put with two men checking a list and making notes. Matt refused to believe one of those bodies might be Caroline's. He hurried over to the men. "I'm looking for a passenger, a blonde woman in her twenties. She boarded at Oklahoma City. I haven't found her anywhere here."

One of the men removed his hat and scratched his head. "Well, she may have been with those already taken into Guthrie. The first ones rescued were taken to the hospital there." He nodded toward the covered bodies. "If she's not with those over there, then the hospital is where I'd check."

"Thanks." Matt scrambled back across the wreckage to the other side, where his horse waited for him. The sun had set, and the going into Guthrie would be rough in the dark, but he had to get to Caroline tonight and make sure she was safe. At least Thunderbolt was familiar with night riding, but Matt still kept his pace slower than he would have in daylight. The moon appeared from behind the clouds to give enough light to see the terrain ahead.

He prayed as he rode, thanking God for the light and praying for Caroline's safety. He remembered the location of the hospital from their trips to Guthrie in the past. When the lights of the town appeared on the horizon, Matt's pulse quickened. He spurred his horse, which picked up his pace to a gallop as though sensing the urgency in his rider.

At the hospital Matt secured his mount then raced inside. He slid to a stop at the desk where a nurse checked off a list and handed it to another nurse. She peered at Matt. "How can I help you?"

"The injured from the train wreck, where are they?"

"The men are in Ward Three and the women in four, but you can't go in there."

He didn't wait for her to stop him but ran to the ward. A nurse there held up her hand to halt him. "I'm sorry, sir, but no men are allowed in the women's ward. Maybe I can help you."

"I'm looking for a woman, Caroline Frankston. She was on the train." *Please let her name be on the list.*

The nurse ran a finger down the names on the paper in her hands. She shook her head and checked again. "I'm sorry, sir, but no one by that name is here."

His throat constricted with fear. Where was she? He didn't even want to consider the possibilities. Holding back his tears, Matt turned to leave.

"Wait, sir. I believe the less injured have been released and taken to a hotel. The railroad is providing housing for them."

"Which hotel?" He'd search all over town to find her if it took him all night.

"Check with the nurse at the front desk. She can tell you."

When Matt asked, the nurse wrote a list of names on a sheet of paper then handed it to him. "I believe these are ones that said they had rooms."

Matt grabbed the list and thanked the nurse. Outside he stood by the door in the light to study the list. He recognized the name of the hotel where he and his family had stayed for the inauguration last month but not the others. He glanced around to get his bearings but recognized little else but the hospital. He should have paid more attention when they had been town before, but with so many people and events going on, he'd paid little heed to his surroundings. The only areas he knew were the hotel, the train station, and the hospital.

The nurses inside should be able to give him directions, so

he headed back to the reception desk. "Pardon me, but could you tell me where these hotels are and how to get to them? I'm looking for someone from the train." He laid the paper on the desk.

One of them scanned the list and smiled. "Oh, this is where they took the patients we released. This is where you'll most likely find them. I'd check them first." She indicated two of the hotels on the list, and neither was the one he knew.

The nurse said, "This one is four blocks over from this corner and about three blocks south from there. If the person you're seeking isn't there, the clerk can give you better directions to the second one."

"Thank you." He walked back outside and mounted his horse then turned in the direction the nurse indicated. Matt shook his head in wonder at the amount of traffic and number of people on the streets for a Sunday evening. Apparently the train accident had the whole city abuzz.

At the hotel he stopped at the front desk. The young man there appeared tired and frustrated. Matt removed his hat and said, "I'm looking for survivors of the train accident. I was told some of them came here."

"Yes, they did, and we've been busy finding rooms, but they're all situated now. What is the name of the person you're looking for?"

"Caroline Frankston. She's from Barton Creek."

The man scanned the list with his finger. "Sorry, but I have no one by that name."

"Can you tell me how to get to the other hotel where some patients may have gone?"

Matt listened to the directions with anxiety beginning to nibble at his soul. "Thank you. I believe I can find it."

Back on his horse, he paused to take in the situation. This was his last hope. *Lord, please let her be at the hotel.* He nudged Thunderbolt forward with his heels. He didn't even want to think about his next destination if he didn't find her this time.

aroline sat on a couch in the hotel lobby while the management scurried around to find rooms for the injured and stranded passengers. With the holidays, the bad weather, and the cancellation of trains, the hotels were full and rooms scarce. At the moment she would sleep on the floor no matter how uncomfortable.

She fought to keep awake as the last of the painkillers wore off. Her arm rested in a cast against her chest, and the stitches on her forehead ached and itched, but the doctor had warned her about touching them, so she kept her right hand in her lap clutching the blood-spattered fabric of her skirt. Blood stained her coat even worse, but she needed the warmth of the coat and ignored the stains.

A wire to her parents was folded in her pocket, but so far she'd found no way to get the news to them. They'd be worried sick by now without any word as to her condition. Not exactly the return to Barton Creek she'd planned, but she had been among the fortunate ones.

When she had awakened in the hospital, gauze covered her forehead, and plaster encased her arm. After an hour, the doctor checked her and decided she could be dismissed. She'd gone to find Prudence Merriweather, who had been admitted for surgery on her ankle. The nurse hadn't allowed Caroline in to see Miss Merriweather, but she gave her assurance that the teacher would be fine in a few days and able to go home.

Caroline thanked her and went to join those headed for hotels in the city.

She'd also learned the elderly couple's name. Mr. and Mrs. Justin had been on their way to visit a daughter. She had found Mr. Justin and offered her sympathy and prayers. Mrs. Justin had been seventy years of age and a wonderful Christian woman according to her husband. Her age and the fact that she was a Christian softened the blow somewhat, but it was the first time Caroline had faced death so close to her.

In the time since the accident, she'd had time to think plenty about her own death and her future. Without a doubt she'd go to heaven, but she still had too much life to live before that happened. God had saved her for a reason today, and she'd make sure she listened to whatever God called her to do. She prayed Matt Haynes would be a part of that future, whatever it was.

Painkillers may take care of the wound on her head and her arm, but nothing could take away the ache in her heart. If she'd been more open with Matt and made sure he knew how she loved him, perhaps she wouldn't be where she was now. She laid her head against the back of the couch and closed her eyes only to have Matt's face fill her thoughts.

Someone touched her arm. She opened her eyes to see the desk clerk standing before her. "Miss, I need to talk to you and the others."

Caroline sat up and rubbed her eyes with her right hand. "I'm awake. Do you have our rooms ready?" How she wished for a clean, soft bed to lie down and sleep for a long time. The reception area of the hotel was filled with those who had been on the train. Some, injured like her, sat waiting for a place to spend the rest of the night.

"First, your baggage has been retrieved from the wreckage.

Some pieces were damaged, but most of it is intact and will be waiting for you at the depot. Second, we have managed to come up with some rooms, but not enough for all of you. We'll start with the injured and the older people first. If any of you who are alone could share a room, it would be a big help." He consulted a list he held. "Mr. and Mrs. Mobley?" An older couple stood. He handed them a key. "You're on the second floor."

Caroline watched them hobble away with their arms around each other. She glanced around at the others. The clerk handed a key to a couple with three children, all of them wearing bandages, and the mother held a child with a cast on her leg. They left, and the young man returned to her.

"We have a room for you next." He held out a key.

Caroline reached for it but stopped her hand in midair. Too many others still needed a room. "Thank you, but I'll wait until some of these others are taken care of."

"But you're injured and have a head wound."

"I'll be all right. I can sleep anywhere, but some of them look like they really need a bed and rest." As much as she'd like to lie down on a soft mattress, she wouldn't be able to sleep peacefully knowing someone else would have to sleep on the floor. She settled back against the deep blue velvet upholstery and closed her eyes once again.

This time when she saw Matt, they were together. He was laughing and smiling and they were riding horses together. Across the rangelands of the Hayneses' ranch then back to the creek and then into town they rode. She wanted to talk with him, but he was always ahead of her and couldn't hear her words.

Caroline pressed her eyes closed to keep the tears at bay. If only he were here now to rescue her and take her home. She sent a silent plea to heaven. *Please, Lord, send someone for me. I want to go home.*

Sometime later the clerk stood before her again. "Miss Frankston, we have a room for you."

Caroline glanced around the room at those remaining without shelter. An elderly man sat on her left, two women huddled together across the way, another gentleman occupied a chair by the window, and a young couple sat near him. The young woman of the couple couldn't have been very old, and her head rested on the young man's chest. He patted her head and whispered to her while tears streamed down her cheeks.

Her heart went out to the couple. They looked so young and scared. "Give the key to the couple over there."

The clerk grinned. "I thought you might do this. They're newlyweds, and this was the first day of their wedding trip to Missouri. I know they'll appreciate your generosity." He headed to the couple and handed them the key with a nod in her direction.

The young woman pulled back from her husband and swiped at her cheeks with her fingers. When they reached her, they stopped. The young husband said, "We can't thank you enough, but are you sure you want to stay here? That cut on your head looks pretty bad, and your arm must be hurting."

Caroline smiled and waved her good hand. "Think of it as my wedding gift to you and don't worry about it. I'll be fine right here on the sofa."

They thanked her again then headed up the stairs to their room. The hotel clerk returned with pillows and blankets for those remaining in the lobby. Caroline thanked him, as did the others. The women immediately went about settling themselves in chairs across from her.

Caroline positioned the pillow on her right side and arranged the blanket with her right hand. The man on her left reached over and smiled. "Here, let me help. That's hard to do with one hand."

In only a minute he had her situated and moved back to his spot. She leaned her head on the pillow and huddled her arm against her body to be as comfortable as possible. The lobby grew still with only the gentle snores from the man next to the window breaking the silence.

For some reason the Lord wanted her to stay right here in the lobby for the rest of the night. Whether it was to make sure the newlyweds had a room or to keep the women company she didn't know, but the reason could be figured out later. At the moment her head ached, and she needed sleep in whatever manner she could get it.

Matt stopped Thunderbolt and scanned his surroundings. This wasn't where the hotel would be. He was lost. He removed the instructions from the clerk at the last hotel and moved under a street lamp. There he read the directions again. His breath expelled in a blast. That last turn was in the wrong direction. In his haste he'd wasted precious time going the wrong way.

He turned his horse around and leaned to pat his neck. "Sorry, pal. I know this street is hard on your hooves, but we have to find Caroline. Then I'll find you a place to rest." He'd worked his stallion hard this night with the ride from Barton Creek and then on to Guthrie. Both of them were tired, but Matt couldn't rest until he knew Caroline was safe.

After several blocks, he turned in the right direction. The streets had cleared since he'd started his search, and whether it was before or after midnight he didn't know. He shook his head in an attempt to rid it of the weariness that slowed his thinking.

Even if he found Caroline in the next few minutes, he

couldn't take her home until morning. He'd have to figure how then. They both couldn't ride Thunderbolt that long a distance. Surely the town still had a livery where he could rent a carriage to take them home. Transportation would be the first thing to do in the morning, that is, if he found her.

Up ahead the lights of the hotel beckoned. At last he'd reached his destination. He dismounted and tied Thunderbolt to a railing then headed inside. He strode to the desk and the clerk there. "I'm looking for a passenger from the train wreck, Caroline Frankston."

A broad grin spread across the man's face. "She's right over there."

He turned to see Caroline asleep on a couch with her hair in disarray and her coat stained with blood. A bandage covered her forehead, and a hand encased in a cast peeked from under the coat. At the moment she looked more beautiful than he'd ever seen her, and his heart felt as if it would burst in his chest with his overwhelming relief at finding her alive.

He trod silently across the room, gazing at her. A lock of hair fell over the bandage on her forehead. Matt knelt at her side and brushed the lock back, then caressed her cheek.

Caroline stirred, and her eyes opened. For a moment she simply stared before a sob escaped her throat. "Matt, is it really you?"

Swiftly he moved to sit next to her, then opened his arms and gently folded her into them. "It's me, and I've come to take you home."

Her good hand clutched his jacket, and she sobbed against his chest. "I was praying you would come. That's why God wanted me to stay here. He knew you were coming for me."

Caroline's head rested just below his chin, and he kissed her hair. "Yes, He did. You're injured, but you're alive." He pulled back slightly to gaze into her face. "What happened to you?"

"When the train went over I was on the up side and tumbled down over the benches. My arm is broken." She held up the cast and grinned through the tears. "I suppose you guessed that already. A piece of glass from a broken window cut my fore-head. I hurt all over, but now that you're here, I'm much better."

"It's been a long journey, but I finally found you. I looked everywhere for you."

"I wanted to send word, but the telegraph office was flooded with messages, so I decided to wait till morning. Mother is probably in a panic."

Matt almost laughed but swallowed it to a grin and whis-pered, "She's in a panic all right, not only for you, but for Becky, who was in the infirmary having her baby. We're aunt and uncle to a healthy boy—at least his lungs sounded healthy."

Caroline's hand flew to her mouth. "The baby, how wonderful. My little brother is a papa, and I'm an aunt." Then she giggled. "Your little sister is a mama, and you're an uncle. What does that make us?"

"I don't know. We'll figure it out later." What he wanted was for her to be his wife, but now wasn't the time for that. He stood. "I have to take care of Thunderbolt, but I'll be right back. Try to get some rest now." He wanted to lean over and kiss her, but he fought the urge because the lobby was too public. Their first kiss would be in private where he could say all the things he'd held in his heart for such a long time.

Matt approached the clerk once again. "Do you have any place I could take my horse for the night? He needs to be unsaddled and rested."

"Yes, we do have a livery out back, but at this time of night, you'll have to take care of him yourself. The men there won't be on duty again until seven in the morning."

"Thanks, I'll do that now." He turned to glance at Caroline once more before leaving. Her eyes were closed in relief and exhaustion. How beautiful she looked even with dirt on her face and her hair hanging about her ears. He turned and strode out to take care of Thunderbolt.

When he reached the horse, he stopped and leaned his head against the saddle. Relief swept over him in a wave of emotion, and he couldn't hold back the tears. The woman he loved could have lost her life before he'd had the opportunity to declare his love. God had been good, and from this moment on, Matt would make sure Caroline knew how much he loved her, no matter what her relationship to Stuart Whittington might be.

Chapter 31

Matt settled down on the floor at Caroline's feet with his head resting against a pillow. This is where he wanted to be for the moment, at the feet of the girl he loved. He dozed off and on all through the night. He awakened to see the pink glow of dawn pushing back the cover of darkness through the front windows. He sat up and stretched, working out the kinks in his back and legs. In spite of their uncomfortable perches, the rest of the guests remained asleep.

The hotel clerk tiptoed to his side and whispered, "If you would be so kind to let everyone know, the dining room will be serving breakfast to all who were stranded. I'm going off duty, but I wish you well for a safe trip home." He walked away, hesitated, and then came back.

"I must tell you, Miss Frankston is one of the kindest, most generous women I have ever met. She gave up two chances for a room last night to give to those she thought needed it more. If she's your sweetheart, then you are one very lucky man."

Matt pondered the words of the clerk, who gathered his belongings and left the building. What he said was just what Caroline would do. She'd always looked for ways to help and comfort others. When Dove had almost lost her life in the prairie fire, Caroline had ignored her mother's wishes and visited her in Doc Carter's office.

Barton Creek needed her kindness and generosity to offset Mrs. Frankston's blunt disapproval of so many. Although the woman had changed some and had given him her blessings yesterday, he didn't expect her personality to change entirely. She would always be brisk and efficient and just a tad superior in her demeanor.

How he longed for a hot bath and a shave right now, but he'd have to wait until they got home for that. He checked his pockets and found a piece of chewing gum and a clove-flavored bark. At least he'd be able to freshen his breath.

A new clerk came on duty, and Matt went over to greet him. "Good morning, I'm Matt Haynes. I trust you have word as to who these people are." He pointed his thumb back toward Caroline and the others still sleeping.

"Yes, we are all very much aware of our unfortunate guests. We have a place for our employees that you can use to wash up. No bathtub, but a sink and a few washcloths may help with the surface dirt, and we can provide for shaving for the gentlemen."

"That would be nice." The Lord was working overtime supplying all their needs this morning, and Matt trusted He wasn't through providing yet. "I have a question about transportation. I must get a young woman here back to Barton Creek and her family. Do you know where I might possibly rent a carriage or buggy to take us?"

"Carriages and such are getting hard to come by. The Carriage Works about four blocks from here is going out of business, so perhaps you could purchase one for a good price. Do you have a team to pull it?"

"No, but I have my own horse, and he would be able to pull a small vehicle. I'll check into it. Thank you."

As soon as they had breakfast and cleaned up a bit, he'd ride over to the carriage place and see what was available. That decision made, he strode back to Caroline, who was just waking up. She smiled up at him, and her dimples flashed.

"So it wasn't a dream. You really are here." Her hand went to her hair then her forehead. "Oh, dear, I must look a fright."

"Considering the alternative, I think you look just fine." He held out his hand to her. "Come, the clerk says they have a place where you can wash your face and tend to your hair. Then we'll eat breakfast. I'm sure you must be hungry. I know I am." His stomach had rebelled during the night at the absence of food since dinnertime at noon yesterday.

"Oh, that sounds heavenly right now." She picked up their blankets from the floor and handed them to Matt.

He folded them and laid them back on the sofa. The clerk then led them to the room he'd spoken about earlier. Matt allowed Caroline to go first and waited outside. All around him employees prepared for another busy day at the hotel, now filled to capacity. Wonderful smells wafted his way from the kitchen. The coffee in particular tempted him with its rich, distinctive aroma.

Caroline appeared with her face freshly washed and her hair smoothed back, although a number of strands still escaped to cling to her neck. The coat now lay over her good arm. "That's better, but it's difficult doing anything with one hand. I had to really work to get my coat off. And I doubt even the laundry at home can get out those bloodstains."

Ten minutes later he'd finished his shaving with the equipment the hotel provided. Matt stepped out of the lavatory and grasped her hand. "Now, Miss Frankston, those tempting smells from the kitchen need our attention."

As they ate scrambled eggs, bacon, biscuits with fresh butter and honey, and coffee, he outlined his plan to her. "First, I'm going to the telegraph office and wire our folks to let them know you're OK. Next, I have to get transportation to take us home. I'll do that while you stay here and rest."

"The hotel clerk told us last night that our baggage had been retrieved and was at the depot whenever we wanted to go and get it."

"Good. When I find a carriage or a buggy, I'll come back and pick you up. We can stop and get your things on the way out of town." That meant there had to be room for luggage on the buggy.

She grabbed his hand. "Matt, let me go with you. I really don't care to stay here."

He covered her hand with his. "I'd like for you to be with me, but it's better for you to stay here out of the cold. We'll probably need to buy you a heavier coat too for when we leave. I don't believe your mother would like seeing all that blood on you."

She glanced down at the coat beside her. "It does look awful, but not all the blood is mine." Caroline moved her hand from under his and fingered the bandage on her forehead. "The doctor put seven stitches here to close this gash." She thought a moment then said, "We'll get a new coat."

Matt finished his meal and pushed his plate back. "I'm going to see about Thunderbolt and then ride over to the Carriage Works and see what I can find to take us home."

He escorted her from the dining room and back to the lobby. Several others from the accident who had been given rooms now joined those already in the lobby. Caroline turned to Matt and placed her right hand on his chest. Her blue eyes peered up at him and churned up all the love he held for her.

"I'll be fine here, but do hurry back."

Again he wanted to lean down and kiss her, but with this many people, he'd embarrass them both. He blinked his eyes and kissed her fingers instead. "I'll be back as quickly as I can. Maybe we can be in Barton Creek around noon, depending on the conditions of the trail between here and there."

He released her hand then strode through the doors. He hadn't yet asked Caroline about Stuart, but by the way she looked at him, maybe he wouldn't have to.

Caroline raised the fingers that he'd kissed to her lips. She had thought he was going to kiss her, but he had lifted her hand instead. How she longed for that kiss and to hear words of love from his lips. So different from Stuart Whittington, Matt's concern was for her and not for what he could get.

She returned to the sofa where she had spent the night. The pillows and blankets had been moved out to be cleaned, and the elderly couple who had been the first ones offered a room now occupied the other end of the couch. The family and the newlyweds had not returned, but several others had. Conversation flowed quietly around her, giving her time to think about the magical appearance of Matt last night.

All through the night she had been very much aware of his closeness. All she had to do was move her hand a fraction and it would have been on his head. The rain had caused his hair to curl even more than usual, and she would have loved to rake her fingers through it. This morning he had brushed it back on his head, but even so, a few dark curls refused to cooperate and fell over his forehead.

The woman next to her spoke. "Dear, was that your young man who just left?"

"He's…he's just a friend from my hometown. He came to take me home."

The woman grinned and winked at her husband. "We're Mr. and Mrs. Watson. We've been married almost sixty years, and I believe I can recognize the signs. He loves you, child. His words, his eyes, his touch all speak of how much he cares for you. And it appears to me you feel the same toward him."

Heat rose in Caroline's cheeks, and she lowered her gaze to stare down at her fingers, picking at the blood spatters on her skirt. If she'd had a grandmother living close by, this woman is who she'd want it to be. Her kind gray-blue eyes and smiling, wrinkled face spoke of wisdom.

Mrs. Watson reached over and stilled Caroline's fingers. "Dear, don't let love slip away. What he feels for you and how he shows it speaks of love that will last a lifetime. If this is what God ordains for you, don't fight it. Let go and let your love flow from you like a fresh spring. Your love will fill him, and his will then overflow onto you and fill you."

Tears sprang to Caroline's eyes. "You sound so much like his aunt Clara. She's a wise woman and has often told me to just tell Matt of my love, but I haven't had the courage. I...I didn't want to be rejected. I've waited a long time to hear him say he loves me, but he hasn't."

She leaned back and smiled at her husband. "I believe he will, and very soon. I'll say a little prayer for you."

"Thank you." He'd been gone only a few minutes, but the time until his return stretched ahead like eternity. If only what Mrs. Watson said could be true, it would be the best Christmas present she'd ever received.

Caroline reached into her purse for one of the pills the doctor had given her for pain. She retrieved the little container and went to the desk. "May I have a glass of water?" she asked the clerk.

"Certainly, Miss Frankston. I'll be back in a moment."

When he returned, she downed the pill and the water in one big gulp. Her head and arm both throbbed with pain now, but this would bring relief. She headed back to the sofa and closed her eyes.

"Caroline, I'm back."

She forced her eyes open to find Matt standing over her. Caroline blinked her eyes and glanced at the large clock over the registration desk. "Oh, I must have fallen asleep."

"You did, and I hated to wake you, but we need to leave." He reached for her hand to bring her to her feet then helped her into her coat. "I wired home and let them know we're coming and then bought a buggy to take us. Thunderbolt is hitched to it outside."

"Will we have time to get a coat? I do want to get rid of this one." She looked down at the stains and shuddered. The sooner this coat disappeared, the better she would feel.

Mrs. Watson spoke to her. "Maybe we'll see you in Barton Creek. Our daughter is supposed to come pick us up so we can go back with her."

Matt leaned over and shook Mr. Watson's hand. "I'm Matt Haynes. Who is your family in Barton Creek?"

Mrs. Watson beamed and held her husband's hand. "She's the wife of the pastor there. Her name is Grace Weaver."

Caroline gasped and looked up at Matt. "He's our preacher. Oh, my, it is a small world."

Mr. Watson said, "They're supposed to come today, but we're prepared to stay another night, so that's not a problem. The clerk sent someone to the depot to pick up our baggage."

Matt turned to Caroline. "I'm sorry. I forgot to tell you. I went by there but didn't know what was yours, so we'll have to stop and pick it up as we leave."

"That's fine. I should have had my name on them anyway. Next time I will." She leaned over to kiss Mrs. Watson's cheek and whispered in her ear, "I'll remember what you said, and if the opportunity presents itself, I will let him know I love him."

Mrs. Watson squeezed Caroline's hand. "God go with you both. We'll look for you in church on Christmas."

Caroline grasped Matt's arm. "We'll look for you in church tomorrow night." She walked beside Matt to the rig he'd purchased. He pulled on leather gloves and said, "I'm sorry this rig isn't a larger carriage so we could have taken the Watsons with us. I know Grace will be glad to hear they're staying in the hotel. Maybe we can get one of the cowboys at the ranch to come back and get them."

Caroline wasn't sorry. It would have been nice for the Watsons to go now, but she really preferred to be alone with Matt. Guilt nibbled at her conscience, and she hoped the couple wouldn't consider her selfish for not at least offering a ride.

Matt helped her up onto the seat then climbed up beside her. Side curtains helped shield her from the wind, which was much colder than she had thought it would be.

She could hardly wait to tell him she'd come home for good and that she loved him, but it would have to be put off until other matters were attended to first. She glanced again at her bloodstained coat. A new coat must be the first order of business.

Half an hour later she had found the coat she wanted, along with a woolen scarf to wear around her head. After she completed the purchase, Matt headed for the station to pick up her baggage.

In the time it would take to reach Barton Creek, she hoped to have a number of things in their relationship out in the open. Caroline retrieved warm gloves from her purse, where she had put them after boarding the train. The fact that her purse had stayed hooked around her arm was a small miracle for which she was most grateful.

As she struggled to put on the gloves, Matt reached over and helped her. "It's going to be awkward for a number of things with your arm in that cast."

She smiled in gratitude for his help. If this trip turned out like she hoped, it would be the beginning of his helping her with many little things. This had turned into a Christmas to remember for more than one reason, and she hoped many more good moments were to come.

Chapter 32

*A*fter finding her suitcases in the jumble and confusion of those brought from the wreckage, Caroline breathed a sigh of relief. Although they were marred with scratches and dents, the bags were intact. She watched as Matt loaded them onto the back of the buggy then lifted her up to the seat. At last they could get on with their trip and they would be alone. He'd already told her he didn't plan to take the route that would lead them by the train wreckage. For that she was thankful. Caroline didn't need any more reminders of her ordeal the day before.

As they rode through the city, the words she wanted to say rolled through her mind faster than the wheels on the rig they rode in. She sat quietly beside him as they rolled past the buildings closer to the edge of town. As soon as they were in the country and away from everything, she'd tell him. She pulled the fur collar of her new coat tighter about her neck. Her arm in the sling rested under the coat, and the left sleeve dangled at the side.

"Are you warm enough? If not, we can get a blanket to spread over your lap."

"No, I'm fine. I'm just anxious to get home." Despite the warmth of the heavy coat and new scarf, a chill coursed its way through her body, but it didn't come from the cold air.

As they left the city, Matt's mouth worked around like Father's when he had something important to say. Maybe she should let him reveal what was on his mind first before she said anything. What he had to say could very well determine what her actions would be.

Mrs. Watson's admonition to just tell him how she felt came back to her, but her courage disappeared like the morning dew in the sun. And if he didn't speak soon, she may never reveal her thoughts to him.

She watched as he took in a deep breath of cold air then let it out. His hands twitched with the reins. "Caroline, I...I have so much to say to you...and I don't know where to begin."

Her heart fluttered with hope. All she wanted to hear was if he loved her or not. Her eyes opened wide, and her lips trembled more from anticipation than from the cold.

"What I mean is, please stay in Barton Creek after Christmas. It's been lonely without you."

The words weren't exactly what she wanted to hear, but it was a start. Surely he wouldn't want her to stay if he didn't care about her. "But I have my job in Oklahoma City. I really enjoy working in the library." She would wait to reveal her plans after he gave her his.

"But what if we had a library in Barton Creek?"

A library in Barton Creek? "The town does need one, and having one would be wonderful, but there's still much to be done in Oklahoma City." Confusion set in as she tried to digest what he said.

Somehow she had to tell him she'd planned to stay anyway. Still she hesitated. She'd much rather for him to make the first move, but if he didn't do so soon, she'd have to take matters into her own hands.

He grimaced, pulled the reins up, and stopped. "Caroline, why did you leave and go off to college?"

Caroline almost choked at his words. She hadn't expected such a question and didn't answer right away.

She placed her hand on his arm. "Matt, I had to go to college. It's what my parents wanted for me." The idea that she'd hurt him by leaving created a new pain in her heart, but at the time she'd had no choice.

"You mean they just wanted to get you away from me. Your mother has never liked the idea of us being together."

Her heart lurched, and she yanked her hand away. So the truth was coming out at last. No wonder he'd been distant. What he said may have been true then, but Mother had changed, didn't he know that?

"But Matt, that's not the case anymore. I saw the difference in Mother when I was home for Thanksgiving. I wanted to tell you then, but you avoided me at every turn, even at church."

He went on as if he hadn't heard her, frustration building in his voice. "And then you up and went off to Oklahoma City. I know Barton Creek can't offer you the excitement of life in the city, but your friends and family are at home. That should count for something." He grimaced again as if in pain. "And then you got all involved with that Whittington guy, and now—"

Caroline held up her hand. "Stop now. I'm not involved with Stuart and won't be in the future."

His Adam's apple moved up and down. Whatever he had to say must be hard. The cords in his neck stood out, and his hands held the reins in a death grip. "Does that mean you will consider staying in Barton Creek after Christmas?"

"The offer of a library in our hometown is certainly an enticement, but what about Susannah?"

His eyes opened wide as if the question startled him. "There's no Susannah. She's with Hawk."

Caroline's heart soared, but if this man didn't come out

and say what he really wanted, she just might reach over and kiss him just to see his reaction. Nothing stood in their way. He knew why she went off to school and that her mother had changed, so what was stopping him now?

Finally he let the reins drop to his lap and turned to her with a grim expression on his face. She forced herself to be still and let him say what he needed to say.

"I'm not good with words like you or Becky, but when we learned about the accident, I was so afraid you were seriously injured or that we'd lost you. I couldn't stand the thought of living life without you. All that stuff about college and your mother and that other guy, those were just excuses I gave for dragging my feet. Hang it all, what I'm trying to say, Caroline Frankston, is I love you. Please stay in Barton Creek. Don't go back to Oklahoma City. We...I need you, and I'm sorry it took so long for me to tell you that."

Her heart leapt with joy, but tears flooded her eyes at the words she had waited so long to hear. "Oh, Matt, I've never loved anyone but you." And that was what she should have told him months ago.

The next thing she knew his arms were around her and his face was inches from hers. Her heart pummeled against her ribs, as though it would burst through at any moment.

"This is something I've been wanting to do for a long time, and especially since last night." His lips met hers, gentle at first then with more pressure.

This is what she'd dreamed her first kiss would be like. She returned the kiss and snaked her good arm around to his back. Warmth flooded her, and she never wanted to let go. This time she'd made the right choice. When the kiss had deepened and she felt it to her toes, he moved his head away.

"I love you more than I can ever tell you. Will you marry me?"

She raised her hand to the back of his head and pulled it closer. "Thought you'd never ask, Mr. Haynes." This time she kissed him.

When they parted, his breath came in short spurts. "I take it that is a yes." Another kiss sealed his love. When he released her, he flipped the reins and shouted, "Yahoo!"

One thing was certain, life with Matt would never be dull, and she couldn't wait to begin it. Barton Creek with all their friends and family would be home for the rest of their lives. She snuggled closer to him, not worried anymore about how cold it might be. His warmth was all she needed now and forever after.

Acknowledgments

My great appreciation goes to Larry Johnson of the Metropolitan Library system in Oklahoma City for all his help is getting me information concerning the inauguration festivities when Oklahoma became a state in 1907.

Another big thank-you to my editor, Lori Vanden Bosch. Without her expertise, I would be lost.

Thanks to my wonderful ACFW and IWA! friends who have encouraged and supported me on my publishing journey.

A big thank-you to the wonderful people of the Oklahoma Tourist Information Center at Thackerville who gave me oodles of information and my interest in the history of Oklahoma.

As always my love and appreciation to my husband, who is my biggest supporter.

Coming in Summer 2011 from Martha Rogers,
Summer Dream,
Book 1 of the Seasons of the Heart series

CHAPTER ONE

1888
Briar Ridge, Connecticut

WHY DID PAPA HAVE TO BE SO STUBBORN? RACHEL Winston stared at the gray clouds outside her window. The dreary weather matched her mood at the moment, and she fought the urge to stomp her foot like a spoiled child. However, a young woman of twenty-one years must behave as befitting her age, as Mama so often reminded her. Perhaps she should have shown the letter to her mother first. Too late for that now, she'd find out as soon as Papa had the opportunity to tell her.

The back door closed with a thud. Rachel shuddered. Papa had left for the church. His departing meant she needed to finish dressing or she'd be late, and then Papa would be even more upset with her.

The paper in her pocket crackled as she moved toward the bed to retrieve her boots. Rachel fingered the crumpled edges of Aunt Mabel's letter. No need to read it, for she knew the words by heart. Her aunt's invitation to come to Boston for an extended visit in hopes of meeting suitable young men for marriage had arrived at a most inopportune time with the winter weather in the northern states at its worst. Even so she shared it with Papa, hoping he might be agreeable to the visit.

A metallic taste soured her mouth, and she swallowed hard in an attempt to squelch it. Papa argued that the unpredictable weather of January made travel from Connecticut to Boston dangerous. If only one of the many Boston trains came to Briar Ridge. Aunt Mabel meant well, but her timing left something to be desired. Papa didn't even want her going to Hartford or Manchester to board a train.

She grasped the wrinkled letter in her hand and pulled it from its resting place. "Oh, Auntie, why did you wait until

January to invite me for a visit? Last summer when I graduated would have been perfect, but you had to travel abroad, and then you wanted to wait until after my birthday. Well, I had it, and now I can't come. It wouldn't have made that much difference to have come in the fall for the social activities then." As if Aunt Mabel could hear her. A deep sigh filled her, but nothing could change her father's mind.

Aunt Mabel believed that after a young woman finished college, she should be thinking of marriage, and Rachel agreed with that, but not that it would have made a difference in her being twenty-one rather than twenty. Of course Papa had thought she should marry and not go off to more schooling, but her aunt's offer to pay and Mama's urging had brought it to pass. Now here she was past the age when so many others had begun their families, but she wouldn't have traded those years at the academy for anyone.

Rachel sighed and sat on the bed to ease off her slippers. Very few boys her age lived in town. The others were too old or just out of the nursery. She bent over for her winter boots, which would protect her feet from the slush. The frozen ground outdoors called for the much heavier ones, not the choice she would have liked to wear to church this morning. Rachel shoved her feet down into the sturdy boots designed for warmth and not attractive appearance.

Once again her mind turned to the eligible young men in Briar Ridge. One young man came to her mind, but then Daniel Monroe didn't count. His sister had been Rachel's best friend since Papa came to be pastor of the Briar Ridge Community Church nearly seventeen years ago. Daniel treated her more like his sister anyway. His knowledge soared high above her own, and keeping up a conversation with him took more effort than she deemed it to be worth. Rachel had finished at the university with good marks, but Daniel's conversation interests leaned more toward science and new inventions like electricity and the telephone than things of interest to her.

Rachel's anger subsided as she pulled on the laces of her boots, and respect for her father rose. Papa loved her and wanted only the best. He had promised that when summer came, he'd talk to her about the trip. Until then she would be the obedient daughter he wanted her to be. The Lord would give her patience, even though that was not one of her virtues.

She smoothed her skirt down over her hips and picked up the letter to place it on the table beside her bed. A response to Aunt Mabel would go out with tomorrow's mail to express her regrets in not being able to accept the invitation. With another lingering sigh, she stood and checked her reflection in the looking glass over the chest across from the bed.

How she wished she could be with her older brother, Seth. Away at the seminary, he studied to be a minister like their father. He had left Briar Ridge and most likely would not return if his ministry took him elsewhere. Not that the town was so bad, but it did seem dull in comparison to Boston or even Hartford, where she had spent her time at school with Abigail Monroe.

She'd met a few young men while at school, but the strict rules and regulations set forth at Bainbridge Academy for Young Women in Hartford had given her few opportunities to develop a relationship. Not that any of them would have been considered, but she would have appreciated the chance.

Mama waited for her in the front hall. Rachel noted the firm set of her jaw and braced for the scolding that would be in order. "I'm sorry to take so long, Mama." She grabbed her cloak from its hook.

"You know how your father hates for us to be late to church. It is unseemly for the minister's family to be the last to arrive." Mama turned and hurried outside.

Rachel breathed a sigh of relief. No time for a scolding now. She set a dark blue bonnet firmly over her hair and fastened the ties. She followed her mother out to the carriage, where the rest of the family waited. As usual, Papa had gone on ahead to open the church and stoke the old stove to provide heat on this cold January morning. Rachel climbed up beside her sister, Miriam, and reached for the blanket.

"What delayed you, Rachel? There's no excuse for not being ready with everyone else." Mama settled in her seat beside Noah, who had taken over his brother's responsibilities until his own departure for college next fall. "Time slipped away from me." No need to tell her everything now. Rachel tucked a blanket around her and Miriam. Mama would find out about the letter later when Papa told her his decision.

Micah piped up from the front seat. "Did you make Papa angry?"

Rachel jerked her head back. "Micah! Of course not." She glanced at her brother Noah and noted the smirk on his face. She frowned to let him know she didn't approve.

His gaze slid to her now. "Oh, then why did he stomp through the kitchen and ride off without a word to anybody?"

Mama clucked her tongue. "Now, children, it's the Sabbath. Papa was late and in a hurry to get to the church." But the look in Mama's eyes promised she'd speak to Rachel about it later, especially when Mama learned the real reason for the tardiness.

Rachel swept the prediction aside. Even though his decision disappointed her, Papa simply wanted to protect her from danger. She should be grateful for his love and concern, not angry because he said no. The promise of a trip to Boston come summer would be enough to get her through the remainder of winter and the months of spring.

A recent snowfall still covered the frozen ground. Most of it in the streets had melted into a hodgepodge of brown and black slush caused by carriages and buggies winding their way toward the church. Rachel breathed deeply of the clean, fresh air that seemed to accompany snow in winter and rain in the spring.

If not for the inconveniences caused by ice and snow, she would love this time of year, even when the leafless branches of the trees cracked and creaked with a coating of ice. She gazed toward the gray skies that promised more snow before the day ended. She hoped it would wait until later in the day so she might visit with Abigail this afternoon.

However, a warm house, a cup of hot tea flavored with mint from Mama's herbs, and a good book might entice her to stay home on this cold winter afternoon. Of course, the weather brought on more chores with keeping the woodpile stocked and the animals in the carriage house warm. Still she enjoyed the winter months, although this year she wished them to hurry by.

Miriam snuggled closer. Rachel smiled at her sister, a little over seven years younger. "I see you're wearing your Christmas dress today. Is there a special occasion?"

Miriam's cheeks turned a darker shade of red. "Um, not exactly."

"Then what is it...exactly?"

Miriam tilted her head to one side and peered up at Rachel. She whispered, "Jimmy Turner."

So her little sister had begun to notice boys. "Well now, I think he's a handsome lad. Has he shown an interest in you?"

Miriam nodded and giggled. Rachel wrapped an arm around her sister as the buggy slowed to enter the churchyard. She stepped down onto the snow-covered ground muddied by all the wagons crossing it, thankful for the thick stockings and shoes she wore to protect her toes. She then reached up for Micah while Miriam raced ahead.

The little boy pushed her hands away. "I can get down by myself."

Rachel couldn't resist the temptation to laugh. At seven her younger brother expressed his independence and insisted on doing things for himself. He jumped with his feet square in a pile of snow and looked first at his feet then up to Rachel. She shook her head and grabbed his hand to go inside the building. How that little boy loved the snow. He'd be out in it all day if Mama would let him.

When she entered the foyer with Micah, she spotted Miriam already sitting in their pew, with Jimmy Turner in the row behind her. Rachel hastened to sit down beside her sister. Miriam stared straight ahead but twisted her hands together in her lap.

When had Miriam grown up? She'd be fourteen her next birthday, but even now she showed signs of the beauty she would one day be. Thick, dark lashes framed deep blue eyes, and her cheeks held a natural pink glow. Papa would really have to keep an eye out for his younger daughter.

Rachel glanced around the assembly room and once again admired the beauty of the old church built not long after the turn of the century. Instead of the quarry stone and masonry of the churches in Boston and even New Haven, Briar Ridge's church walls were of white clapboard with large stained glass windows along the sides. On bright days, sunlight streamed through them to create patterns of color across the congregation.

Brass candelabras hung from the high vaulted ceilings, and the flames from the candles danced in the breeze as the back doors opened to admit worshipers. As much as she loved her church here in Briar Ridge, she remembered the electric lights she'd enjoyed in Hartford. How long before electricity would become as widespread in Briar Ridge as it was in the larger cities? Probably awhile, since Briar Ridge wasn't known for its progress.

When the family first came to town, Rachel had been three years old, so this was the only home and church she could remember before leaving for school. Familiar faces met her everywhere she gazed. A nod and smile greeted each one as she searched for her friend Abigail and the Monroe family.

Unexpectedly a new face came into view a few rows back. A young man with the most incredible brown eyes stared back at her. Rachel's breath caught in her throat, and the heat rose in her cheeks.

She felt her mother's hand on her arm. "Turn around, Rachel. It's not polite to stare."

With her heart threatening to jump right out of her chest, Rachel tore her gaze away from the stranger seated with the Monroe family. Papa entered from the side door and stepped up to the pulpit. The service began with singing, but Rachel could barely make a sound. Everything in her wanted to turn and gaze again at the mysterious person with the Monroe family, but that behavior would be unseemly for a daughter of a minister.

However, her thoughts refused to obey and skipped to their own rhythm. Rachel decided that whoever he was, he must be a friend of Daniel's, because Abigail had never mentioned any man of interest in her own life. In a town like Briar Ridge, everyone knew everyone's business as well as their own. She hadn't heard any talk of a guest from Daniel or her other friends yesterday.

A prickling sensation crept along her neck as though someone watched her. She blinked her eyes and willed herself to look at Papa and concentrate on his message. However, her mind filled with images of the young man. Why had the stranger come to Briar Ridge?

Nathan Reed contemplated the dark curls peeking from beneath the blue bonnet. When she had turned and their eyes met, he swallowed hard. He had never expected to see such a beauty in a town like Briar Ridge. His friend Daniel's sister was attractive, but nothing like the raven-haired girl ahead.

When she turned her head back toward the front, he stared at her back as if to will her to turn his way again. With a sigh, he turned his sights to gaze around the church, so much like others he'd once attended. He wouldn't be here this morning except out of politeness for the Monroe family. He'd arrived later than intended last evening and welcomed Mrs. Monroe's offer to stay the night with them. The least he could do was attend the service today.

Nathan had no use for church or things of God. He believed God existed, but only for people who needed something or someone to lean on. God had forsaken the Reed family years ago, and Nathan had done quite well without any help.

He shook off thoughts of the past and concentrated once more on the blue bonnet several rows ahead. Perhaps Daniel would introduce him to the dark-haired girl. She would be a nice diversion from the business he must attend to while in town. He blocked the words of the minister from his mind. All the times he'd been in church before, the messages always seemed to be the same. God loved everyone, but unless one repented of his sins, he'd spend eternity in hell. Nathan sighed. The thought of hell, if it existed, didn't bother him, because his life had been bad enough in the past. Now he enjoyed good times in the company of attractive women who had no more desire for commitment than he did.

He glanced again at the young woman. The little boy next to her seemed restless, so she lifted him onto her lap. The child couldn't be her son. She didn't look old enough. Then the older woman next to them reached for the boy and settled him in her arms. In a few minutes the boy's head nodded in sleep.

Nathan resisted the urge to pull his watch from his pocket and check the time. Surely the service would end soon. Two potbellied stoves in the front and back of the church provided warmth, and the additional heat of so many bodies caused him to wish he had shed his coat. He fought the urge to nod off himself. Oh, to be like the young lad in his mother's arms.

Finally the congregation rose, and the organ played the final hymn. None too soon for Nathan, for he had grown more uncomfortable by the minute. Long sermons only added to his distaste for affairs of the church. The singing ended, and people began their exit, but he kept his eye on the girl in blue until the crowd blocked her from view.

He stayed behind the Monroe family, who stopped to greet the minister. Mrs. Monroe turned to Nathan. "Reverend Winston, this is Nathan Reed, our houseguest from Hartford this week and a friend of Daniel."

The minister stretched forth his hand in greeting. "Very nice to have you in our services today, Mr. Reed. I hope you enjoy your stay in Briar Ridge and that we'll see more of you."

"Thank you, sir. I look forward to my visit here." But the minister wouldn't be seeing any more of him unless they possibly met in town.

When they reached the Monroe carriage, Nathan turned and spotted the girl coming down the steps. He nudged Daniel. "Could I get you to introduce me to the pretty girl in blue headed this way?"

Daniel grinned and slapped his shoulder. "Delighted, old friend." He waved to the young woman, and she waved back. Abigail ran to greet her, and the girls hurried over to where Nathan stood with Daniel. Abigail tucked her hand in the girl's elbow. "Nathan, this is my best friend, Rachel Winston. Rachel, this is Daniel's former roommate in college."

Rachel Winston? Nathan's hopes dashed against the slushy ground on which he stood. Could she be the preacher's daughter? He didn't mind a young woman being Christian, but he drew the line at keeping company with one so close to the ministry.